PENGUIN (P) CLASSICS

PATHS OF GLORY

HUMPHREY COBB (1899–1944) was born in Siena, Italy, on September 5, 1899, to Alice Littell Cobb, a physician, and Arthur Murray Cobb, an artist. He attended boarding school in England during his childhood. Cobb was kicked out of an American high school and he never returned to graduate. At seventeen he decided to enlist in the Canadian army. After serving in the army for three years during World War I, he returned to the United States to work by turns in the stock trade, the merchant marine, publishing, advertising, and the Office of War Information (precursor of the OSS, the CIA predecessor) writing overseas propaganda. During his lifetime he wrote *Paths of Glory* (1935) and *None but the Brave* (1938) and was the lead screenwriter on the movie *San Quentin* (1937).

JAMES H. MEREDITH is an internationally respected scholar on the literature and films of twentieth-century wars. He is a retired U.S. Air Force lieutenant colonel. He was a graduate English professor at Colorado State University and now develops, teaches, and presents the writing-across-the-curriculum program to doctoral learners at Capella University. He is also the president of the Ernest Hemingway Foundation and Society and is a contributing editor of *War, Literature, and the Arts: An International Journal of the Humanities.*

DAVID SIMON, a longtime journalist, author, and television producer, was born in Washington, D.C. He was a reporter for the *Baltimore Sun* for thirteen years before leaving the paper after the publication of his first book, *Homicide: A Year on the Killing Streets*, which was later adapted as a television series. Simon is the creator and executive producer of the critically acclaimed HBO TV series *The Wire.*

HUMPHREY COBB

Paths of Glory

Introduction by
JAMES H. MEREDITH

Foreword by
DAVID SIMON

PENGUIN BOOKS

PENGUIN BOOKS
Published by the Penguin Group
Penguin Group (USA) Inc., 375 Hudson Street, New York, New York 10014, U.S.A.
Penguin Group (Canada), 90 Eglinton Avenue East, Suite 700, Toronto, Ontario, Canada M4P 2Y3
(a division of Pearson Penguin Canada Inc.)
Penguin Books Ltd, 80 Strand, London WC2R 0RL, England
Penguin Ireland, 25 St Stephen's Green, Dublin 2, Ireland (a division of Penguin Books Ltd)
Penguin Group (Australia), 250 Camberwell Road, Camberwell, Victoria 3124, Australia
(a division of Pearson Australia Group Pty Ltd)
Penguin Books India Pvt Ltd, 11 Community Centre, Panchsheel Park, New Delhi–110 017, India
Penguin Group (NZ), 67 Apollo Drive, Rosedale, North Shore 0632, New Zealand
(a division of Pearson New Zealand Ltd)
Penguin Books (South Africa) (Pty) Ltd, 24 Sturdee Avenue, Rosebank, Johannesburg 2196, South Africa

Penguin Books Ltd, Registered Offices:
80 Strand, London WC2R 0RL, England

First published in the United States of America by The Viking Press 1935
This edition with an introduction by James H. Meredith and a foreword by David Simon published in
Penguin Books 2010

LIBRARY OF CONGRESS CATALOGING-IN-PUBLICATION DATA
Cobb, Humphrey, 1899–1944.
Paths of glory / [by] Humphrey Cobb ; introduction by James H. Meredith ; foreword by David Simon.
p. cm.—(Penguin classics)
Includes bibliographical references.
ISBN 978-0-14-310611-1
1. World War, 1914–1918—Fiction. 2. Trials (Treason)—France—Fiction. 3. Mutiny—France—
History—20th century—Fiction. 4. Military discipline—France—History—20th century—Fiction.
5. France—Politics and government—1870–1940—Fiction. I. Title.
PS3505.O1385P38 2010
813'.52—dc22 2010013185

Set in Adobe Sabon

146028962

Contents

Foreword

Humphrey Cobb gave us our last, failed century in a single, basic narrative. He told us of men devoured by the very institutions they served, without recourse, and for purposes petty, mechanical, and abstract. Indeed, given how little mankind truly learned from the charnel house that was the twentieth century, Cobb may have given us a blueprint for human suffering that will carry us through the next hundred years as well.

To say that *Paths of Glory* is a novel ahead of its time is problematic, however. Cobb's careful representations of the state of humanity, the use of institutionalized terror, and the savagery of modern war making are all appropriate reflections on what he experienced as a young man in the trenches of World War I. His novel was right on time; it's the rest of us who have been late to grasp its implications.

An American who was an early volunteer for the Great War's western front with Canadian forces, Cobb comes to his story with a veteran's wary eye and with little of the flummery and sentimentality that accompanies so many war narratives. He rightly suspects even the most earnest antiwar literature of harboring the sustaining seeds of heroism and nationalism in its depictions of quotidian suffering:

"Where all these *Journey's Ends* and *All Quiets* fail utterly as anti-war propaganda, indeed where they become pro-war propaganda, is in the stoicism, the self-abnegation, the idealism and romantic nobility which they portray," wrote Cobb in early 1933, only two years before the publication of his own masterwork. "How the actors hate war, etc., but Christ, how nobly they suffer! And a regiment marching down a street behind a good band—

everybody knows what that does to your reasonableness and logic. The only available effective anti-war propaganda that I know is photographs of butchered bodies—the more horrible the better."

Cobb's own words do not waste themselves on pathos or the stoic heroism of the everyman. No, he is about the practical facts, and *Paths of Glory* has its focus on the chain of command. The target is the army itself as an institution, an unwieldy and unyielding organism that lurches from one murderous horror to the next, guided only by whichever combination of ambitions and vanities are in play at any moment. No human presence is larger than the institution; none has agency enough to transcend it. Sudden, inevitable death is the great constant in *Paths of Glory*, its omnipresence mitigated only by random chance.

This is indeed a book for a world in which men fly airplanes into buildings and think of themselves as religious martyrs, in which beheadings and car bombings are grist for YouTube video making, in which the flick of a switch thousands of miles distant sends a missile into a village market or wedding party.

Despite all of our warm, humanist hyperbole, this is the fundamental outcome of the twentieth century. Mass exterminations and total wars have made a mockery of the Napoleonic Code and the Geneva conventions; venture capital, an international corporate culture, and modern automation have brought organized labor to its knees. And while the lucky and talented among us are, perhaps, worth more than ever, the average human soul has never been more expendable than it is right now.

Human beings, Cobb's work argues, are worth less every day.

This singular truth suffuses the experience of World War I and its aftermath, and it is this truth from which Cobb, writing in dry, crisp sentences, refuses to turn. The debacle of the Great War laid bare the fraud behind so many institutional ideals. Nationalism was a butcher; religion, ever more useless amid the unending horror. And the institutions of state to which one might appeal for a reprieve—the government, its diplomats, its ministers, its army commanders, its clergy—were all complicit in granting normalcy, even a certain inevitability, to the daily cavalcade of violent death.

In *Paths of Glory*, Cobb finds the proper allegory to drive this point home. He uses the true story of the Corporals of Souain, in which four corporals of the French 136th Regiment were executed at random *"pour encourager les autres"* following the failure of a March 1915 attack against a hill near Souain in Champagne. The senselessness of the action, coupled with the callow ambitions of those in command, is indeed ripe with portent for the century ahead—an epoch in which barbarity would fall as much on the civilian occupants of a Warsaw, a Dresden, or a Nagasaki as upon armed combatants. As the generals bicker over the number to be shot in order to cover their own failure, we can already hear the cold calculations a century hence, the arithmetic of terror that is in play every time a suicide bomber steps onto a Tel Aviv bus, or, for that matter, every time a helicopter fires a missile into a crowded Gaza street.

It is a century in which we calibrated our most powerful institutions against the very idea of innocence, and Cobb, reflecting on only the bloody beginning of that epoch, takes pains to portray the institution of the French army not as an unfeeling, unthinking monolith but as a living, functioning organism, ever greater than the sum of its parts, moving from certitude to certitude, expediency to expediency, and chewing up lives in the process.

It is a general's ambition. It is a colonel's sense of duty. It is a lieutenant's cowardice. And it is a sergeant's inability to refuse the most amoral order. It is all of these things, operating simultaneously, sometimes in conflict, sometimes in concert, each small part of the killing mechanism playing its role and no more. But in the end, the death of innocents is the fixed outcome.

To write his great tragedy, Cobb needed no archvillains, no great evils. As the machine guns and poison gas of the new century bring forward the possibilities of mass extermination, the story requires only ordinary ambitions and commonplace vanities in order for good men to die. And it is not so much a solitary and vile decision by any one scoundrel that condemns the innocent, but the absence of a decision by so many others. The inertia of the modern, layered bureaucracy is immutable. The institution demands blood, and then, by and large, the individuals who constitute that institution simply shrug, incapable of resistance or rebellion.

This is not to say that Cobb was ready to absolve from blame the architects of his war. In describing the Chateau L'Aigle, where his novel reaches its climax, the author dances a few half steps from the ordinary plotting to name names. Citing the mansion's history, the author is pointed in saying that von Kluck, John French, and Foch had stopped there, not to mention Joffre, who had "dined there, silently but with gusto, and then gone to bed and slept undisturbed by any nightmares of Verdun. Haig had sat his charger at the lodge gates and had taken the salute of the Canadian regiments on the way up to the Passchendaele butchery. . . ."

And yet Cobb knew that what he had witnessed in the war was too diffuse, too nuanced, to rest solely on the Great Men of History. In his own writings, he expresses his own complicity and that of his fellow veterans in the savagery:

"I have often had the feeling that a man writing a personal war book was editing it into conformity with post-war fashion and post-war trend," he wrote in 1933. "It is pathetic in a way because it expresses so clearly the feeling of shame at having, whether as a victim of deception or not, made a jingoistic ass of oneself, of having been awfully gullible. What I feel and have felt for some years is pride in my physical and mental stamina, shame in my mental blindness, in my ignorance."

Nor does Cobb's outlook spare the bystanders to the Great War, the multitudes who were able to pick up their ordinary lives as if something extraordinary had not happened to humanity in the trenches of the western front:

"Saw some war pictures—movies taken at the time," he wrote in 1933. "I was glad that several shots of dead and mangled bodies were shown. I went out of the theater inwardly very angry at war, and all the more so because I have been reading—saturated as they are with pettiness, lousiness, and bickerings—of the men who sent those other poor devils to that frightful butchery. But I went out of the theater right into the Broadway crowd, the pasty, unhealthy fishy eyed throng of pimps and chorus men

and I wished they could all be mowed down by a fine clean rat-
tling machine gun."

An angry fellow, and rightly so, given what he had seen. But
Cobb's contempt for what humanity had done to itself never
reads white-hot on the pages of his novel. Indeed, it is in its re-
straint that *Paths of Glory* finds its clarity and, indeed, its
passion.

No wonder that a fourteen-year-old Stanley Kubrick would
read the book and remember it deeply enough to return to its
story. No wonder that Kirk Douglas—an actor with most any
part for his asking—would risk his own money to bring it to the
screen.

It is no slight to Cobb's creation that Kubrick and his screen-
writers managed to tease out even more political implication
than the novel itself offers. It is the 1957 film version of *Paths of
Glory* in which the lieutenant is compelled to face, in the last
moments, the man he has sent to his death. And it is the film
version that parses between the generals, with one turning on
the other as the unlawful order to fire French artillery on French
positions is revealed. These were nuances upon nuances—the
gamesmanship of ambition and command brought to even
greater heights by an auteur operating against the darker strain
of the cold war.

Similarly, it was Kubrick who would use the character of Colonel Dax as the moral center of the tale, allowing Kirk Douglas
his star turn, and making it possible for him to both lead the
doomed charge against the German position and then defend
his men passionately in the ensuing court-martial.

Tellingly, Cobb offers no such overarching hero in his original
telling. No grand villains, no epic heroes; just the slow tyranny
of a self-preserving, self-aggrandizing institution. When asked
why he had made an antiwar film, Kubrick reportedly said he
hadn't. He had made a political film, a film about authoritarian
ignorance.

And of the few liberties that Kubrick took in adapting Cobb's
masterwork to the screen, there is no arguing with his extraordinary final scene, in which dog-faced French soldiers first jeer
and mock a captured German girl's song, only to see their cru-

elty dissipate into grief and empathy. Cobb did not write that moment, but every line in the film version of *Paths of Glory* tells us that Cobb would have recognized himself in those worn, sad faces. Indeed, he recognized all of us in those trenches, staring at the shards of our common future, measuring our thinning odds, and enduring, somehow, nonetheless.

DAVID SIMON

Introduction

Humphrey Cobb's *Paths of Glory* came out in June 1935, six years after the publication of the great class of 1929 World War I novels that included *All Quiet on the Western Front* by Erich Maria Remarque and *A Farewell to Arms* by Ernest Hemingway. Cobb was a veteran of World War I, but unlike the works of his contemporaries from that era, *Paths of Glory* has neither been taught routinely in courses nor been prominent in informed conversations about literature of that war. Stanley Kubrick's 1957 movie version of the novel, however, has become a classic. In fact, the movie, starring Kirk Douglas in one of his first major roles, may arguably be the best American antiwar film ever made and certainly one of the best before the great antiwar films came out following the Vietnam War era. No matter how one ranks the movie, *Paths of Glory* as a film is a classic, and now it may be time to reach the same conclusion about the book as well. Due to the fact that the war and the novel both took place in the early part of the last century and much of the context is either forgotten or not understood, the best way to reintroduce this potential classic is to provide the larger context and history of its publication.

THE FRENCH ARMY, 1914–1918

On May 27, 1917, large portions of the French army mutinied along their sector of the western front. World War I scholar Martin Gilbert writes, in *The First World War: A Complete History,* that on that date:

a dramatic change [occurred] . . . where a growing number of desertions turned, on May 27, to mutiny. At the Front itself, along the Chemin des Dames, as many as 30,000 soldiers had left their trenches and reserve billets and fallen to the rear. Then, in four towns behind the lines, the troops ignored their officers' orders, seized buildings, and refused to go to the Front. On the following day, at Fere-en-Tardenois railway station the mutineers tried to get to Paris, but the trains were prevented from leaving. Two days later, at the Front, several hundred French infantrymen refused to move into the front-line trenches, where they were needed to go to the support of French Moroccan troops, already in the line.[1]

Humphrey Cobb's *Paths of Glory* does not refer to this mutiny in particular; however, this event is a part of the book's historical and moral background. Although the French soldiers did not actually mutiny in *Paths of Glory,* they were unable to proceed in the face of overwhelmingly superior military resistance and, as a consequence, unable to take their objective; yet these soldiers were unjustly punished as if they had mutinied. This punishment forms the basis of the novel's injustice (in this particular fictional case, three men from the regiment are unfairly selected to face a firing squad to pay for the whole unit's "crime"). Quite simply, because of the profound ignorance of how to manage the war, the World War I military system was unjust to the common soldier and the cost of this mismanagement was extremely high. Martin Gilbert puts this cost into perspective by stating, "If each of the nine million military dead of the First World War were to have an individual page, the record of their deeds and suffering, their wartime hopes, their pre-war lives and love, would fill twenty thousand [enormous] books."[2]

Because the common French soldiers were particularly mismanaged, it is not coincidental that Cobb chose the French army in which to set this novel; the *poilu,* as the basic French soldier was called, remained restive practically throughout the war—and certainly for good reason. No such mutinies ever occurred within the English army, including the Canadians, or within the relatively green U.S. forces, who arrived en masse only in late 1917 and 1918, or within the German army, for that matter. On the western front, the French army was the only restive Allied force. But of course there were other armies that had their weak moments, too: the Russian army collapsed on the eastern front, and the Italian army had a decisively weak moment as well along their own front, especially during the great retreat from Caporetto, which formed the historical basis of Hemingway's masterpiece *A Farewell to Arms*. However, the western front is where Cobb served and is where most American readers centered their attention about that war. For these reasons, Cobb's decision to set his novel within the French army makes perfect sense.

However, Cobb was not alone in this choice. William Faulkner did it, too. It has always been an understanding that the greatest compliment to any writer is attribution. As such, Faulkner was impressed enough by Cobb's *Paths of Glory* to borrow the setting and situation for his own World War I novel, *A Fable* (1954). While this introduction is primarily about Cobb's novel, it would be very informative to examine how another author dealt with similar material. Faulkner emphasized the actual French mutinies more than Cobb did in his novel, and he turned the event into a Christian allegory, thereby forming the thematic basis of his novelistic fable. It seems to be this Christian allegory that has bothered both modern scholars and general readers alike, as this ancient genre has not been transferred into the contemporary era successfully. Despite this critical difficulty, Faulkner's *A Fable* does convey the moral dilemma that modern war, with its vast numbers of casualties and horrors, has created for the common soldier, the conscript who was ripped out of his normal civilian life to be made cannon fodder for the killing machine in the hands of the generals and political leaders who were in charge of the enormous military apparatus that World War I quickly morphed into. Yes, there is an inherent injustice about modern war toward the common soldier, who generally comes from the country's heartland, and while these soldiers had been responding to their nation's call to arms for generations, World War I proved to be different. In his novel, Faulkner describes these common men during World War I and where they came from:

And most of its [the French regiment's] subsequent replacements had been drawn from this same district, so that most of these men were not only veterans of it in their time, and these male children already dedicated to it when their time should come, but all these people and kin, not only the actual old parents and kin of the doomed men, but fathers and mothers and sisters and wives and sweethearts whose sons and brothers and husbands and fathers and lovers might have been among the doomed men except for sheer chance and luck.

So, while for generations these men had served their country in previous wars, something changed radically during World War I, especially in how these men were treated by those in charge of the modern bureaucracy. And both Faulkner and Cobb were correct in depicting the reaction of the common French soldier as a consequence.

WORLD WAR I

World War I began in the summer of 1914, following the assassination of Archduke Ferdinand, the heir apparent to the throne of the Austrian Empire, in Sarajevo,[3] and ended with the November 11, 1918, armistice and the notorious Treaty of Versailles, which was signed on June 28, 1919.[4] While history moves toward the centennial anniversary of World War I, and with it a forthcoming revival of material about the war, little is generally known by the average reader about this conflict beyond trench warfare and the images of mud, barbed wire, and human suffering. Yet this war was far more complicated than that, especially as one particularizes the vast human suffering, which Cobb's *Paths of Glory* does so well. Joseph Stalin has been credited with saying that in the twentieth century, one death is a tragedy but a million deaths has become only a statistic. At its most basic level, this paraphrase conveys the bitterly dehumanizing effect of mass warfare. In normal life, very little is more personal than the act of dying; however, in modern warfare, particularly conflicts that occurred in the first half of the twentieth century, when armies numbered in the millions, death has become more of a management problem than anything else. While casualty rates have significantly fallen in recent conflicts, the bureaucratic bean-counting mentality inherent in large organizations (or corporations in civilian life) has become intrinsically pervasive. This mentality emerged for the common man during World War I when the various conflicting nationalities had to organize themselves to fight one another on a massive and global scale. The nineteenth-century Napoleonic Wars and American Civil War were preludes to what would come in the next century, and the dehumanizing reliance on the hierarchical management of large and complex organizations instead of direct human contact. In essence, World War I sealed mankind's tragic fate in that it manifested a sense of alienation in the depersonalized modern world. On a basic level, the common man was often led to death by men he barely knew. As large armies and organizations grew in number, it became increasingly impossible for the man at the top to know the common man or to even be known by him as well, and as a consequence, life-or-death decisions were made by those who had little or no direct human contact. While it certainly does not justify General Assolant's attitude, as the division commander and the man at the top of the hierarchy, it at least explains why he is so able to punish otherwise innocent men as a consequence of the regiment's failure to reach the unattainable objective of the Pimple.[5] Adding to the dehumanization was that for the first time in history, armies ended up not fighting each other face-to-face and standing up man-to-man, as they primarily had done in the past. Warfare in the trenches meant not only living and dying often in muddy squalor, but also fighting the enemy lying on one's belly in order to avoid getting killed by high-powered and accurate rifles and machine-gun fire and high-explosive artillery shells as well.

Although few people realize it now, World War I actually began much like the Napoleonic Wars, with mobile warfare, cavalry charges, and antiquated elaborate uniforms and military equipment, which led to enormous casualties in the face of modern machine guns and artillery. In fact, France suffered the largest overall percentage of casualties during the first few months of the war. The result of this large number of casualties so early in the conflict was that the embattled countries soon discovered that because their prewar troop strengths were so depleted, they had to start relying more on the citizenry, the common conscript, to keep fighting the war. After the assassination of Archduke Ferdinand, the two conflicting alliances that had divided Europe ignorantly stumbled toward the inevitable conflict, ultimately leading to the deaths of approximately nine million men.

The diplomatic bungling that ensued began when Emperor Franz Joseph of Austria presented Serbia with demands that were so severe that no sovereign nation could fulfill them, although it desperately attempted to do so. As a consequence of Serbia's rejection of his demands, Joseph asked German emperor Wilhelm, an Austrian ally, for support. Russia, a diplomatic ally of Serbia, then countered Germany's implied intervention by mobilizing its vast citizen army, which unnerved the highly influential German army's high command. War was eventually declared on August 1, 1914.

Concerned about the superior size of the Russian mobilized army (although this army was poorly equipped and trained), the German army high command soon initiated the Schlieffen Plan, which called for a two-pronged invasion of France, an ally of Russia's since 1892,[6] through Belgium and across the Alsace-Lorraine frontier. For Germany to avoid being caught in a two-front war between Russian and France, the basic strategy was to strike quickly—to take Paris before the French army could be mobilized for war. Germany subsequently invaded France through Belgium, where it soon met unexpected resistance that significantly slowed its invasion. In the meantime, Great Britain, which had previously formed an alliance with Belgium, intervened and fought a difficult battle at Mons and then began a delaying campaign to slow the Germans' seemingly inevitable advance toward Paris. For its part, France had thrown together its own armed resistance both along the Belgian border and in Alsace-Lorraine. And Russia had finally mobilized its army and was attempting to engage in the war as well on the eastern front. During this time, the large armies engaged in rather dramatic and sweeping combat that eventually led to the German invasion being halted at the first battle of the Marne, and what followed after that were the initial stages of trench warfare, a form of combat radically different from what had gone before. After being stopped on their drive toward Paris, the Germans, instead of retreating to their own country, which would have been the traditional thing to do, dug in on French and Belgian soil. And, to counter them, Britain and France dug in, too, forming the infamous western front. This stalemate is what is preeminently known about World War I. While death on the battlefield is always tragic, especially for the families of the fallen, it was the dehumanizing effects of trench warfare, men living like rats in mud trenches, bodies of the fallen piling up around the scarred battlefield, that dramatically changed the entire attitude of the modern world. Injustice is always an inherent consequence of a dehumanized world, especially when soldiers are continually asked to do much, much more than is humanly possible by generals who are detached from their own humanity.

As these two warring factions continued to face each other in their trenches over the next four years, heavy casualties started to mount in battles such as Verdun, which lies in France near the border with Germany. Verdun was a model for the battle in *Paths of Glory*. No single battle of World War I more fully exemplifies the futility and utter waste of humanity than does the one fought at Verdun. The historical significance of Verdun dates back to the Romans, who gave the city its original name, Virodunium.[7] What made Verdun such an important location was the series of fortresses that surrounded the city and had shielded the French heartland from attack by the Germans for generations. As a consequence, Verdun had become a sacred place in "the hearts and minds of the French people," who would defend the city at all costs.[8] The Germans knew of its importance and decided to attack Verdun because they wanted to kill as many French combatants as they could. "In five months, more than twenty-three million shells were fired by the two contending armies at Verdun, on average more than a hundred shells a minute. Verdun itself remained in French hands, but the death toll there was 650,000 men."[9] The battle for Verdun began on February 21, 1916, and lasted for ten months.

For the most part, French soldiers had been poorly led early in the war, and they were needlessly slaughtered more often than not. Verdun was the most catastrophic battle of the war for the French, as well as for the Germans, if not the most catastrophic battle for all of historical time. While the historical aspects of Verdun do not actually coincide with the novel, that battle, more than anything else, is an emblem of the war's seemingly futile experience for the French soldier. In Verdun, Cobb found the crucial thematic foundation for his story and emblematic justification for the bitter injustice his novel so poignantly conveys.

PUBLICATION HISTORY

Paths of Glory was first published in 1935. Its title comes from Thomas Gray's "Elegy Written in a Country Churchyard," in the line "The paths of glory lead but to the grave."[10] While this eighteenth-century poem was written during a much more heroic age than the modern period, the idea in Gray's line reflects a less-than-heroic attitude toward dying for the sake of glory. However, in this twentieth-century World War I novel, Cobb's modern perspective is much, much more ironic and bitter. While Gray describes the individual's paths of glory leading to the death of one man, Cobb focuses on the hubristic paths of the generals' glory leading to the graves of millions of common soldiers, those who were just trying to do their job and survive, to go home and enjoy their ordinary lives. The countryside of Belgium and northern France is littered with military cemeteries and monuments to the dead. One could say that the modern context requires a whole new sense of mathematics that was not even contemplated in the eighteenth century, primarily because the calculus of war dramatically changed in the twentieth century. Despite all these crucial thematic underpinnings embedded in the title, *Paths of Glory* was not actually titled by Cobb, but came out of a publisher's promotional contest that attracted significant interest.[11] The book initially stayed on the bestseller list for several weeks and was a Book-of-the-Month Club selection. *Paths of Glory* was also turned into a play by Sidney Howard.

Despite this early boost, however, the novel did not sustain momentum, and sales subsequently declined. The novel was republished by Avon in 1973 and the University of Georgia Press in 1987.[12] While Cobb's novel has been somewhat neglected over the years by academia, more recently, Kubrick's movie version has received a somewhat more scholarly examination, especially after the death of the filmmaker in 1999.

THE MOVIE

Cobb's novel was adapted into a film in 1957 by the great filmmaker Stanley Kubrick.[13] Tim Dirks writes about this film that

> the suicidal attack on an impregnable fortress named "Ant Hill" in the film (against an unseen German enemy) was inspired by and loosely based upon the six-month bloodbath in 1916 during the Battle of Verdun for Fort Douamont, a French stronghold eventually captured by the Germans. (The same battle was frequently referred to in Renoir's *The Grand Illusion* [1937]). . . . Due to the film's raw, controversially offensive and critical assessment of hypocritical French military and bureaucratic authorities who callously condemn and sacrifice three randomly chosen innocent men with execution (for cowardice) for their own fatal blunder, it suffered poor box-office returns, and was banned in France and Switzerland for almost twenty years (until the mid-1970s) following its release.[14]

To term this film antiwar, a commonly misused term, is not quite accurate because the film and the book do not necessarily criticize war in a pacifistic way as much as they deride the bureaucratic apparatus that is organized to fight modern war. More than any other feature, the movie goes to great and obvious lengths to contrast the elaborate living conditions of the generals, who reside in magnificent châteaus, with those of the common soldiers, who live in cramped and rustic trenches. However, those are not all of the differences between the book and movie. For his part, Kubrick "adds at least four scenes that were not in the novel, and which ameliorate Cobb's almost totally bitter picture of humanity."[15] One significant outcome of these changes is that the film depicts Colonel Dax in a much more heroic way. In the book, Dax equivocates in his support of his troops; in the movie, he does not. In Kubrick's hands, the moral focus is on the heroic actions of one man, Colonel Dax, fighting a corrupt and self-serving bureaucracy. In Cobb's version, there are no heroes. The difference between these two versions of Dax is that the movie forms a much more simplistic examination of bureaucratic moral corruption than is depicted in the novel. One could say that the movie version veers somewhat toward the Hollywood Western hero morality play, with Dax playing the tough-guy hero and Assolant the scar-faced villain. Although ultimately Dax fails to get his men out of harm's way, his motives have remained pure throughout, and, yes, he does manage to get the bad guy in the end. The novel, however, creates a more complex and yet bitter indictment of the military bureaucracy during war, possibly too complex and too bitter for film-going audiences in the mid-twentieth century.

PATHS OF GLORY AND THE AMERICAN WAR NOVEL TRADITION

The American war novel tradition began with Stephen Crane's *The Red Badge of Courage,* which was set during the Civil War. This tradition primarily depicts the plight of a common soldier in the face of modern combat, specifically involving not necessarily the first taste of combat as much as the initial comprehension of one's own mortality in war. While the protagonist in *The Red Badge of Courage,* Henry Fleming, runs like a rabbit during his first taste of combat, it is actually his encounter with a corpse that initiates his moral development as a character. The ultimate issue concerning the eventual moral development of the protagonist is whether to stay in the war and possibly die as a consequence or instead run away from the killing and save oneself. The protagonists in this phase of the American war tradition always choose to flee. Other representative novels, which include Joseph Heller's *Catch-22* and Tim O'Brien's *Going After Cacciato,* have their protagonist choose similar moral actions in the face of mortal danger.

Paths of Glory does not fit neatly into the American war novel tradition, primarily because it is entirely about French soldiers in the French army, and the novel does not focus on the individual. None of the soldiers involved in the novel is American. Although the main protagonist in Hemingway's *A Farewell to Arms,* Frederic Henry, belongs to the Italian ambulance corps, the story itself is essentially American because he is an American. While Cobb did serve in the Canadian army, he was actually an American citizen, born in Italy to American parents, and spent most of his early life living in England. The point is that Cobb did not necessarily have French sensibilities. Yet all the men in Cobb's novel are French because they are a better fit for his moral tale within the context of World War I. *Paths of Glory* is more an emblematic moral tale than the highly personalized, realistic novel Hemingway wrote about World War I. Moreover, unlike Cobb's novel, *A Farewell to Arms* is a love story more than it is about the conditions of war. Cobb's novel is grounded in the idea that modern war is an ignominiously dangerous experience.

Despite all of these considerations, there is one very prominent aspect of *Paths of Glory* that does fit into this tradition, and it is the fact that the novel has a strong antiwar, or antimilitary, strain in it. While other features of the American war novel tradition do not necessarily apply, this particular one is very important. Serious American war fiction never conveys a prowar stance (while there is plenty of bad fiction that certainly does). And because the ultimate moral issue in the novels from the American war tradition concerns the survival of the individual, these novels always convey an antiwar message, because while war may be helpful for a nation's political survival, the experience is often harmful for the individual, especially the common soldiers, who are the ones doing the dying. Moreover, Cobb's novel does not focus specifically on the moral example of an individual, but rather on that of several individuals; *Paths of Glory* does not completely fulfill this aspect of the tradition. While *Paths of Glory* obviously conveys a moral message, it is representative of the effect of the war overall more than of the individualistic experience of one specific soldier, which is a major distinction.

In *Paths of Glory*, the moral focus is on the men, plural, who are in charge of the military bureaucracy rather than on the men who are sentenced to death. Didier, Langlois, and Férol are victims more than anything else. Instead, it is the men who have to make moral choices about the condemned who are under examination, the ones who are making the decisions and giving the orders. And the ones following the orders are the modern apparatchiks. Cobb points to General de Guerville, the army commander's chief of staff; General Assolant, the divisional commander; Colonel Dax, the commander of the 181st Regiment; and the lower-ranking leaders at the company level, Jonnart, Renouart, Roget, and Sancy. Except for Captain Renouart, who acts upon his Christian conscience and refuses to select a man, each one of these men responds within the narrow moral confines of a military bureaucracy. General de Guerville is the quintessential bureaucrat, who attempts to find a solution that serves everyone's needs, especially the command apparatus that runs the military, and Assolant is the perfect self-serving tyrant. Although Dax initially tries to defend his soldiers, in the end he acquiesces to the dictates of the bureaucracy when he realizes that if he continues to defy orders, he may be sticking his neck out a little too far. Yes, he could have done more, but in the end he does not. Jonnart is simply following orders unthinkingly, and leaves his selection literally up to the luck of the draw. Lieutenant Roget of course uses the situation to his own personal advantage by eliminating a potential adversary. Sancy deludes himself into thinking that he is doing the right thing, when in fact he is attempting to play God instead.

COBB'S WAR DIARY AND
HIS LATER REVISIONS

During the war, Cobb kept a war diary, starting it, as he says, on "the day I enlisted."[16] He was eighteen at the time, in military age, but Cobb was actually seventeen, and he continued working on the original text "until a year or so after the war."[17] Cobb later revised and annotated the diary at the age of thirty-four. The diary has remained unpublished since.

In the revised foreword to the diary, Cobb describes his manuscript: "It was written mostly in indelible pencil in a small leather covered diary bought with an eye to its fitting into the breast pocket of my tunic—the pocket over which all the medals were to dangle. It was against orders to keep a diary, so I went ahead and kept it."[18] Cobb continues to describe the diary by stating that he has read it only twice. The first time was in 1919, when, as Cobb writes, he was "brooding that year over my lost status as a hero and, apparently, consoled myself by thumbing over the record of my gallantry."[19] The second time he read the diary was fifteen years later. In doing so the second time, Cobb states that he "found that my memory, like the indelible pencil, was beginning to fade."[20] He goes on to say that it was then "time, therefore, to annotate those staccato, laconic lines. Time to unlock the cryptic references before I lost the combination. Time, too, to catch and peg down those fading memories, some of them at least, before they were gone forever."[21]

Cobb's revisions are revealing about the perils of World War I duty. He writes:

"On post," "Down for rations" meant danger. "Good dugout" meant safety. "Rain and rations" reflected degrees of bodily comfort—hellishly important. "Moonlight" was, usually, less an aesthetic note than a workaday one. It was a great advantage in the line because it saved you a lot of unnecessary bumps and floundering around. It easily outweighed the disadvantage of your being more visible to Fritz. But on patrol the moon was a thing to curse. In No Man's Land you'd sooner take the bumps and let the ability to see and be seen go. "Shells" meant a flock of particularly close ones. It registered a definite scare, the kind that, when it was over, left you panting because you found you had been holding your breath.[22]

In this description of the World War I battlefield landscape, the ordinary events of life, moonlight and rain, for example, have transmogrified into nightmarish experiences, and the words of the quotidian have become surreal modifiers for extreme pain and suffering.

The pain and suffering of the war helps shape the language of modern literature. Frederic Henry, in Hemingway's *A Farewell to Arms,* states that "abstract words such as glory, honor, courage, or hallow were obscene beside the concrete names of villages, the number of roads, the names of rivers, the numbers of regiments and dates."[23] In his foreword, Cobb indicates why this desire for linguistic concreteness is so important for a veteran: "Names of places and villages are noted down systematically. It was not only because they were the only thing which distinguished one pile of ruins from another, but also because I was always keenly interested in knowing what place I was in."[24] Interestingly, Cobb himself pays tribute to Hemingway's words in his foreword. The language of specificity that the World War I combatants used to describe their experiences separates them significantly from those who had not even been close to the battlefield, and the reason is quite simple. No one who went through the horrors that occurred around the city of Verdun could ever feel normal about those particular places again. Moreover, particularities are also a way to control the emotional experience, to remain focused on the thing itself instead; concreteness abreacts the trauma of war by putting a name to the feelings. Once you put name to something you have gone a long way psychologically toward controlling the memory of the experience. This linguistic abreaction and transformation in part formed the drive toward the specificity of language in modernism away from the more abstract nature of Victorian literature.[25] Since World War I, the concrete language of war has increasingly become the language of normal life.

To put all of this into perspective: despite the best efforts of many high-minded individuals, war continues to be an inevitable part of the human condition. Until mankind truly figures out a way to live in peace, wars will continue to occur, and as long as there are wars, people are going to die unjustly. In order to fight wars, nations are going to have to manage large organizations, meaning that the few people at the top are going to continue to make tough decisions that will directly affect the lives of the many soldiers at the bottom. Cobb's *Paths of Glory,* therefore, serves as a cautionary tale about how bureaucracies tend to take on lives of their own outside the normal moral attitudes of civilized society. Even ordinary soldiers, who would never consider such actions in civilian life, are capable of very inhumane actions when put under the pressure of war. As mankind moves forward in the twenty-first century, Cobb's novel should continue to stand the test of time and remain relevant to an informed public. *Paths of Glory* will finally become the war classic that it truly deserves to be.

—JAMES H. MEREDITH

NOTES

1. Martin Gilbert, *The First World War: A Complete History* (New York: Henry Holt, 1994), 333–34.
2. Gilbert, xxi.
3. James H. Meredith, *Understanding the Literature of World War I: A Student Casebook to Issues, Sources, and Historical Documents* (Westport, CT: Greenwood, 2004), 11.
4. Meredith, 165.
5. In the book the German fortification is called the Pimple; however, in the movie it is referred to as the Anthill.
6. Gilbert, 4.
7. Meredith, 63.
8. Meredith, 63.
9. Gilbert, 299-300.
10. Thomas Gray, http://www.thomasgray.org/cgi-bin/display.cgi?text=elcc.
11. Stephen E. Tabachnick, Afterword to *Paths of Glory* (1935; repr., Athens, GA: University of Georgia Press, 1987), 237.

12. Tabachnick, 269.
13. Tim Dirks, http://www.filmsite.org/path.html.
14. Dirks.
15. Tabachnick, 303.
16. Humphrey Cobb, Foreword (an unpublished diary).
17. Cobb, I.
18. Cobb, I.
19. Cobb, II.
20. Cobb, II.
21. Cobb, II.
22. Cobb, IV.
23. Ernest Hemingway, *A Farewell to Arms* (New York: Scribners Paperback Fiction Edition, 1995 [1929]), 185.
24. Cobb, IV.
25. Meredith, 2.

Suggestions for Further Reading

Dirks, Tom. Review of *Paths of Glory*. http://www.filmsite.org/path.html.

Faulkner, William. *A Fable*. New York: Vintage Books, 1978.

Gilbert, Martin. *The First World War: A Complete History*. New York: Henry Holt, 1994.

Meredith, James. *Understanding the Literature of World War 1: A Student Casebook to Issues, Sources, and Historical Documents*. Westport, CT: Greenwood, 2004.

Tabachnick, Stephen E. Afterword, *Paths of Glory: A Novel by Humphrey Cobb*. 1935. Reprint, Athens, GA: The University of Georgia Press, 1987.

A Note on the Text

The appendix to the Penguin Classics edition of *Paths of Glory* includes excerpts from the previously unpublished "Diary of Humphrey Cobb (October 1917–November 1918): Annotated by Him in 1933." The text was provided by Annie Cobb and selected by James H. Meredith.

Paths of Glory

I

"They're marching pretty sloppy," said the younger one.

"So would you, if you'd been through what they have," the older one answered.

The two soldiers were standing, partly concealed, behind a roadside clump of trees. A light wind from the northeast brought a sound of distant gunfire which the older one recognized as the dying notes of the dawn bombardments. The attention of both men had become fixed on the body of troops which was approaching them down the road. It was a regiment of infantry, and, as it drew level with them, the uneven tramp of many feet that were not wholly in step grew louder and blotted out the sound of the distant artillery. The younger one began again:

"How d'you know they've been through anything?"

"There are several ways of telling," said the older one, getting ready to do the telling with a pause which expressed at the same time his boredom with the obvious and his pleasure in an opportunity to exercise his didactic impulse. "It's not that they're dirty and need a shave. You don't need a war to get that way. No. But look at their faces. See that sort of greyish tint to their skin? That's not from sitting in a café on a Sunday afternoon. Then look at some of those jaws. See how the lower jaw looks sort of loose, how it seems to hang down a bit? That's a reaction. It shows they've been clenching them. Take a look at their eyes. They're open, but they have the look of not seeing much of anything. They've had it tough, all right. Their eyes are glazed. They're nearly all of them constipated, of course, but it isn't so much that as . . ."

"Now I know you're fooling me. Everybody always says the front line acts on you just the other way."

"Is that so."

"Yes, it is. Why, only the other day I went to the medical officer for a pill. He said, 'You're going to join your regiment, aren't you?' I said, 'Yes, sir,' and he said, 'Well, here's your pill, but it's the last one you'll need till the war's over. The German artillerymen will keep your bowels open for you from now on.'"

"That doctor was a fool. And what's more, it's clear he's never been near the line or he wouldn't talk that way."

"But everybody—"

"Yes, I know. But don't forget this—all the hot air in this army isn't stored only at the balloon sections."

"What d'you mean?"

"I mean this. The Germans have got all our trench latrines registered. And we've got theirs, too. Now a soldier doesn't like to go to a place that's registered. What's more, he doesn't like to take his breeches down because when his breeches are down he can't jump or run. So what does he do? He bakes it. I've been out on this front for nearly two years and I haven't seen a case of diarrhoea yet. And the reason is that when men get scared they get tense and things inside them solidify. Functions stop. Secretions dry up. When you hear a shell coming straight at you, you hold everything, even your breath. You can't help it. That's why those fellows' faces look grey. Their skin is dry. So are their eyes, and from lack of sleep too. That's why they look glazed. For some reason their jaws seem to relax first. Every time a man comes out of the line something happens inside him like the mainspring busting in a watch. Besides, I happen to know those fellows have taken a terrible pounding up in the Souchez Valley."

"You know a lot, don't you?"

"No, not so much. I just keep my ears and eyes open, that's all. But I do know for a fact that they've had it tough because that's my regiment and I met a sergeant down at railhead who'd been wounded up there and he told me about it."

"What regiment is it?"

"I don't know that I ought to tell you. You ask so many questions you're probably a spy. That's the 181st Regiment of the line—or what's left of it."

"Say, that's the regiment I'm ordered to join. Let's follow

along. We'll save ourselves a fifteen-kilometre hike to Villers and back again. Come on, grab your stuff—"

"Hey there, wait a minute. There's no hurry. Let me handle this and we'll be all right."

"Funny, I saw your numerals but somehow I didn't take it in. Excitement of going up to the front and all that, I suppose. . . . Say, my name is Duval. What's yours? Where are you coming from, anyway? Hospital?"

"No. First-Class Private Langlois. Late of Paradise, otherwise known as leave."

The two men shook hands, looked each other quickly and deeply in the eye for the first time, then smiled as their glances disengaged. The regiment in horizon blue—at that distance the blue of a horizon upon which a storm is gathering—was already passing out of sight and merging into the poplars which lined the road. The sound of their tired, uneven tread had moved away with them too.

"Well, what'll we do?" said Duval.

"Somebody said that a good soldier is one who knows when to disobey. He was right, and I'm a good soldier. Now we're ordered to join our regiment at Villers. But they've apparently just come from there, so we'll save ourselves a thirty-kilometre hike for nothing. But we won't hot-foot it after them either. Got any money? All right. Then we'll go back down to that *bistro* we passed at the crossroads and have a couple of drinks and spend some time. They'll tell us there which way the regiment went and we'll start out so as to catch up with them in time for evening grub. Let's get going."

They heaved their packs on, slung their rifles, and clambered over to the road. Turning to the left, they moved off in the wake of the regiment, taking their time and exchanging bits of information about themselves. Langlois learnt that his companion worked in a Belfort bank and lived with his parents in the suburbs. His class was just beginning to be sent to the front, and he had somehow got left behind by the detail ordered to the 181st. That was why he was alone. It was a complicated story of confused orders and Langlois didn't pay much attention to it. Duval, glancing involuntarily at Langlois's ribbons, said he hoped he would win a medal, wondered what the chances were of his getting a commission when he was a year or so older. Langlois told him the chances were good if you weighed them on the basis of time and officer casualties alone. He himself, he said, didn't want a commission. He had enough to think about looking after his own skin without worrying about a lot of other men too. He was an engineer, he told Duval, and added derisively that that was no doubt the reason for his being in the infantry. Duval pointed out that Joffre was an engineer, but Langlois only laughed.

A thin rain began to fall and the conversation soon died out. Langlois asked himself why rain always seemed to put a stop to talk on the march. He welcomed the silence and used it to enjoy the relief of finding himself walking away from the front. Duval, on the other hand, was rather disappointed with the direction they were taking, mildly resentful of it. He consoled himself with the sound of the distant gunfire. At last, he reflected, he had heard the noise of war—The Orchestration of the Western Front. The phrase stood in his mind's eye, capitals and all, just as he had seen it in a headline. Soon he would see war. His romanticism and inexperience insulated him from the thought that he might feel it, too.

They walked along. Already both men had the feeling that they were pals. Langlois wondered how soon this friendship, abruptly begun, would, like so many others, be as abruptly ended. The question came aimlessly into his head and he let it dissolve there. As soon as he had a chance he must send his wife a note to tell her that his regiment was going to the rear for a rest and that she could count on his being out of danger for a week or ten days more.

It was a morning in early spring and the shower had passed over. The countryside was refreshed by the rains and the landscape seemed just on the point of breaking out its delicate greens. The two men stopped to light cigarettes, then went on again, taking their time and finding an unexpected pleasure in doing so. They had plenty of time anyway.

The regiment came to the crossroads, made a quarter circle round the café which stood there, and swung off the main road to the right. Some of the men lifted their gaze from the calves of the men ahead of them and looked at the Café du Carrefour. Their interest in it was not an abstract one, for it was the first house they had seen in three weeks that was intact; more than that, it was a drinking place, forerunner of similar drinking places, farther on, among which they hoped to end their march.

"We're almost there," said Didier.

"Where?" said Lejeune.

"Where we're going, of course."

"How do you know where we're going?"

"I don't. But I know we're almost there because when a regiment marches down a main road for four hours on end and then suddenly turns off it, it's getting somewhere."

Other voices were heard in the ranks.

"Ah, rest! I could do with a bit of rest . . ."

"Me too, my boy. You're not the only one . . ."

"Sleep, that's what I need, sleep; long, quiet sleep . . ."

"And to get my clothes off. They're stiff. I've got a strong stomach, I tell you—you have to have in this war—but I can hardly stand my own stink . . ."

"You have my sympathies, my friend," said the man behind him. "I don't find it any too sweet either."

"At that, I prefer mine to yours," the first one retorted.

The lieutenant, marching alongside the sergeant at the head of the platoon, said to him:

"That sounds better. Now they're beginning to come out of it. It's when the men give up joking that it makes me anxious."

"Yes, sir," said the sergeant without fully getting the officer's meaning.

A light rain began to come down, and the talk, which had bubbled up suddenly at the turn off the main road, began to dwindle away. The men lowered their heads to keep the rain off their faces, then hunched their shoulders to keep it from going down their necks. Little waves of private verbal sighs beat up upon the lieutenant's ears: "Rest . . . my feet . . . rest . . . what a march . . . sleep . . . rest . . ."

"Their resistance is certainly low," the lieutenant said to himself. "So's their morale. But who can blame them? How much farther have we got to go? If they'd only tell you beforehand how far you had to go, you could brace yourself for the march. You might know it would start to rain just as we got on the dirt road . . ." Suddenly furious with the eternal minor perversities of life, the lieutenant stopped thinking and began instead to let a series of blasphemous and obscene words tumble about in his mind, and, when they had exhausted themselves, he started to force them through again. His lips moved in time to his vehement inner language, but no sound came from them until, soothed by his silent outburst, he turned once more to the sergeant and said:

"They'll have to give us ten at least, I should think."

"At least ten, sir," the sergeant agreed.

They spoke elliptically, as men do when powerfully absorbed in a vital and pervasive subject, as they will when it does not occur to them that anyone could be thinking of any other than the common topic. Neither one, however, quite succeeded in convincing either himself or the other that they would really get ten days' rest.

The regiment passed through a hamlet and over a stream, then up a wooded hill where the mud lay rutted on the road. Men stumbled, slipped, jostled each other, and swore, and the ranks lost what little formation they had had. The wood ended abruptly and neatly on the brow of the hill and they came out onto a low plateau of fields. They crossed the plateau, cursing the road for leading them on an S-shaped route instead of going straight. Quick to note that no natural obstacle had caused its deviation, they cursed it all the harder for having curved itself into an S wantonly.

"Things like that do make you angrier than the devil," the lieutenant reflected. "The hostility of inanimate objects begins to seem a real thing, especially when you're tired out. And the angrier you get the more exhausted you get, and vice versa." He was just beginning to wind himself up for another convulsion of private profanity when the regiment turned sideways and began to fall away down a road into a shallow valley. Voices broke out behind them:

"Here we are at last."

"Interesting ruins, no doubt . . ."

"Ruins nothing. Look! The houses have roofs."

"Then they're not for us."

But this time, as always sooner or later he was likely to be, the professional sceptic was wrong. The village on the floor of the valley was to be their village; the houses with the roofs were to be their houses. The pace quickened as the men slithered down the road to a destination finally in sight. Talk became general, and louder than it had been for many days. What with the slope of the road and its sliminess, the men were going almost at a run in their eagerness to get there. Then suddenly the mass of blue buckled, closed up like an accordion, and came to a dead stop. The colonel, at the head of the column, was talking to the billeting officer who was standing by the roadside with his billeting party drawn up behind him like a guard of honour.

Soon the line began to move again, slowly and in jerks. As each company came up, a man of the billeting party detached himself from it, saluted the company commander and said: "This way, sir. I'll show the platoons their billets, and then they can fall in again at once to draw a hot meal from the rolling kitchens. The colonel's orders are, sir, that the men are off duty till noon tomorrow."

At the Café du Carrefour Langlois wrote a note to his wife. He took some pains to convey his information in such a way that it would be vague enough to ensure the letter a quick passage past the censor.

Just a line, my dearest, to tell you that I shall not be going up to the front for a week or ten days more at least. So you need not worry about me for a while yet. In fact you need not worry about me at all for, as I have often told you, I have an absolute conviction that I am destined to come through this war alive. Some of us are bound to, you know, and I am certain that I am one of them. There is no German shell or bullet that has my number on it . . .

He quite knew the fatuousness of writing such stuff, also its futility. But what was a man to do when he caught that look in his wife's eyes; when he felt those spasmodic pressures of her hand clasped in his; when he saw her, more and more often, sud-

denly drop whatever she was doing, come to him, take him in
her arms and hold him, hold him with terrible tenderness?

   . . . *I'm glad we decided as we did last Thursday.* [He counted
on his fingers.] *Perhaps you will have a hint for me by the time
we come out of our next trip into the trenches?* [He thought for
a long time, staring at his letter without seeing it, then decided
to risk the phrase, so filled with implications.] *I hope it will be
a girl. No more now. I'll write again soon. All my love, my
darling . . .*

   He sealed the letter and put it away in his pocket-book, in-
tending to mail it at the regimental field post office that evening.
"I hope it will be a girl." He wondered if the censor would consider that as evidence of defeatist tendencies. He wondered what
his wife might read into that hope, what conclusions she might
draw. Perhaps he shouldn't have said it after all. It had been her
wish, broached unexpectedly two days before his leave was up,
to have a child. It was a complete reversal of their previous feeling and agreement about the subject, but he quite understood
her change of heart—all the better because she had refrained
from giving any reason for it.

   The door of the café opened, and a corporal came in. He was
covered with mud, the spattered mud of the roads though, not
the caked mud of the trenches. He took in Duval and Langlois
at a glance, his eye lighting first on their insignia, then shifting
to their faces. He seemed to be in a hurry.

   "Where's your regiment?" he said, instinctively discriminat-
ing between the recruit Duval and the veteran Langlois, and
addressing himself to the latter. "I've been looking for them all
up and down the front."

   "I don't know," said Langlois. "I've been trailing them myself. The old woman here says a line regiment turned down that
road this morning. Sounds as if that's our gang, all right. What's
up anyway?"

   "Have a drink," said Duval who had had enough of it himself
to make him feel friendly to a stranger.

   It is doubtful if the corporal heard him, however, for he was
already half-way out the door (which he didn't stop to close)
when Duval spoke. And, if the roar of his cut-out and the skid

with which his motor cycle took the corner was any indication, it is still more doubtful if he would have accepted the offer, even if he had heard it.

"Whew! What a tornado!" said Duval. "What's eating him, anyway?"

"He's a dispatch rider," said Langlois. "They always act important. Sometimes they are."

"What's all the rush about? D'you think the Boche have broken through somewhere, or what?"

"My God, no. It's probably an invitation to our Old Man to dine at the Divisional Mess. Or maybe it's a flock of medals for the lottery . . ."

"So that's how you got yours, eh, in a lottery?" said Duval, expecting a prompt denial and slightly shocked when it didn't come.

"Practically, yes. Listen, young fellow, don't get the medal bee in your bonnet. It makes you do foolish things, and if you're patient you'll probably get the medal anyway without doing the foolish things for it. Don't look so indignant. What else can it be but a lottery? All those men deserve medals, if you're going to give medals at all, for what they stood at Souchez. But only some of them will get them. So it's a lottery, isn't it?"

"Well, you've been pretty lucky, drawing down a *croix de guerre* with two palms, not to mention your *médaille militaire* also. You shouldn't complain about it."

"I'm not. I simply say it's a lottery. But it's different from the usual lotteries in this way—your chances of winning prizes increase each time you win a prize. Anyway, that's the way it seems to work. Or perhaps it's more like making money. After the first million, the rest comes easier. . . . Say, it's getting late. Let's shove off."

Duval paid for the drinks, and they went out into a landscape upon which the declining sun was laying long shadows side by side with strips that had a golden glow. The air was soft, and the light, too, was becoming imperceptibly softer. The evening had the ephemeral quality of a caress, and Duval expanded himself to it, opened his city eyes, his city lungs, his city flesh to its grateful touch. "What a country to fight for!" he thought, his sensibilities made keen by just the right amount of wine. One more drink, he realized, and he might have spoilt it all, made himself ridiculous, by shouting *"Vive la France!"* But that was the way he really felt, he admitted privately.

Langlois purposely took a couple of steps out of his way to satisfy the whim of planting his boot on the scar which the whizzing motor-cycle wheel had left in the mud. "What the devil did that fellow have in his dispatch case?" he wondered. "I've never known a corporal to pass up a drink before, especially if it's free. Oh, well! We'll soon find out. Or, better still, we'll never find out."

Rounding the corner, the two men set off along the dirt road. They passed through a hamlet and over a stream, then up a wooded hill, falling one behind the other and picking their way through mud which lay rutted underfoot. The wood ended abruptly and neatly on the brow of the hill and they came out onto a low plateau of fields. The road led them, now walking side by side again, on an S-shaped route across the plateau. That, Langlois thought, was a pleasantly informal habit for roads to have. The slight elevation on which he found himself had the effect of bringing back the evening, which had already made one departure while he was in the wood. The curving of the road seemed to prolong the second leave-taking, and he was grateful to it for doing so.

On the far side of the plateau the road began to fall away downwards to a shallow valley. Langlois stopped at this point and turned for a last look at the twilight before moving down into the shadow that would soon be night. He gazed, but not as long as he wanted to, at the silent, lovely countryside upon which the afterglow of the sunset lay so peacefully.

"That's it," he formulated the thought, "peace, peacefulness. This that I am looking at is the very essence of it. I myself am the only evidence that the picture is an illusion." Turning away, and forgetful of Duval's presence for the moment, he looked down at his own uniform as if to verify its inharmoniousness. He saw the butt of his rifle pushing itself forward on the sling, he saw the bluish cloth on his knee, then his black army boot. He watched his boot far enough along on its first step to see that, on its second, he could bring it down again on the track of a motor-cycle wheel.

"What the devil did that corporal . . ." his thought began once more. But, before it had been completed, the question was this time answered by a bugle call which came up to him from the valley below.

It was sounding the assembly.

Had the notes of the bugle been resonant enough to carry some ten kilometres to the southward, they would have reached a divisional headquarters installed in the *mairie* of a town there, and they would have told the elder of two men alone in a ground-floor room that his orders were being obeyed.

He was a man in that period of life when appearance can be the most distinguished because although mature, it is not, at the same time, in the least decrepit. That he was aware of this could be seen in the decorousness of his uniform and in his way of wearing it; also in the correctness of his face, clean-shaved except for his moustache—a dash of white on a background of healthy pink. His eyes were blue, steady, and kindly, yet there was no hint there of the sanguine spirit which lay behind them. His mouth and chin were not quite strong, yet by no means were they weak. There were two rows of ribbons on his left breast, and on his right four little loops to which the star of a Grand Officer of the Legion of Honour could be attached for formal or ceremonial occasions. He was the Commander of the Fifteenth Army.

The other man, General of Division Assolant, did not at the first moment look as though he deserved the nickname by which he was known among the staffs—General Insolent. His attitude was too respectful, and it surprised the Army Commander, who had expected something different in this formidable subordinate, well known to him by report, unseen till today. The Army Commander looked at Assolant with an interest which he took little pains to disguise.

What he saw was a stocky body set firmly on a pair of solid cavalry legs, legs whose heels could meet but whose knees couldn't. He saw a uniform that was as unconventional as it was serviceable. The boots and spiral puttees were those of the rank and file, and the breeches had obviously come from an artillery quartermaster's stores. The tunic was second-hand but of good vintage; it looked enviably loose and comfortable. No one glancing at the uniform would have thought the wearer an officer until his eyes had chanced to light on the three stars worn in a triangle just above the cuffs. But the face was the face of a man of action, of a man who would be satisfied only with a position of command. It was distinctly of the type that is called strong; that is, it was hard, aquiline, brutal even. A close-cropped black moustache suggested that the slit beneath it was a mouth. The slit bent downwards at the corners, the moustache following along, and gave the impression of forcing the flesh of the jaws down with it. This helped to square off a chin that was already square. The nose was arched and prominent, and hairs bristled in a pair of impertinent nostrils. The eyes were bent downwards at the ends and accentuated the scornfulness of the expression. Thick black hair, brushed to an erect pompadour, began at a level which seemed a trifle too near the line of the eyebrows. The Army Commander did not miss the point that the pompadour was there to add height to a forehead which could have been higher.

"No," the Army Commander was thinking, "respectful attention does not suit him. It's temporary. He's all right, though. He'll do." Aloud he said:

"I think you served under me in Algeria, didn't you, Assolant?"

"Yes, sir. When you were chief of staff of the Nineteenth Army Corps. I was a major then, stationed at Aïn-Sefra."

"Ah yes, I remember now," said the Army Commander, then moved quickly away from the subject before it became apparent that he didn't remember at all. "This is what I came to see you about. I couldn't go into it over the telephone. By the way, are all your troops on the move?"

"All the ones that are available, except the 181st, and they should be getting off by now. My messenger had a hard time finding them. If I may be permitted to say—"

"Yes, yes, I know. But just wait till I've outlined the situation to you, then I'll hear you. Did you read this morning's *communiqué*?"

"I don't read *communiqués,* sir, I make them," said Assolant with a smile which he hoped would temper his impudence.

"Humph," said the Army Commander, ignoring both the smile and the impudence. "Well, a regrettable error has occurred, which I shall explain to you. You know that the C.-in-C. has for some time been complaining because the Pimple wasn't captured. Lately he's been insisting on it for a reason which I'll tell you presently. Several attempts to take it have been made, the last one yesterday morning by the Tirailleurs. They've all failed."

"No wonder, it's a miniature Gibraltar."

"The reason I asked about the *communiqué* is that it seems that through some mistake the Pimple was reported as having been taken yesterday. I don't want you to misunderstand me. I mean that that has nothing to do with—"

"I understand only too well, sir. You are going to ask me to take with my bayonets what a G.H.Q. ink-slinger has already inadvertently captured at the point of his pen!"

"That's exactly the conclusion I didn't want you to—"

"So it's come to this, has it?" Assolant went right on, warming to his pet phobia of the *communiqué.* The Army Commander, who had heard of these tantrums wherever Assolant's name was mentioned, decided to sample one for himself.

"So it's come to this, has it? G.H.Q. is no longer satisfied with attacks for the purpose of window-dressing their *communiqués.* They must now go the limit and make their infernal literature an objective in itself! I must read the *communiqué,* must I, because that's where I shall find my operation orders? My reputation as a fighting commander is secure enough in this army to warrant my refusal—"

"That's enough, general," the Army Commander's voice cut in drily. "No need for any dramatics here, and less than that if you will be so good as to listen to me."

"I must apologize, sir. I was carried away . . ."

"That's all right," the Army Commander said soothingly, and not entirely displeased with his subordinate's outburst. On the contrary, he admired the genuine fire of the man, a quality Assolant would need above all others for the job that was going to be assigned to him.

"Now this is strictly secret, this part of it I mean. It positively must not go further than your chief of staff, and not even to him unless you are sure of his discretion. A group of armies is forming on this front for an attack about three weeks from now which the C.-in-C. is determined to make a complete break-through. No attack can succeed, however, as long as the Boches hold the Pimple. As you know, it's a key position which can hold up and cripple our advance from the moment it starts. It must, therefore, be captured—and held. I saw Joffre a couple of days ago and he gave me formal orders to take the Pimple not later than the eighth, which is day after tomorrow—"

"But, Name of God, sir—"

"I've entrusted this job to two generals already and, as you know, they've both failed me. If there's one man in this army who can do it, you can, Assolant. I'd have called on you first, but you were up to your neck in it at Souchez."

"Well, I must say, sir, that you couldn't have called on me at a worse moment than the present. My division is cut to pieces, and what's left of it is absolutely exhausted. No, it's absurd. I'm in no condition to hold the Pimple, much less to take it. It's out of the question. Can't you get the C.-in-C. to assign some troops from G.H.Q. reserve to do the job? They'd be fresh and—"

"Yes, but they wouldn't be assault troops, and the success of this engagement is going to depend on assault troops."

"Well, mine aren't assault troops any more, and they won't be again until they've had a thorough rest and refitting."

"I can give you all the artillery you want, within reason."

"Artillery isn't going to be much use on the Pimple, sir. I know that place. It's a boil, not a pimple. It's honey-combed with subterranean machine-gun emplacements and it's connected with the rear by an underground passage having several exits. No. Shells just bounce off it; we've seen that before. It's a fortress."

"How do you propose to take it then?"

"I don't. I propose that the C.-in-C. take it with some of the troops he's going to use for the main attack. Why doesn't he use the Moroccans? They're good with the bayonet, which is what the place will have to be taken with, hand-to-hand. And besides, they're black and our losses will be heavy."

For a moment the Army Commander thought of protesting vigorously against a cynicism which could arouse such a repugnance in him. Then he realized that Assolant wouldn't know what he was talking about.

"He won't hear of it. I told you he expects a complete breakthrough. Do you know where the first day's objectives are? Twenty kilometres off. He won't use a man on these 'minor operations'—as he calls them—whom he has reserved for the offensive. They must be absolutely fresh so they can exploit the break-through—indefinitely, if necessary. He really thinks this attack will be the last one of the war."

"Well, the attack on the Pimple will be the last one of my division."

"Come, come, Assolant, you've got a crack division. It may be a bit tired, yes, but it ought to be refreshed and revived by the new class that has just joined it."

"Now, sir, you're not going to tell me that recruits are the proper material for a job of this kind . . ."

"Why not? They're young, strong, healthy—full of youthful ardour. All they dream about is making a bayonet charge. They won't even know the attack is a bit—hmm—a bit—unusual." The satisfaction the Army Commander derived from finding that last word was enough to dispel the slight distaste he felt for his own cynicism until Assolant tactlessly brought it home to him.

"That's true enough. And they'll never have a chance to find out."

"Which one of your units is in the best shape?" The Army Commander was again moving quickly away from a subject he didn't want to get entangled in.

"I suppose the 181st are. Owing to the messenger's stupidity, they should have gotten five or six hours' sleep," said Assolant, unconscious of his irony.

"Ah, the 181st, yes. I've seen them cited in Army Orders more than once. Put them in the first wave, then, and let your other regiments support them and consolidate the position."

"It might be done," said Assolant, half to himself.

"Of course it can be done. Anyway, it's got to be done. A first-class regiment which is, precisely at this moment, at the top of its form, made up half of recruits and half of seasoned veterans. The recruits will have the *élan*, the veterans will temper it. There couldn't be a better combination. And, as I told you, you can have all you want in the way of guns." The Army Commander knew he was being specious but he noted with satisfaction that his enthusiasm was beginning to infect Assolant, always susceptible to offensives, and to make him oblivious of the speciousness.

"I'd rather have rest than artillery just now, sir. Still, this is a new experience, to be offered unlimited ammunition. How many rounds of gas could I have? If the wind is right, I'd want to smother that Pimple in gas . . ."

"Call de Guerville in, and your chief of staff too—what's his name? Couderc. We'll go over it all thoroughly. Now no weakening in front of Couderc, no reservations. That sort of thing gets around."

"Don't worry, sir, my mind is made up. I'll take the Pimple for you, if you'll give me a free hand and plenty of grenades besides the artillery."

"I'll give you more than that, Assolant, after it's over, I'll give you a Corps. Do you think you could possibly snatch the Pimple off tomorrow?"

"Impossible, sir. But the day after, you'll have it for lunch. In fact you can put it in the *communiqué* now. Oh, no! I forgot. It's already in the *communiqué*. Well, I'll make it official. You may have heard, sir, that I've never said I'd take a position that I didn't take."

"And you may have heard that I've never made a promise I didn't keep."

"Yes, sir. And that leads me to wonder if . . ."

The Army Commander waited for the sentence to be completed, then realizing it wasn't going to be, he sought out Assolant's eyes. But he could not engage them, for they were staring with deliberate significance at the four little loops on his own jacket, the four little loops to which the start of a Grand Officer of the Legion of Honour could be attached for formal or ceremonial occasions.

"Perhaps . . ." said the Army Commander, concealing his contempt. "Now to work! Ask the staffs to come in, please." Then he added to himself: "What vulgarity! What a bounder! But he'll take the Pimple."

It was after dark, now. The sudden noise of their hobnailed boots striking on cobblestones, and its equally sudden ending, conveyed to each company of the 181st Regiment of the line, as it followed the preceding one, that it was crossing a main highway.

Didier, in Number 2 Company, was, perhaps, the only one of the three thousand rank and file who knew or cared where he was. And perhaps he didn't care so much either, for he was as tired and preoccupied with his aching muscles as the rest. To know his whereabouts, however, was an automatic function for a former frontier guard and night prowler, and that function continued to exercise itself in spite of his fatigue. Nor did it do so any the less keenly because it was dark. On the contrary, senses which had been submerged during the day-time but which had not, for that reason, failed to absorb impressions, came to the surface at night and intensified perceptions which, after all, had been deprived of only one of their number—and that one only partially in Didier's case—sight.

His sense of direction was a strong one; so strong, indeed, that it inclined him to be intolerant of those who did not have it and to be contemptuous of their laziness, to which he attributed their deficiency. Didier knew exactly where he was; it was a question of pride for him to know this. He knew the regiment had left the village shortly after nightfall on the same road by which it had entered. He knew he had walked up a hill. He had felt the open fields of the low plateau, and the road curving back through them. He had not been able to discern the outline of the wood into which he had been plunged abruptly, but he knew he was in a wood because he had felt space and sound confined about him. His sixth sense of the out-of-doors told him that these places were the same places he had passed through that morning. The order to break step, which was relayed back down the column as it approached the bridge over the stream, merely confirmed his certainty of his position, and the slight tonal change in the echo of the marching regiment, shortly thereafter, made him aware that he was now walking between walls of brick instead of walls of trees—the walls of the hamlet.

Thus, when he heard the boots of the company ahead of him strike on the cobblestones, resound on them for a space, and then go soft again, he automatically noted the fact that the regiment was cutting straight across the highway, past the Café du Carrefour, and that it was heading towards another sector of that front which it had, in his opinion, only too recently quitted.

"So, that's it," he said to himself. "Combat order, and this direction. Something doing, all right. The moon ought to be up soon and then I can get some idea of the lay of the land."

The regiment tramped on in silence. Even the newly joined recruits had had some of their spirits taken out of them by the marching and counter-marching. The others were too weary and dazed by unfinished sleep even to swear. There comes a degree of numbness in fatigue and exasperation which can be expressed only by a sullen silence. Five hours' sleep had been just enough to stiffen all those men's muscles but not enough to begin the work of reviving them. Equipment, boots, clothing had stiffened too and, worst of all, their boots had all been made a size too small by the swelling of their feet which they had hastened to release from them. . . .

The tail of the regiment vanished on the other side of the highway, enlarging at each step the gap between itself and the Café du Carrefour.

"To the trenches, again," said the old woman as the last hobnails of the column went silent on the continuation of the dirt road beyond the cobblestones—her cobblestones, as she was in the habit of thinking of them. She was sitting by her stove in the carefully shuttered café, sipping her bowl of black coffee. "To the trenches, again." She did not add "Poor devils!" because no such commiserating thought came into her head. She merely made an oral note of a fact. She had sat there, like that, for the better part of two years, ticking off to herself the mysterious and aimless movements of the armies which fluctuated around her crossroads. At first she had sat at her door and watched them. Then winter had driven her inside, and she had stayed on there, alone and without curiosity. There was, moreover, no need for her to come out any more for, as she soon discovered, she had learnt the significance of sounds and her ears now gave her almost as much news of what went on around the crossroads as her eyes had formerly done. She could, for instance, make a fair estimate of the size of a body of troops by the duration and spacing of its tramp. She knew the difference between the rumble of an artillery train and of a convoy of motor lorries, and she could tell whether the latter were loaded or empty. She could distinguish between the noises of a staff car and an ambulance and, more remarkable still, between a troop of cavalry and patrol of mounted military police. When questioned about it, she explained this last accomplishment by issuing the following ultimatum: "The keeper of a *bistro* must be able to smell police, or go out of business." Soldiers stopped off there at the Café du Carrefour on purpose to ask that question and to hear the reply. They were never disappointed, unless they happened to be police.

So she sat there, on the high-water mark of the war in those parts, sometimes within the heavy artillery zone, sipping her bowls of black coffee and enumerating to herself the various fragments of the army that beat up and down past her café, enumerating them not from any interest, patriotic or other, in military affairs, for she had none, but as so many good customers lost.

There was a rumble on the road outside which drew nearer as she finished her bowl of coffee. She gave the stove a poke or two, lighted a candle, and blew out the lamp. She moved over to a door and, candle in hand, paused for a moment, listening.

"Rolling kitchens," she said. Then she went down into her cellar and climbed into bed.

Colonel Dax was marching at the head of his regiment with the officer commanding its First Battalion, Major Vignon.

"It always looks like a distant thunderstorm, doesn't it?" the major said. He was referring to the effect of sheet lightning produced by the flares along the front and the reverberating overtone of gunfire.

"Not so distant, at that," the colonel answered in a voice that did not encourage any further small talk. The major took the hint and relapsed into silence. But why, he asked himself, had he been invited to walk with his chief? Was it merely for the purpose of keeping step with him?

"It's too bad," the colonel was thinking, "that you can't ask a man to walk with you without his jumping to the conclusion that you want him to talk to you too. Why can't I say to a man, 'Look here, I'm getting into a blue funk, as I always do at this point, and I really need your companionship. But it must be your silent companionship. I just want your bulk, your flesh near me, within touching distance. It takes the edge off my funk and helps a lot.' But Vignon wouldn't understand at all. He'd think I'm mad. He just hasn't the faculty for knowing what I'm going through now. If he suspected the crisis I'm getting near, he'd consider it his duty, probably, to pull his pistol and put a bullet through my head. As a matter of fact that's exactly why I need his presence so badly at these times. He hasn't any nerves."

He was right, too. Neither Vignon nor anybody else suspected for a moment that Dax, colonel of the 181st Regiment of the line, of the crack Assolant Division, next on the list for a general's stars and a promotion in the Legion of Honour, four times cited for bravery in Army Orders—no one suspected for a moment, so well did Dax conceal the fact, that he was in a state of fear which was rapidly turning into panic.

This fear of his was, so far as he knew, an idiosyncrasy, one which grew with each step forward he was now taking, one which became more acute every time he had to perform the duty of leading his regiment into the trenches. Once the men were in the trenches, the crisis would evaporate. He quite realized that his fears were unreasonable, even groundless, to a certain extent, but that did not make it any easier for him to master his rising terror. All he could think of was the compact mass of living, human, vulnerable flesh, strung out for two kilometres or so behind him. All he could think of was that in another half hour that whole two kilometres of compact, living, human, vulnerable flesh would be well within range of the German guns. The thought appalled him; it also prevented the saliva from forming in his mouth.

"Flesh, bodies, nerves, legs, testicles, brains, arms, intestines, eyes . . ." He could feel the mass of it, the weight of it, pushing forward, piling up on his defenceless shoulders, overwhelming him with an hallucination of fantastic butchery. A point of something formed in his stomach, then began to spread and rise slowly. It reached a level near his diaphragm where it became stationary and seemed to embed itself. He could not dislodge it or budge it up or down, but he recognized it for what it was: the nausea induced by intense fear.

"Three thousand men. My men. To run the gauntlet of open, registered roads with three thousand men. All neatly packeted for the slaughter. It's too much for one man to bear. I can't give the order to space out now or they'd know I'm in a funk. They're quick to sense it when an officer has the wind up. At any moment . . . This strain is intolerable. What an awful racket they make. Where the devil are those guides going to meet us? I'd look like a fool arriving with the regiment in single file, all spaced out. Think of it, I can't order the fire-zone intervals yet because it wouldn't look right. What a relief it would be though . . . Keep up appearances, no matter how many lives it costs. What torture this is, and that fool Vignon strolling along as if he's on a boulevard. Good old Vignon! Why can't I have some of his . . . Three thousand men, two kilometres of massed flesh. What a target! What's that light over there? . . ."

His imagination suddenly side-slipped, then righted itself in front of another mirage. He saw, way over there across the lines, German gunners, grotesquely helmeted figures, moving in quiet efficiency around their guns. He saw them ramming shells and charges home and closing the breeches, reading gauges, twirling wheels. He saw the great cannon, mouths still smoking from the previous salvo, rising, slow and erectile, until their muzzles were pointing at just the right spot in the sky. He saw the gun crews step down and away and put their hands to their ears, all except one man to each gun who was clutching a lanyard. He saw the officer raise a whistle to his lips. He saw all of them bow their heads a little and turn half away. He saw the lanyards go suddenly taut, looking as if they had jerked the guns backwards, so instantaneous was the explosion and recoil.

"Flesh, bodies, nerves, legs . . ." Things were getting all mixed up in his mind. It seemed to be filled with flesh, cloyed with the sweetish smell of flesh that is torn open and over which blood is pouring. It was his flesh, their flesh, lying about still alive, but dying, dying so slowly, dying so fast . . .

"Marching, marching, marching. Slowly, as in a dream. Slow march, funeral march . . .

"The naked road. The hard-surfaced road. The ditch too shallow to shelter even a rabbit from the whizzing, centrifugal metal . . .

"The neat, fatally compact mass on the fatally neat road, so neatly marked on the map . . .

"The neat German captain in his compact dugout. His fatally neat figures, the fatally neat co-ordinates of the naked road . . .

"The lanyards going suddenly taut, looking as if they had jerked the huge guns backwards . . .

"The rush of terrifying sound . . .

"Two kilometres of compact, living, human, vulnerable flesh behind him. Three thousand men paralyzed in their tracks . . .

"The blinding flashes of the detonations . . .

"Whizzing, centrifugal metal . . .

"Shambles . . .

"And then smoke, billowing, acrid smoke, settling slowly . . ."

The hallucinations reeled in his head, then fell to pieces as words broke in and shattered them.

"Why, it's the moon coming up. I thought it was a searchlight at first. I'd forgotten about the moon . . . Watch out for that shell-hole!"

"Ah! Thanks, old man, thanks." Even to Vignon, who was not usually given to noticing such things, his chief's tone of intense gratitude and relief seemed all out of proportion to the commonplace service of warning him not to step into a hole—so much so, indeed, that he could not help giving his companion a side glance. Dax, feeling the glance rather than seeing it, decided he'd better pull himself together and create a diversion of some sort.

"Pass the order back to put out pipes and cigarettes, will you, major? Also gas respirators at the alert." His voice sounded quite normal again, he was pleased to note; he was pleased to note, too, that Vignon seemed reassured by its customary tone of decisiveness.

"Silly," Dax thought, "but the mere issuing of a command always inspires confidence. It doesn't matter whether it is a necessary command, or even a correct one." Then, a little later, an afterthought came to him: "It inspires self-confidence even in the man who issues it."

The regiment tramped on. The moonlight made marching easier, not only because it showed up the irregularities of the road, but also because it brought shapes into being, gave the men something to look at. The exercise itself, too, had begun to make muscles, boots, and straps more limber. The equipment was no longer such a dead refractory weight. It was moving, now that it was alive with some suppleness of its own again, to the movement of bodies, arms, and legs. The rhythm of men on the march was gathering uniformity once more.

The order to stop smoking and to adjust their gas masks was a message the men understood well enough. Their understanding of the message was reflected in an almost imperceptible change in the rhythm of their marching. It was not so much that they quickened their pace (which they didn't), as that they tightened it—tightened it, perhaps, in response to an inner visceral contraction which swept, like the order, back over the advancing column. Waves of expectancy, of a kind of nervous expectancy, seemed to fluctuate over those pale, moonlit faces, and the men had a tendency to step on the heels of those ahead of them.

Major Vignon's distant thunderstorm was appreciably nearer now. It seemed to have been brought nearer, in one bound, by the order to stop smoking. The rumble of artillery was no longer a rumble, for it had broken up into its component parts of battery salvos. The Very lights were on the other side of a hill and they still produced their collective rather than their individual effect, an effect no longer quite like sheet lightning, however, because it now seemed to die out too slowly.

Colonel Dax cursed the moonlight. He knew it was childish of him to do so, but he couldn't help feeling that his regiment must be more visible to the enemy gunners. Anyway, he wanted to curse it, and he didn't care how unreasonable he was. Vignon, on the other hand, and most of the rank and file felt quite the other way about it. They welcomed a visibility which would spare them the minor, but none the less exasperating accidents of a relief made in pitch darkness.

"Hey there! 181st?" The hail was at the same time a challenge and a question; it came from behind the glow of a burning cigarette in the roadside shadow.

Colonel Dax swung round in his stride and shouted "Halt!" Then he added in an even louder voice: "Don't close up. Keep your intervals. Company commanders forward, at the double. Pass the word back!" He turned towards the roadside shadow.

"181st, yes. And put that cigarette out." The cigarette dropped to the ground and went out under a boot.

"Guides from the Tirailleurs, to take you in, sir. Lieutenant Trocard speaking."

"All right, lieutenant, you stay here with me and the headquarters details. Headquarters details, fall out on the right. Fix bayonets. Pass the word back to fix bayonets!"

A noise of clicking metal broke out at once and spread off down the road. Here and there the sound of a rifle breech being opened and closed showed that there were, as usual, some men still shy enough of firearms to postpone loading them until the last possible moment. Desultory machine-gun fire could be heard on the other side of the low hill, now and then a muffled crump. There was a certain amount of furtive sibilance in the air, a weird, ghostly sound to which no one paid any attention. A star shell, rising higher than the rest, burst and began to fall gracefully, outlining the crest of the low hill. Four doors banged suddenly, not quite in unison, but so near they made everybody start.

"Where the devil are they?" the colonel asked.

"Just a few paces down the road, sir. There are two batteries of seventy-fives there."

"Fools," said the colonel. "Don't they know there's a relief on tonight? They'll draw fire. Herbillon! Herbillon! Where's that adjutant?"

"Here, sir."

"Go down and see if you can get that idiot to stop firing till this relief is over. And tell him not to stir up any more trouble than he—"

The four doors banged again.

"Hurry up, please . . .Whose signal is that?" The colonel was pointing at three coloured lights which were rising from the other side of the hill. "Red over green over red. That's not ours, is it, lieutenant?"

"No, sir. That's the Boche signal for a barrage."

"Just as I thought. I knew that fool would start something."

To be exact, it was not just as the colonel thought, but more how the colonel felt. He was an old enough soldier to know that the greater part of those barrage signals were, as often as not, prompted by the nervousness of an outpost or a sentry who had heard a rat moving and thought he was going to be fallen on by a raiding party. The S O S rocket was a straw that a man could not resist clutching in a moment of panic. The lieutenant of Tirailleurs reminded the colonel of this, obliquely:

"It's a jumpy sector, sir, especially after these attacks we've been making on the Pimple."

"Here are the officers. Let's get started. Paolacci, are you there? Captain Charpentier? All right, lieutenant, any particular instructions?"

"Only this, sir. There's a chalk pit about a kilometre up the road, where the narrow-gauge track crosses it. The Boches shell it from time to time with five-nines. They've been quiet so far this evening, but that S O S will probably start things up. The shells usually come at thirty-second intervals. There's nothing to do but to try to rush it, a half a section at a time, between shells. You can't go round it, the ground's all chewed up and tangled with old wire. Are you ready, sir?"

"Yes, yes. You heard that, gentlemen. Act accordingly then, and positively no closing up. Report to my dugout in the Tranchée des Zouaves as soon as you have completed your reliefs. Password tonight is—what's the password, lieutenant?"

"Calais, sir."

"Calais. Back to your posts, gentlemen. Charpentier, you stay with me. I have a job for you. First Company forward, by sections!"

The column began to move again, this time in single file. The guides came out one by one from the roadside shadow and took their places with the company commanders as each one drew level with the headquarters group. Colonel Dax personally held up each detachment until the preceding one had created an interval to his liking. Then he released it: "All right, forward! Remember, no bunching up. Keep your distances!"

The machine-gun fire on the other side of the hill was no longer desultory. The interims between crumps were getting shorter, too, by the time half the regiment had disappeared up the road. The crest of the hill was now almost a constant outline against the festoons of star shells, and the air was filled with a profound uneasiness, an uneasiness which communicated itself to the men, made them fidgety and made their words, actions, and thoughts even, come in jerks.

Three bright-red flares rose perpendicularly and deliberately into the sky. They reached their zenith, paused there for an instant, then, losing their alignment, they began to sink sedately back to earth.

"Red over red over red," said the lieutenant of Tirailleurs. "That one's our S O S. It's going to be a bad night." Then he added to himself: "And I've got to pass that chalk pit twice . . ."

"At last they're spaced properly, and in single file," the colonel was thinking. "The worst is over, for me anyway. Soon they'll be between the protecting walls of the communication trench . . ." A feeling of deep relief came over him.

Eight doors banged, not quite in unison. They were answered by eight others, farther away. The first eight banged again . . . and again . . . and again . . .

The colonel was shouting at the top of his lungs now, trying to make himself heard: "Intervals . . . chalk pit . . . bunching . . . intervals . . ."

The chalk pit was a circular excavation situated in the southeast right angle formed by the intersection of the road and the narrow-gauge track. Had a balloon been placed in it, it would have looked like a good-sized egg in its nest. As you went up the road towards the Pimple sector, the chalk pit was on your right. It was near enough to the road for you to spit into, if you wanted to. Many of the men who passed it did want to do so, for it was an inviting spittoon. Also it had an evil reputation, and spitting into it was one way of expressing your opinion of it. Few did, however, because even the trivial act of spitting made it necessary to turn the head and the attention away, for an instant, from the exceedingly important business of getting past the place as quickly as possible. To turn your head aside, moreover, was to lose your acoustic orientation for a moment, and, no matter how short that moment might be, it might easily prove to be too long.

The regimental formation being in numerical order, the first section of Number 1 Company was the first to approach the chalk pit. The Tirailleur was walking in front, with the section strung out in single file behind him. Duval, who had been separated from Langlois and assigned to this section, was near the end of the line. As the detachment drew near the chalk pit, the Tirailleur's pace increased. He was crouching a little, and he walked as if he were treading barefoot on pebbles. He was tense throughout his body, the blood was throbbing in his head and pounding in his heart. His breath came quickly because he was too preoccupied to draw it down deeply into his lungs; it also tasted sour. His eyes were focused straight in front of him, but his head was turned slightly to the left so that his right ear could better catch any sound which came to him from that direction. He had adjusted his acoustic orientation nicely, and he was now straining to keep it attuned.

By the time the guide had reached the chalk pit, he was going at a jog-trot. The narrow-gauge line was crossed at a run, the section keeping pace with him and cursing him for a panicky fool. Even if their curses had reached him, he wouldn't have heard them, for his ears were busy with other sounds and his thoughts were too engrossing:

"Twenty metres more and I'll be past the place, safely past it. Fifteen . . . twelve . . . ten . . . eight . . ."

Already his run had slowed to a jog-trot, already his jog-trot was slowing to a walk, for he could see banks begin to rise ahead of him, the protecting banks of what would soon be a sunken road. The tenseness of his whole body eased a little, all except that of his ears. They were still straining to remain attuned to the first warning sound. . . .

A sibilance began high in the air above them. It had hardly begun before it had grown to a piercing whistle, it was hardly a whistle before it became a tremendous, fearful sound, rushing with terrific speed straight at the section. Everyone flattened out in his tracks, including Duval who had the feeling that something enormous was going to hit him. The terrifying thing seemed to pass right down the length of each cringing spine, then it went off with a roar to burst behind them. The explosion seemed to Duval to be strangely far away for something which had been right on top of him. He raised his head, preparing to get up now that it was all over. He had just time to note that the rest of the section was still flattened out on the ground when the air around him became alive with pieces of flying, humming metal. He flattened out again and listened to the flying metal being abruptly silenced by the earth into which it embedded itself.

"Baptism of fire," he said. He bestowed the accolade upon himself without self-consciousness but with a passing surge of pride.

The minute the flying metal had subsided, the men got up and made off along the road, without pausing to look back, all except Duval. He turned to look at the spot where he had been lying as if to preserve it in his memory. Then he ran after his section. He had a feeling that he was, somehow, a different person. Time, however, had to pass before he could define the change, and only then did it come to him that that spot on the road was the place where he had ceased to be a boy.

Lieutenant Paolacci, temporarily in command of Number 2 Company while Captain Charpentier was being detained by the colonel, approached the chalk pit in his turn. He had the reputation among the men of being strict but brave, among the officers of being conscientious to the point of foolhardiness. He prided himself on never flinching or ducking under fire if he could possibly help it. He also prided himself on the care he took of his men. So it was that, while most of the other officers contented themselves with giving the necessary orders and then letting their sections manage the chalk-pit obstacle as they chose, Paolacci considered it his duty to remain at the danger point himself so that he could personally direct the rushes of his men. This he did so skilfully from his position on the lip of the excavation that he was able to pass three sections safely through the shellfire— shellfire to which he himself was constantly exposed during the running of the gauntlet.

He was passing his men across a half section at a time. The last shell had burst on the other side of the track, a little to the side of the road. The range, he had noted, seemed to be a bit short of the track, so he eased his sections up nearer to it before giving the word to go. His last section was now lying in single file, prone to the road. He was waiting for one more shell.

"Are you ready there? After the next one then, when I give the word, run for it."

The next one came and burst squarely on the track.

"Go!" he shouted.

The file rose and started to run forward, crouching. The second half of the section rose at the same moment to move up closer to the track.

A whistling began high in the air above them. It came down with terrific speed, swelling to a tremendous roar. The men wavered, sensing a direct hit, then closed in together, instinctively seeking protection from each other's flesh. Paolacci watched them, transfixed, unable to utter a sound. He saw some of them sprawl headlong, some turn their backs and cower, others start to run, in any direction. He saw that in the few seconds it took the shell to come down, the two half-sections had, incredibly, managed to form into a confused bunch.

There were two detonations, so nearly simultaneous that they seemed to be one. The flash of the explosions photographed a fantastic picture of hurtling chaos on his mind. A chunk of jagged, revolving metal was travelling with speed and precision in Paolacci's direction. It tore through his pelvis, carried his whole right hip away, and knocked him over the edge into the chalk pit. He tumbled down, down, down. . . .

When the smoke cleared away no one was left to see that, where the section had been, there was now nothing but two tangent, smouldering holes in the centre of some scattered bundles of motionless clothing.

The relief had been completed by midnight, and the high tide of a double congestion of men in the trenches was already ebbing fast. Thirty-two men of the 181st had been killed on the way in, and seventeen Tirailleurs were being killed on the way out. None of them were killed as a result of the crowding caused by the other regiment, but everybody, from the two commanding officers down, entered into the passing and automatic sophism of blaming the casualties on the congestion, notwithstanding. Reason told them that the chances of a certain man being killed at any given moment were the same, whether he was standing alone or in a group. Reason, however, was not uppermost, but feeling was. And feeling was too strong to take heed of the paradox it engendered, the paradox of men rushing together for protection in the face of shellfire, and their being convinced that if they were in a group, no matter how invisible to the enemy, they would attract shellfire and suffer the more from it.

The 181st had lost thirty-two men, the Tirailleurs seventeen. It wasn't a bad record for a relief made during a heavy bombardment, nor did it make the slightest difference to the conduct of the war. Every day and every night men were being killed at the rate of about four a minute. The line remained the same, everything remained the same—uniforms, equipment, faces, statures, men. Men standing at the same posts, listening to the same sounds, smelling the same smells, thinking the same thoughts, and saying the same words. Forty-nine men had been killed, and one set of collar numerals had been replaced by another. Rats weren't interested in collar numerals, so it made no difference to them either.

Intelligence officers, on the other hand, were interested in collar numerals, interested in learning those of the troops opposite and in concealing those of their own.

Towards one in the morning, when the artillery duel had died down somewhat, Captain Charpentier sent for Paolacci. A quar-

ter of an hour later Lieutenant Roget entered the captain's dugout to tell him that Paolacci could not be found.

"Yes," said Charpentier. "I heard one of his sections got it at
the chalk pit. I saw some bodies there when I passed. He's probably gone back to see about them. Anyway, we're short of officers and I can't wait. So you'll have to do. By the way, have you
ever been on patrol before?"

"Only once, sir, when I was in the ranks."

"Well, you'd better take Didier then. He's an old hand at it.
The colonel wants a reconnaissance patrol to go out. Hand me
that map over on the bunk there. Look at this, that's the Pimple.
This is our frontage, see, from here to here. There's the Boche
wire, about five hundred metres or so from our line. You are to
go out on the left and work your way down to our right boundary where you can come in through our post, see it here, Post
Number 8. Division is very anxious to know the depth and condition of the German wire. This map is not up to date and the
Tirailleurs report that the Boches have been strengthening their
wire. That's your main job, to find out about the wire. But you
must also look for any Boche outposts. This is really just as important as the other because we want to know where they are so
we can knock them out of action before the attack. The moon is
bright, so if you find any you shouldn't have any trouble placing
them exactly. Take a luminous compass and use the Pimple's
summit for a landmark. And don't forget to bring back identifications of any German bodies you find."

"Yes, sir. But how will I know where to re-enter my own
line?"

"Let me see. You ought to be out about two hours. All right
then, two hours after you leave I'll have Number 8 Post send up
flares. One red flare at five-minute intervals until you come in."

"And how many men shall I take?"

"Take two, besides yourself. Remember, this is a reconnaissance patrol, pure and simple. You are to avoid a fight at all
costs and you're not to let the Boche get wind of you, if you can
possibly help it. Go out, reconnoitre, and report, that's all. But
do it thoroughly. You can depend on Didier. He's an ace at that
sort of thing."

"If you don't mind, sir, I'd rather take someone else."

"What's the matter with Didier?"

"Well, er—er. Well, if it's the same to you, sir, I'd rather take some other man."

"No, it isn't the same to me at all. As a matter of fact, Roget, if it weren't that the report had to be made by an officer, I'd be only too glad to put Didier in charge of the patrol. What have you got against him, anyway?"

"Me? Nothing. But what has he got against me, that's what I'd like to know?"

"Well, what has he got against you?" Charpentier had often wished he could put his finger on just what it was that officers (including himself) as well as the men seemed to have against this lieutenant.

"How should I know? I suppose because I was given a commission and he wasn't. We used to bunk together, you know, and it's quite contrary to custom, my being assigned back to the same company again. I don't know how that happened. He probably resents my being an officer now. He's a sullen, envious fellow. I just thought that if you . . ."

"That may be. But he's a first-class scout, and you're going to take him along. You may be very glad you did before the night's over. Now study that map carefully. Learn it by heart."

As the moon moved higher into the sky, the shadow it cast moved lower on the side of the chalk pit down which Lieutenant Paolacci had fallen. Most of the bottom of the chalk pit was still in the shadow, a pestilential-looking place. Had Paolacci turned his head from where he lay on top of and athwart an entrance to a gallery, he might have seen the reflection of the moon in the pool of stagnant water which covered the floor of the pit. Much as he may have enjoyed seeing the moon, even in reflection, he did not turn his head. He did not do so for several reasons, none of which took form as such in his mind. First, the effort was too much for him. Second, the mere moving of his head already made him vomit each time he had tried it. Third, he didn't know there was a reflecting pool of water below him; in fact, he thought he was on the bottom of the pit as it was. Fourth, he

could feel that his left check was wedged against some obstruction, something that smelt of horse dung.

"Tell me," he said out loud and discursively, "tell me if you
please, how it happens that there is horse dung in the bottom of
this pit? How could a horse get in here? Easily enough; the way
I did. But how did I get here? How could the horse get out
again? He couldn't, the sides are too steep. Then there must be
a horse down here somewhere. That's obvious."

The simplicity of his logic, the clarity of his mind amazed him.

"This is a real pleasure," he went on, "to find my thinking
apparatus working so beautifully. I must make the most of it
and dispose of some of my perplexities once for all."

He fell to hunting for his perplexities, but he couldn't find any
of them. They were there, he knew, but just once out of reach,
exasperatingly so.

"Well, let's start over again. Where was I? Ah, yes, here it is.
Horse dung, horse dung . . . But how the devil did I get here?
Confound it, it isn't working at all now. All mixed up. Wait a
minute and it'll clear up again. . . ."

He moved his head, trying to shake the confusion out of it,
then choked. Bile welled up into his mouth and trickled out the
corners. He tried to spit, but couldn't, so he was forced to swallow the rest. Darkness closed in on him and he was unconscious
again.

The moon moved higher into the sky, the shadow moved
lower on the side of the chalk pit. It moved imperceptibly across
the figure of the lieutenant, then dropped away quickly from the
roof to the threshold of the gallery entrance. A stone came
bouncing down the side of the chalk pit and fell into the pool
with a plop. There was a rustle of scurrying rats.

Paolacci came to with the smell of horse dung in his nostrils.

"Ah, yes. A horse down here somewhere. But he can't get out
unless I help him. I'll see about that later, not now. Ha-ha-ha-
ha-ha . . ."

The thought of a horse down there had suddenly and inexplicably become a tremendously funny one. Paolacci was roaring
with laughter, a laughter which came from his throat only. Imperceptibly as the movement of the shadow, Paolacci's laughter

was transformed into tears, and from tears into deep, intestinal sobs. These sobs shook him in a way the laughter hadn't. A fiery pain took form in his left shoulder and he raised his hand to it. It came back stained and sticky. Panic burst in him.

"Help! Help! I'm hit. Help! Help! Stretcher-bearers! Get me out of this! Down here! For the love of Christ! Help! Help! I'm dying. I'm all alone. Down here! Here, in the chalk pit! Jesus! Stretcher-bearers! Help! Help! Help! . . . Help . . ."

His shrieks echoed back and forth on the walls of the chalk pit. Each time he paused long enough to hear an echo, he mistook it for the voices of rescuers and redoubled his cries.

The moon faded from his sight, and he was still for a while. A rat climbed noiselessly up the jamb of the gallery entrance and looked at Paolacci for a long time. Then it turned and went down again. Two shells burst along the opposite wall, and a shower of gravel fell upon the unconscious lieutenant. . . .

Paolacci began to feel the pain in his shoulder. He also felt a lump between his shoulder blades. He realized he wanted to get up and climb out of the pit, then waited for the desire to become more impelling. While waiting, his right hand began to move in exploration. It came in contact with the obstruction wedged against his cheek. He pushed, and it gave way, the smell of horse dung receding with it. He moved his head gingerly to look at the thing. It was his own boot, unmistakably. But how did it get there, near his face? He formulated the will to straighten his leg out, but there was no response. His hand moved downwards, feeling over his own body. He could feel his body, but his body, below the third or fourth button of his jacket, didn't seem to feel his hand. He pinched, and his pinch closed on air. He groped for his thigh and couldn't find it. Instead, his hand entered an enormous, sticky cavity which seemed lined with sharp points. . . .

Gradually, with weary patience and a persistence which was constantly being thwarted by waves of silent delirium, he untangled the chaos of his life. He had been hit by that shell. One wound in his left shoulder and another, a much worse one, in his right hip. In falling into the chalk pit, his leg had been buckled back diagonally under him, and he was now lying on it, with his left cheek against his own heel.

"I must have been standing in some horse dung," he said. The voice, which he did not recognize as his, startled him, it sounded so loud, but his surprise lasted only a moment, for death was bringing its own anæsthetic with it. Fever was rising in him, giving comfort to his body and ineffable peace to his mind. The terror of being alone and helpless had gone. He closed his eyes the better to appreciate the delights of his hallucinations. . . .

Later his eyes opened, and his jaw relaxed.

Later still, when the shadow cast by the moon was rising again on the side of the chalk pit, a rat climbed noiselessly up the jamb of the gallery entrance and watched Paolacci for a while. Then it stepped forward daintily, jumped onto the lieutenant's chest and squatted there. It looked to the right and to the left, two or three times, quickly, then lowered its head and began to eat Paolacci's under lip.

Lieutenant Roget went down the trench, looking for Didier. He found him standing on the firing-step, his rifle lying in a groove across the parapet, a little pile of hand grenades on one side and a Very pistol on the other. Another figure sat huddled on the firing-step, a figure which coughed at the lieutenant, as he came around the corner of the traverse, instead of challenging him.

"What's the matter, you two asleep?" said Roget.

"Yes," said Didier, recognizing the voice.

"Sir," said Roget.

"Sir," Didier replied, emphasizing his reluctance.

The figure answered with another cough.

"Well, I've got something that'll wake you up. You two are going out on patrol with me."

"Not him," said Didier.

"Why not?"

"Because he's got a cough."

"That's too bad. And I suppose you've got a pain in your tail?"

"Yes, I have. But that's different."

"How's it different?"

"Because my pain in the tail is silent and his cough is a big noise in the face."

"Well, I don't care which end you're indisposed in, you're both going on patrol. Now get started, will you? We haven't any time to lose."

"Listen, Pierre, you know as well as I— "

"You Pierre me once more and I'll put you under arrest. I've had enough of it, see?"

"All right, lieutenant, I was only trying to tell you. You know how Marchand got killed, don't you?"

"Yes, on patrol. And served him right too, he was almost as insolent as you are."

"Yes, on patrol. But why? Because he had a cough. So he coughed in a Boche's face that night, see? Well, that was the last cough he ever coughed. The Boche cured him of it on the spot. And that cough cost us three more men, two wounded and another killed, when they started to bomb us."

"All right then, have it your way. But get a move on and stop jabbering. Get somebody else, anybody you want."

"I'll bring Lejeune. He's been out with me before. He's a good man."

Didier pulled his rifle in and stepped down. The man with the cough replaced him and set his rifle carefully in the groove.

"The S O S rockets are here," said Didier. "They're not to be fired except on orders from an officer. Understand? We'll send up a man to take my place." The use of the "we" pricked Roget. Decidedly, this fellow needed taking down a peg. But how was it to be done? Roget's vanity prevented him from admitting it in so many words, but he knew none the less that he had never gained an ascendency over Didier.

The man with the cough was staring into no-man's-land as the other two went off along the trench in the direction of their dugouts. The lieutenant was walking in front and talking to Didier over his shoulder:

"Reconnaissance patrol. Only three of us. German wire and machine-gun posts. Identifications of bodies, if possible. Go out on the left. Come in through Post Number 8 on our right. They'll send up red flares. Get Lejeune and get ready. Then go up to Number 8 and see that they understand. Then report to my dugout. And warn all the sentries on your way back that a patrol will be out. We'll tell the rest of them as we go along to the left.

Now hurry up. And by the way, see to it that you make your behavior more respectful to me, especially when there are others around. None of that Pierre stuff, understand?"

"Yes, Pierre. I mean, sir."

"I'm not fooling now. I mean it. It just makes things worse for me. And it will for you too, if you're not careful. This is my dugout. Report back here."

Roget bent down, stepped sideways into the wall of the trench and disappeared.

"He looked as if he was bowing to me," Didier said to himself. "What a louse he is, with his little gold stripe. Why the devil didn't they send the Corsican with us? He's the kind of man you want on patrol."

Didier went on down the trench until he saw two boxes of rifle ammunition protruding from a niche in the wall. He passed the boxes, stooped suddenly, and also disappeared from the trench. He went down three or four steps, groping, until his hand touched a blanket. The blanket felt damp, slightly oily and heavy. He pulled it aside and adjusted it carefully behind him. There was a dim light, far below him, a smell of charcoal and of men, and the sound of voices. He went down thirty or forty steps more and came into the main gallery of the dugout. It was warm and comfortable there, and it seemed very remote from the war. A double tier of bunks lined one wall. These were occupied mostly by N.C.O.'s. The men were stretched out on the floor. All of them were asleep, except a group of three who were sitting around a candle stuck in a wine bottle, talking. The dugout was not crowded, and most of the men who were there were old-timers. Didier, who always read the signs, put two and two together and noted that the recruits were being used for the working parties, ration details, and other front-line duties. This was as it should be.

"What's new?" said one of the men near the candle.

"Patrol. Where's Lejeune?"

"He's that fog-horn, down the end there." Turning back to his companions, he went on, ". . . No, by God, they're not as mad as that. Why, we haven't had any rest. I heard we were going in for a day or two while—"

"Well, why have we taken over only half a regimental frontage then? The same one the Tirailleurs did for their attack. We're as thick as fleas around here. And now this patrol . . ."

Didier had found Lejeune and was working over him, trying to wake him up.

"Come on, show a leg. We've got to go on patrol."

"What?"

"You heard. Patrol."

"I can't. I'm all in. Get somebody else. Leave me alone."

"Come on, get up, will you? I can't get anybody else. Captain's orders. You and me and the lieutenant."

Lejeune began to skirmish for time:

"Who? Paolacci?"

"No. Roget."

"That bastard!"

"Yes. Come on. We're late now."

"What time is it?"

"About two-thirty." Didier, joining in the skirmish, purposely advanced the hour.

"Two-thirty, eh . . ."

"Yes, two-thirty. And if you don't get a move on, we'll get caught by the dawn and have to spend the day out there." Didier gave Lejeune a slight kick. Because of his impatience, the kick turned out to be less slight than he had intended.

"If that's the way you're going to act about it, you know where you can stick your patrol," said Lejeune.

"And if that's the way you're going to act about it, you know where I'm going to stick my bayonet. Come on, Paul, get up. I asked the lieutenant specially for you."

"Oh, you did, did you. Nice of you that was." Where shakes, commands, and even kicks had failed, flattery was successful and Lejeune responded to the compliment by finally heaving himself to his feet, not, however, without further protests.

Didier went back to the space near the candle and began to make himself ready. This he did with the solemnity and precision of a ritual.

He took off all his equipment, including his gas mask and trench helmet, and stacked them by his rifle in a corner. He took a knitted cap and a polished steel mirror out of his haversack and put them aside on a shelf. He emptied all his pockets, pausing to light his pipe, and put the contents into the haversack. He unwound his puttees all the way down, then scratched his calves for a full minute. He undid his boot-laces and tied them again, carefully knotting them. He put his puttees back on and tied them with a knot, too. He looked around the floor of the dugout until he found what he wanted—a cork. He burnt the cork in the candle and began blacking his face and hands methodically, stopping now and then to look at the results in the steel mirror. When he was through, he impaled the cork on the tip of his bayonet, caught Lejeune's eye and informed him by a gesture that the cork was at his disposal. He looked around once more until he again found what he wanted, this time a revolver holster. He took the revolver out, unwound the cord attached to its butt, then held it up so the revolver could dangle freely and straighten out the cord. He opened the noose in the cord, passed it over his left shoulder and under his right armpit, then pulled the noose in and caught it tight by slipping the revolver back through as if it were a stitching needle. He yanked the gun up and examined it with care. He cracked it open and dumped out the shells, then looked down the barrel. He snapped it shut again, pulled the trigger several times, sighted it on the candle flame and clicked it once or twice more. Satisfied that it was working properly, he reloaded it after having examined the shells. He took some more shells from the pouch near the holster and put them in the left pocket of his jacket. The gun went into his trousers pocket. He put on the knitted cap, looked at himself once more in the mirror, knocked out his pipe, then put the mirror and pipe away in his haversack and closed it.

"If the sergeant wants his gun," he said to the group near the candle, "tell him I borrowed it. He can have my rifle in the meantime. Here are my things, here. My personal belongings are in the haversack. There's no money, so you needn't start fighting over it as soon as I go. Anyway, I'll be back. Ready, Paul? Come on, then. We'll pick up some bombs at the lieutenant's dugout when we come down again."

"Say, I thought this was a reconnaissance patrol."

"So it is, but we're going to take some bombs just the same."

"Why not some machine guns too."

"Come on, shake a leg. See you later, you dugout pimps."

"Good luck!"

"Bring me a spiked helmet!"

"Come and get it yourself."

"Keep your rump down, Paul, or you'll draw a barrage of heavies."

"And don't tread on my feet when you come in."

"Good luck! . . . As I was saying. The doctor says to him, 'What a beauty! Where d'you get it?' It was a beauty too, I saw it myself. That long. 'I got it from the cannon,' he says, 'the 155-mm.' 'You must be a very passionate young man,' says the doctor. 'But I wasn't thinking of your dose just then. There's only one way to get that, you know.' 'Yes, sir,' says the fellow. 'There was a man in my squad who had it and I must have caught the infection off the gun.' What a fathead! And did the doctor roar! Take it from me, boys, calomel ointment's all right against the syph, but you can't be too careful when it comes to . . ."

Lieutenant Roget saw the flame of his candle waver and knew, even before he heard the footsteps, that his gas blanket had been pulled aside and closed again. He put the bottle he had been drinking from under his overcoat on the bunk.

"Well, you took your time about it," he said.

"It's only ten past two," said Didier, guessing.

"Anything to report?"

"Yes. Sentries are all warned, down to here. There's some shelling going on up there on the right, also some gas. Number 8 will start sending up flares at four-thirty. But they'll send them up at ten-minute intervals, not five. And not from their post, but fifty metres to the left of it . . ."

"I see. Perhaps they'd rather go to a cinema instead."

"The sergeant says every five minutes is too much. It's sure to start the artillery going again. Ten minutes is plenty too, he says. It'll give the position of his post away and he figures that after the third or fourth flare there won't be any post left. So he's going to send a man down the trench to shoot the flare off at a distance. All we have to do is to bear to the left of it as we come in."

"Quite a strategist, that sergeant. What's his name?"

"I don't know."

"You're a liar, but it won't do him any good. I'll get it later. Did he have any other observations to make?"

"No," said Didier, privately relishing the malice of his evasion. He had omitted to tell Roget that the sergeant had covered himself by getting permission for the changes from his company commander.

"All right, you two go up and get some bombs. I'll join you directly."

"We've got the bombs."

"Where are your gas masks?"

"You don't take gas masks on patrol," said Didier. "They get in the way, get caught in the wire . . ."

"Well, go ahead anyway. I'll be up in a minute."

Didier and Lejeune climbed up the dugout steps, passed the gas blanket and stood on the other side of it, waiting.

"He's fortifying himself," said Didier. "See the bottle under his coat?"

"No, but the place stank like a *bistro*."

"You can always tell when he's had a few. He gets sarcastic."

"He might have passed it round, the swine."

"There isn't enough even in a barrel to give him guts. Listen, Paul, if he gets funny, or starts kicking up a noise . . ."

"I understand."

Lieutenant Roget felt fine, just about right, he thought. His condition was so nearly perfect that he reasoned he ought to have one more shot of the cognac to go on, and now that those two were out of the way, he could take it. He reached for the bottle under his coat and took a long pull at it, then set it down on the table. He lighted a cigarette and looked at the map again.

"Very simple," he thought. "Go out up here where the beginning of the wood marks the boundary, crawl over to the German wire, there, then along it for a few hundred metres until we reach this old communication trench, and that will lead us to Post Number 8. In fact, Number 8 is behind a block in that trench, about fifty metres from our front line."

It was simple, too, on the map. The nice smooth strip of white, which was no-man's-land. The German wire, neatly marked by double rows of x's. The outskirts of the village that straddled the German wire and then, farther on, the thin, winding, blue line which joined the two fronts and represented the unpossessed communication trench. There were no shell-holes marked on the map, no corpses, no stray wire, no obstacles of any kind. There were no symbols for the men who stood behind that wire, nor any signs to indicate that they were armed with rifles, bombs, machine guns, and flares.

"It'll be easy," said Roget out loud, and belched. He picked up the bottle to put it away, felt that there was still some liquid in it, and held it up to the candle for appraisal.

"For when I come in," he said, and continued to look at it. By the time he decided to stop looking at it, he found, as he had expected, that his mind had changed.

"Might as well," he said. His tone had that mixture of apology and joviality which it would have had if some other person were present. He tossed the empty bottle onto a bunk, trod on his cigarette and blew out the candle, then went up the dugout steps, bumping the braziers and boxes there and cursing them. He found Didier and Lejeune sitting on the firing-step.

The three men made their way along the trench, Roget in front, Didier in the rear. The lieutenant was stepping out, and it wasn't long before he had left the other two behind, for they were delayed in each traverse by stopping to warn the sentries that the patrol was going out. Sometimes the sentries were a bit thick and Didier had to waste time explaining what it was all about. He didn't consider it a waste of time at all, but Lejeune did. He was for hurrying on and trying to keep up with the lieutenant. Didier, however, insisted on seeing that the sentries understood.

"Go ahead, if you want to," he said. "But I'm going to see that these fatheads know we're out. One of the most dangerous parts of a patrol, you know, is trying to get back into your own line. And we might be driven in anywhere."

Not far from the left boundary they came around the corner of a traverse and found Roget rooted there, his arms raised over his head, furiously cursing the sentry. The sentry's bayonet was brushing the lieutenant's chest.

"Calais! Calais!" said Didier, taking in the situation at a glance.

"All right," said the sentry. "Come through. Where are all you Senegalese coming from? Here's a fellow all dressed up like an officer and he doesn't know the password. He can talk French, too. Say, send the sergeant up, will you, you'll find him down the line there. I know my orders. I'm no fool, you know . . ."

"As it happens, you are this time," said Didier. "We're not Senegalese in spite of our faces. Put your bayonet down, this is our lieutenant. We're going out on patrol, and we'll be out a couple of hours. So watch what you're doing, will you. Understand? I said, do you understand?"

"Yes, I understand. But how was I to know? Orders are orders, you know, and the officers make them themselves. A black-faced devil comes around the corner and when I challenge him . . ."

"All right, forget it. You only did right. Remember we're going to be out there. And remember to tell your relief."

Roget had gone on ahead again. They found him, a few minutes later, in conversation with another officer, and Didier was pleased to hear the officer saying:

". . . it wasn't my sentry anyway and it certainly isn't his fault if you forget the password."

"Here they are," said Roget. "Didier, you look around for a place to get through the wire."

"Perhaps the captain knows a place . . ." Didier began.

"Yes, I do. Come along and I'll show you."

They retraced their steps through two traverses. In the third one they found half a dozen men, three of them standing near a machine gun which was on the parapet.

"There's a lane through the wire here," said the captain. "That gun is pointing to the opening and straight down the lane."

"Thanks, Sancy," said Roget. "Keep your fingers off that coffee grinder till we get out of the way. All right, you two. Come on!"

All three got their revolvers into their hands, unbuttoned the flaps of the pockets which held the bombs, then one by one, with Roget leading, they climbed the parapet and made quickly for the opening in the wire, crouching. They crawled into the lane and followed it as it led them obliquely away from the front line for a few metres. Half-way through the wire, the lane turned at right angles and led them obliquely in the other direction. Just when they thought they should be coming out of it, they found themselves wired in. Roget started to swear.

"Keep quiet," Didier whispered. "It's only a block in the lane. Follow me. We can crawl through here." He went off down a slight incline, wriggling under the wire, laboriously detaching the barbs from his uniform when it got caught. As soon as he was clear, he raised himself on his knees and looked around, then made for a nearby shell-hole. Standing in the shell-hole, he examined his surroundings with care, noting the position of the wood behind him and its relationship to his own and the German line. He was looking attentively at the moon when Roget and Lejeune joined him.

"Who are those two?" asked Roget, pointing to two figures already occupying the shell-hole and apparently asleep.

"Can't you smell? They're dead."

Lejeune went over to them.

"Tirailleurs," he reported.

"Come on then!" said Roget, getting up and starting to walk off briskly, as he thought, towards the German front. He was feeling very fine indeed, very brave and very clever. The cognac had given him a sense of being disembodied and immune. He wished he had a rifle, for he wanted to lead a bayonet charge, a bayonet charge by moonlight. The idea appealed to him immensely. . . .

"Hey! Not that way!" said Didier. "You'll be back in our wire again in a minute. This is the way over here. Keep the moon on your right. And crawling. We're not in the Champs Elysées."

"Well, those two are," said Roget, laughing at his own joke.

"And we'll be joining them soon, if we keep on making all this noise," Lejeune added, shooting the lieutenant a glance.

Roget oriented himself and moved off over the lip of the shell-hole, Didier and Lejeune falling in behind him so that he made the point, they the wings, of an inverted V. Roget continued to set a fast pace, even when crawling, so fast, in fact, that Didier pulled himself up to him twice and caught him by the ankle. The last time, he drew level with him and whispered in his ear:

"Not so fast. We're getting near their wire. I think that's it over there. Yes, now you can see it. Take it slowly, a few metres at a time, and then stop and listen. They may have a patrol out too. And if they're doing any wiring, they're sure to have a covering party out here somewhere."

Roget belched.

"And cut that out too. You make a devil of a lot of noise. Watch where you're going, and don't kick tins and things."

"Who d'you think you're talking to?"

"You. If you can't run a patrol properly, I will. I know my business, and I'm not going to have my head blown off just because you don't."

"You'll hear more about this later."

Didier said nothing, and Roget started off again, bearing a little to the right. Didier waited for Lejeune to come up with him. There were several corpses scattered about and they stank.

"What's the matter?" Lejeune whispered.

"Plenty. Roget's drunk and doesn't give a ———. We'll be lucky to get out of this without a mess of some kind."

"How about . . .?"

"No. He may sober up."

Roget was working along the German wire now, with Lejeune behind him and Didier a couple of metres off on the flank. The Pimple loomed on their left, an enormous-looking bulk, cutting cleanly into the moonlit sky. They felt as if they were crawling on its base; actually they were about three or four hundred metres from it.

Roget belched.

Instantly a flare went off, so close it seemed as if they had fired it themselves. A machine gun started to rattle, and they lay still as death, pressing themselves into the unyielding earth. The flare burst right over them, the machine gun was firing over them too, and they felt huge and naked on a naked plane. They held their breaths and their minds were emptied of all thought.

The flare went out and the machine gun, after two or three more bursts, stopped firing. Didier could hear a little bunch of shells travelling by quietly, high overhead.

The German wire began to bulge and to force them over in

the direction of their own line. They crossed a series of shell-
holes linked by shallow trenches. The earth seemed quite fresh
to Didier, and he wondered if Roget had noticed it. A little farther on, they came to an area thick with French corpses. The
smell was nauseating. Roget started belching again, speeding up
his pace, going forward heedless of the noise he was making and
reckless of the danger he might be running into.

Didier started to close in on him from his flank position and
succeeded in catching him by the leg.

"Name of God! Don't do that!" It was almost a shriek.

"Another sound out of you, and I'll kill you," Didier
whispered.

"Well, don't sneak up on me like that then. It's enough to
make anybody jump out of his skin. Hurry up and get me away
from these bodies. I'm going to be sick."

"Go ahead and vomit, you swine, and be quiet about it. We're
right in front of a strong point here."

There was a low gurgling sound while Roget gave up his cognac and spread it in a puddle under his nose.

"Come over in this direction," said Didier.

They drew away from the bulging German wire and moved
out towards the centre of no-man's-land. They gathered for a
while in a shell-hole to take stock of things and to give Roget a
chance to pull himself together. Then they went on again, in V
formation, Didier on the lieutenant's left now, Lejeune on his
right. Roget's feeling of immunity had flowed out of him soon
after the flowing out of his liquor. He now had an imperious
need to be done with the patrol and to get back to the safety of
his own dugout. His sense of well-being had evaporated, leaving
him defenceless and afraid in a hostile world. His nerves came
to life again from their alcoholic anæsthesia. They were jumpy
and hard to control.

A large mound of what looked like kindling wood appeared
in front of them. Roget turned and threw lumps of earth at his
companions, the signal to close in. They lay on their stomachs
and put their heads together. Roget's breath was sour.

"What d'you make of that?" he asked Didier.

"Ruins of some houses."

"All right, then, Lejeune, you work around the right of the pile. Didier will come with me on the left. We'll meet on the other side."

"Not on your life," said Didier. "Split a patrol? You're crazy!"

"Shut up. Do as you're told, Lejeune."

"Don't do it, Paul, it's madness."

Roget turned his wrist slightly and Didier found himself looking into the muzzle of the lieutenant's gun. Lejeune saw the movement too and checked a remark he was on the point of making. He searched for Didier's eyes, the question he wanted to ask him plainly to be seen in his expression. Didier, however, was staring down the barrel of the revolver, his own weapon uselessly pointing away from under his left armpit. Lejeune was baffled. He decided the safest way out of the dilemma would be to obey. He started to crawl off to the right of the mound.

When Roget could no longer hear Lejeune, he dropped the aim of his gun and smiled—an unpleasant smile—then started off towards the left. Didier followed him, straining to make all his senses alert, and silently raging at the lieutenant for making the double blunder of splitting the patrol and leading him into the zone between the ruins and the enemy wire. Roget, too, soon felt that he had made a mistake in getting himself into the corridor, however short it might turn out to be. He stopped to borrow a couple of bombs from Didier and put them in his breast pockets, leaving the flaps unbuttoned, then went on again, taking infinite pains not to disturb the loose debris of the ruined houses. The place was in shadow there, and no matter how careful he was, it was impossible not to make some noise in the mass of litter which was strewn about. The lieutenant's heart was, therefore, constantly in his mouth. Didier wondered what they would find on the other side of the mound. The signs all indicated that there would be some kind of outpost thereabouts. In fact, he was surprised and made increasingly anxious by the fact that they hadn't yet seemed to disturb anything but loose bricks and timbers. Was he being led straight into an ambush? How was it Lejeune hadn't flushed anything? Or had he, and was he now lying with a bayonet through his throat? . . .

They came out of the shadow of the ruins after what had seemed a long journey in both space and time. Actually they had been about fifteen minutes in covering the frontage of three or four houses. They advanced a few metres more until they were clear of the mound. Roget stopped to examine his surroundings. . . .

Didier, lying just back of him, was sweating. Now for the excessively delicate business of gathering Lejeune into the patrol again. The patrol, which had been a defensive unit, was now a doubly dangerous offensive two units. The reunion had to be accomplished under the most agitating circumstances possible. The tension would be terrific for some seconds, the seconds during which Lejeune would be trying to make himself known, known to men whose identity he himself was no longer sure of. "This ought to cure him of splitting his patrols," Didier said to himself. "Where the devil has Paul gone to? . . ."

There was a sound of boards tumbling, nearby, on the right. Didier raised his head and quietly cocked his revolver. He saw Roget rise to his knees. He saw his arm start to swing . . .

At that moment Didier fired at Roget's head, and missed.

The arm completed its swing. He saw a roundish shape detach itself from the hand and fly upwards, describing the arc of a lob.

There was a detonation, a cry of surprise and pain, then silence.

The silence lasted four seconds, long enough for Didier to hear his name called. Then the air was filled with a deafening roar and lighted by three star shells which burst simultaneously overhead. He saw Roget on his feet, his mouth open, gesticulating. He saw him start to run, still gesticulating wildly, back the way he had come. He watched him disappear behind the mound of ruins and hoped he would be killed. The roar stopped suddenly, then opened up again, the sound wavering as the machine gun was swept from side to side. Didier looked around with the utmost caution and caught the flash of the gun. It was up there in the ruins, within a stone's throw of him. He noted he was in dead ground and he crouched down again, reprieved. Two green flares went up from the top of the mound. Didier wriggled sideways carefully towards the mound and got into a shallow hole.

He waited. The machine gun continued to roar. Then it would
stop while a new belt was being put in. Then it would roar again.
Within five minutes the protective barrage had come down in
front of the machine-gun post. Didier lay still, while the ground
trembled around him, and watched the barrage. As soon as he
had made out just how far away it was falling, he started to
crawl towards it in search of Lejeune.

"Stand to! Stand to! Up on the step, there! Out of the dugouts! Come up! Come up! To your posts, all of you! Stand to!
Stand to. . . ."

Officers and N.C.O.'s, from Switzerland to the sea, were going up and down the front lines, routing out their men and lin-
ing them along the firing-steps. The two armies faced each other,
tense and alert. Not a man was asleep, not a man was unarmed,
not a man had his boots off as the lines waited, staring into
space at each other, waiting, staring, waiting. . . .

Duval, standing on the firing-step from which Post Number 8
had sent up the red flares, found himself in a fantastic world.
The air flickered with the constant illumination of star shells, as
if a celebration of some sort were going on. He heard, behind
him, the rat-tat-tat-tat of the brigade machine guns. Farther
back, the seventy-fives were banging their doors again. Now
and then, from still farther back, came the ponderous sounds of
the heavies. The air was full of noises, the weird, shuddering,
moaning noises of countless shells in their flight. Nearer to the
ground, too near to be comfortable, there was the swish-swish-
swish of machine-gun bullets as they made the earth spurt along
the parapets and parados. Men ducked, and now and then some
were hit.

"Get up there! Up on the firing-steps! Keep your heads low!
Stand to! Stand to! Push that machine gun farther up, there!"

The noise increased. It became a din, the din an uproar, a
crescendo of sound so deafening that you had to shout in a
man's ear to make yourself heard. "The Orchestration of the
Western Front." The phrase again came into Duval's head. "And
I've got a front-row seat. It's glorious! Magnificent!" Duval, beside himself with excitement, was yelling at the top of his lungs,

shouting with an exuberance which did not reach his own ears even, so deafening was the noise of the bombardment. Shells dropped in the traverses, machine-gun bullets continued to clip the line of the parapet, but Duval went on yelling, intoxicated almost to the point of hysteria by the vibration of the gunfire, oblivious of all danger.

The star shells were becoming fewer, but a light remained none the less. The bombardment was now drumfire, and the air was heavy with the smell of explosives. It was getting harder to see the flashes of the detonations because the darkness of the night was thinning. But the earth continued to jump and rock, and whole sections of trench caved in, crumbled and lay still, smoking a little. The wire zinged to the flying metal and chunks of it, thrown aloft by the shells, came down and fell into the trench.

The horizon began to widen slowly, swept back by the dawn which was now advancing with gathering speed. Men looked at the debris around them, and at each other, searching for the faces of friends, then turned again to wait and to stare. . . .

A fire began to burn, over in the German lines. The fire grew brighter and revealed its shape: the sun. Slowly it raised itself out of the earth, red and hostile-looking, but welcome to the men who watched it. It swelled to enormous size, then paused in delicate contact with the rim of the world like a dancer waiting for the first notes of the ballet. For a moment the two edges were tangent and seemed to cling. Then the sun stepped off the edge of the earth and was instantly floating in its own space.

The bombardment began to die down slowly and the holocaust was gradually extinguishing itself. The earth seemed to relax from its fearful punishment of steel. Men, too, relaxed a little and began to talk in monosyllables, elliptically. Later, it seemed very quiet after the fury of the paroxysmal gunfire. Later still, when all danger of a dawn attack was over, the order came along the line, from mouth to mouth:

"Stand down! Stand down! Stand down. . . ."

Duval stood down, on the right; so did Langlois on the left. Didier stood down too, near the centre, where he had been overtaken by the bombardment. Everyone stood down, except some scattered sentries. Everyone silently nursed the inner bruising he had received from the drumfire.

The sun, to whose coming all this inferno had been but a prelude, moved higher in the cloudless sky, unmindful, so it seemed, of the havoc caused in honour of the event. Day was full now, and Langlois saw that it was really spring. He saw the delicate blades of grass which the bodies of his comrades had fertilized; he saw the little shoots on the shell-shocked trees. He saw the smoke-puffs of shrapnel being blown about by light breezes. He saw birds making love in the wire that a short while before had been ringing with flying metal. He heard the pleasant sound of larks up there, near the zenith of the trajectories. He smiled a little. There was something profoundly saddening about it. It all seemed so fragile and so absurd.

It was about an hour after sunrise when General Assolant's car arrived at Number 5. Number 5 was the place where the Tirailleurs guides had met Colonel Dax the night before, and the spot where Colonel Dax had been standing was now marked by a very large and quite fresh shell-hole. It was this shell-hole, in fact, that brought the general's car to a stop. Had it not been there, the general would have driven right on without seeming to see the officer who was saluting him from its farther lip. He would, to the dismay of his chauffeur and of the aide-de-camp who was with him, have driven right up to the entrance to the communication trench, a few hundred metres beyond the chalk pit, and he might easily have driven right into his own front line. It was the sort of thing the general liked to do. He felt that he owed dashing exploits of this kind to his reputation for dash, a reputation which he spent a good deal of time trying to live up to.

The chauffeur brought the car, skidding, to a halt on the edge of the shell-hole. There was an expression of relief on his face when he turned and said:

"We can't go any further, sir."

"All right. Wait for us here, then. Come on, Saint-Auban, we'll have to walk it."

The aide-de-camp got out and held the door for the general,

then both moved off round the edge of the shell-hole. The officer on the other side of the hole remained at the salute and, as
the general approached him, he pivoted on his heels so that he
could keep the salute full in the face of the man for whom it was
intended.

"All right, captain. I consider that I have been sufficiently saluted. You may carry on."

"Colonel Dax sent me to meet you, sir, and to escort you
to his headquarters. I am the adjutant of the 181st, Herbillon, sir."

"Doesn't Dax think I can find my way about my own
trenches?"

"Oh, no, sir, yes, sir. Everybody knows that the general is always to be found in the trenches." It was not an answer to the
question, but it was just the right thing to say.

"You'll be an aide-de-camp some day, if you can keep that
up," Saint-Auban said to himself.

"Tell me, Herbillon, why is this utterly undistinguished spot
on the road called 'Number 5'?" Place names, especially military ones, were a hobby of the general's. In fact he was keeping
some private notes with the intention of publishing a book on
the subject after the war. "Just 'Number 5.' That's queer. Number 5 what? Battery? Regiment? What?"

"I—er—I don't know, sir. A map co-ordinate, perhaps. . . ."

"Nonsense. Who ever heard of a map co-ordinate in one
figure?"

"Yes, sir."

"I say no, sir."

"Yes, sir. No, sir." Herbillon floundered, trying to get back
into verbal step. The aide-de-camp, having waited to make sure
that he would not be contradicted by the adjutant, intervened
with a brilliant answer, an answer no less brilliant for being a
spontaneous invention:

"Number 5 kilometre, sir," he said softly, with a smile which
he strove to make as brilliant as his answer.

"Of course," said Assolant. He made a mental note of the fact
and was so pleased with the information that he failed to notice
it was incomplete—Number 5 kilometre from where? Saint-

Auban could not have answered that, for the place was actually not five kilometres from any other particular place. It always had been, and it continued to be—except in the general's private notes—Number 5, nothing more, nothing less.

The morning was cloudless and fresh with spring. The dawn bombardment had died down and there was nothing to show for it but some new shell-holes, in some places linking, in others superimposed upon the old ones. The general walked along the road enjoying the cool and fragrant morning. Now and then a whiff of a less fragrant smell would filter through the bristles of his nostrils, and he enjoyed that too, in a way. Casualties were a part of war. Where there were no casualties, there was no fighting. It would be unthinkable not to have fighting under a fighting commander. The smell of the dead reassured him on this point.

"And how did the relief go off, Herbillon?"

"Quite well, sir. We lost only about thirty men. A direct hit on one section. An officer apparently missing."

"And the bombardment?"

"The reports hadn't come in when I left, sir."

"Did the patrol find out anything?"

"Nothing we didn't know. The Boche wire is heavy and his line seems well-manned. They found a machine-gun post in some ruins on our right centre. The lieutenant is at headquarters to report to you personally, if you wish to see him, sir."

"Well, we'll have the artillery blot it out during the hurricane barrage. . . . Ah, this must be the famous chalk pit. A bad place all right. I suppose they think we've got some guns or a headquarters in it. They might know the position is too obvious."

"Yes, sir, this is the place the section got it. See, there are the bodies."

Assolant glanced at the bundles of motionless clothing without pausing in his stride. He noted that one group wore the uniform of a line regiment and that another, a smaller one, wore that of the Tirailleurs. Large blue flies were buzzing indiscriminately over both groups, and clusters of them were busily feeding at eyes, nostrils, mouths, and open wounds.

"The fatally gregarious instinct of troops in the presence of the enemy." There was no pity in the general's apostrophe, only a slight contempt. Herbillon thought the remark was very good. More than anything else, perhaps, it reconciled him to the mystery of why Assolants were generals and Herbillons were not.

"That's it exactly, sir," he said, making no effort to conceal his genuine admiration for such remarkable powers of definition. Saint-Auban said nothing. He had heard the phrase before, and he knew the source to which the general had overlooked crediting it—a military text-book.

The road, beyond the chalk pit, became a sunken road. They met a detail from the 181st going down to fill their clattering petrol tins at the water tanks. The corporal in charge carefully saluted Herbillon who, to him, was the ranking officer of the three. He had failed to notice the stars on Assolant's sleeves, the only indication that a general was present. Assolant was pleased with the corporal's error and accepted it as a tribute to his own soldierlike appearance.

The officers came to a place where the horse dung and the shell-holes lay a bit thicker on the road, indications that they were at a rendezvous of some sort.

"Here's the entrance to the communication trench, sir. Boyau des Perdus."

"Confound these sniveling names!" said Assolant, petulantly. "Why can't we have names with some inspiration to them, names that express the offensive spirit of the troops? But it's always something about death, almost a defeatist propaganda. Boyau des Perdus; Tranchée des Supplices; Carrefour de la Mort. I'm getting tired of it. Boyau des Perdus! Bah! And look at that, will you! They don't even know how to spell it. What was there, a whore-house around here?"

The general was pointing to the wooden signboard on the side of the road, and he was referring to the feminine spelling of the word "perdu." The sign was written thus: BOYAU DES PERDUES, and below it was an arrow pointing in the only direction the trench went, namely, straight off into the embankment, on the right-hand side of the road.

"Yes, sir," said Herbillon, "that is wrong. I'll see that it's changed at once. What name would you suggest, sir? Would the general permit—I mean—er—would the general allow us the honour of naming the trench after him? . . ."

"Certainly not," said Assolant, flatly, so flatly indeed that Herbillon sensed, Saint-Auban knew, that nothing would have pleased him more. "You can't go around changing names here and there. It would cause too much confusion, to say nothing of the work on the maps. But when I get a chance I'm going to take the matter of these defeatist names up with Army. However, if you want to wallow in perdition in the meantime, you might at least spell it right."

"As a matter of fact, sir," said Saint-Auban with a suppressed excitement which indicated that a great moment had come in his career of aide-de-camp, "the error in that sign is actually one of omission, not of spelling."

"What are you talking about?"

"If you will permit me to explain, sir?"

"That's what I'm waiting for you to do."

"Well, sir, originally there was another word there, a word that is at the same time feminine and masculine. That is to say feminine in grammar, masculine in anatomy." Saint-Auban was again turning on that brilliant smile of his, the smile which was to supply the brilliance in case his wit did not.

"Stop grinning and making riddles and get on with the point."

"Yes, sir, yes, sir. What I mean is that this trench was named after a legendary wound that is supposed to have taken place up here. The sign read originally: Boyau des Couilles Perdues—in memory of the emasculation of a sergeant. Somebody or other took exception to the sign and the objectionable word was deleted. The spelling of the adjective remained, however. So the story goes, at least."

"Ah, that's interesting, very interesting indeed, Saint-Auban. No, on no account must the name of the trench be changed. Ha, ha, ha! D'you suppose that sergeant feels compensated for his sacrifice by having a trench named in commemoration of it? When all is said, it is an honour, a eunuch honour!"

They all laughed uproariously and went into the trench, Herbillon leading the way.

—————

As soon as the order to stand down had been given, Didier went on along the trench to his company. He went down into the dugout, struck a match and found his equipment. The match went out and he felt around in his things until his hand came in contact with a clasp knife, a hunk of bread, and a box of sardines. He took his canteen with him and groped his way up the stairs. He sat down on the top step and worked over the sardine tin with the can-opener in the knife. When he had got the lid curled half-way back he closed the can-opener and opened a blade. He uncorked the canteen and took a drink of the sour, red wine. The wine puckered his mouth and he made a face, then began to eat. He ate quickly and deftly, using the blade alternately as a fork for the sardines and a knife for the bread. Each mouthful was washed down by a swig of wine. He was hungry and the food tasted good to him. Other men were squatting up and down the dugout steps and in the traverse outside. They too were eating their breakfasts, talking between mouthfuls.

"Hey, Blackface! How was the patrol?"

"Good. How was the dugout?"

"Dugout my ————! I was carrying grenades all night."

"Where's that Boche helmet you promised me?"

"You can get it yourself, tomorrow."

"Yes. Where?"

"Over on the Pimple."

"That official?"

"Absolutely. Latrine Gazette."

"What'd you do with Lejeune?"

"Killed."

"Well, his troubles are over."

"How'd it happen?"

"Bomb."

"And the lieutenant?"

"I don't know."

"A fine patrol, all right!"

"Yes, it was."

"I saw the lieutenant here at stand-to."

"Did you? When'd he come in?" Didier began to show interest.

"How should I know? He just showed up, that's all, but he left before the bombardment started."

"That's him all right," said Didier.

"Say, what makes you think we're going to attack, Didier?"

"I read the signs."

"Or the Latrine Gazette!"

"Well, you said you were carrying bombs up all night, didn't you?"

"Where did Lejeune get it anyway? How . . . ?"

"For God's sake, let me eat."

"You're a chatty bastard!"

"Oh, go sell your fish in some other street."

"Lejeune wasn't a bad sort. The trouble with him was his feet stank."

"Say, Didier, are you sure he was killed? He owed me three francs, you know."

"Well, you can collect it tomorrow, when you go where he's gone."

"Thanks. And I hope you're there to see him pay me."

"I probably will be."

"Jesus, don't say that. That's a sure way to get it."

"He'll get it all right. Look! His face is already in mourning! Ha, ha, ha!"

"Don't talk that way, it's bad luck!"

"Luck my ———! If you stay here long enough you'll get it."

"I won't. They haven't got my number over there."

"I say don't talk that way. It's bad luck. It's tempting God . . ."

"Fat lot he has to do with it."

"He's with the Boche anyway."

"If we attack, the Boche'll never know what hit him."

Didier looked up and found, as he expected, that the remark had been made by one of the new class.

"Don't talk through your hat," he said.

"The boy's all right," said one of the older men.

"I say he's all wrong," said Didier.

"A lot you know about it."

"More than you, anyway. I saw the Boche wire. Also what he did to the Tirailleurs."

Didier got up and began collecting his things.

"Say, Didier. About those three francs. Show me where Lejeune's things are, will you . . .?"

"No," said Didier, without trying either to conceal or to emphasize his contempt.

Didier went down into the dugout again and began changing himself back from a scout to a soldier of the line. The place was crowded now, crowded with men who were already sleeping the sleep of exhaustion. Didier took pains not to disturb them. As soon as he was fixed up he left to report to his company headquarters.

Roget was alone, sitting at Charpentier's table, when Didier entered the company headquarters dugout. He was in the act of reading over his report of the patrol. This was giving him a good deal of pleasure for he found both his handwriting and prose smooth and admirable.

He felt the presence of a man in front of him but continued for a while to absorb himself in his report. Didier waited, tolerantly. He felt he could afford to be tolerant under the circumstances, circumstances the existence of which gave him the upper hand, and the explanation of which he was looking forward to with curiosity. Also he was amused by the lieutenant's obvious pleasure in his own composition.

"Well?" said Roget at last, without looking up.

"Well?" said Didier.

Roget gave a start at the sound of the voice, then looked up. The expression on his face was one of unpleasant, almost angry surprise.

"Well, I'll be . . . I thought you were killed. In fact I reported here in the . . ."

"But you didn't wait to make sure, did you, Roget?"

"Now look here . . . What d'you mean, anyway?"

"When you ran away. After killing Lejeune."

"Have you gone out of your head? Killing Lejeune, what are you talking about?"

"You know. You threw the bomb."

"Certainly I threw the bomb. What d'you want me to throw? Bouquets?"

"Well, that bomb killed Lejeune. And if you hadn't been drunk—"

"I've had enough of this!"

"I don't doubt it. You've gotten yourself into a bit of a mess, Roget."

"Well, if that's your attitude, I don't mind telling you that you've gotten yourself into a worse mess."

"How's that?"

"I'll tell you," said Roget. "I've been thinking about it. First, general insubordination. Second, threatening to kill your superior officer. That's mutiny number one. Third, refusing to obey an order and inciting others to do the same. That's mutiny number two and three. Fourth, firing at your superior officer. That's attempted murder and mutiny number four. How d'you think those charges would look on paper?"

"Well, since you mention it," Didier answered, "I say they wouldn't look half as good as these. Drunk on duty. Endangering the lives of your men through drunken recklessness. Refusal to take counsel. Wanton murder of one of your men. Gross incompetence in general and finally, Roget, cowardice in the face of the enemy. Don't forget you ran away. How did you explain that in your report?"

Both men were silent for a few moments, then Roget began to smile that unpleasant smile of his.

"I see. So that's it, is it? I didn't explain it in my report. But I'll explain something else to you, and I advise you to think it over carefully. It's simply this. I'm an officer and you're a private. It's my word against yours. Whose do you think is going to be believed? Or let me put it another way, if you like. Whose do you think is going to be accepted? Have you ever tried bringing charges against an officer? Just think it over for a while."

The two men fell silent again. Roget went back to his report and pretended to read it. Didier looked at the top of the lieutenant's head.

"That'll make him think twice," Roget told himself. "Lucky for me I did kill Lejeune, if I did. He would have made a devilishly inconvenient witness. As soon as I get him out of here I'll write up charges, just in case his tongue starts to wag. In fact, I'll tell him I'm going to do it. Yes, I'll certainly tell him. It may stop him from getting funny in other ways. The fool, bringing such accusations against an officer. He hasn't a chance. Hope he realizes it. Quits all round or I'll take the jump on him now and have him arrested. I hope to God he gets killed tomorrow. Dangerous fellow. Suppose he gets drunk and starts to talk. Arrest him now and nip things in the bud? But if he's killed? Yes, that would be the best. Oh, God, kill him, kill him, kill him. . . ."

"All right, Roget, I've thought it over. What do you propose?" Didier had, as a matter of fact, done no thinking whatever after the first instant of silence, the instant which it had taken his thoroughly practical mind to register the thought: "He's got me. I can't do anything." He had been merely staring, killing time, instinctively putting off his capitulation in the hope that it would seem a less complete one.

"Just this. If you keep your mouth shut, I will too. And don't forget to keep it tight shut. Then we'll agree on a story about the patrol. And that will end the matter. What d'you say?" Roget was almost affable. He had the air of a business man who has just concluded a shady but profitable deal. He was also congratulating himself on a second thought he had about telling Didier that he was going to make a record of the charges. He decided he wouldn't tell him after all, shrewdly surmising that it might put the idea of doing the same thing in Didier's head.

"All right," said Didier with a reluctance which did no justice at all to the inner pain of his surrender. "But you know what I think of you."

It was Roget's turn to be tolerant now and he exercised the privilege by ignoring Didier's remark. "Very well," he said, picking up the last page of his report and beginning to read from it. "This is what happened, then:

"I signalled the men to follow me to the left of the mound of ruins. I came out on the farther side and stopped to have a look and to listen. I heard a noise of moving timber on my right and I saw a Boche helmet distinctly. I threw a bomb at the Boche and killed him. At that moment a machine gun somewhere near the top of the ruins opened up while at the same time three flares burst over-

head. I looked around for my men but could not find them. I real-
ized they had mistaken my signal and had gone round the right of
the mound. Two green flares were sent up by the machine-gun
post and in a few minutes the protective barrage had come down
in front. I withdrew from my position by the way I had come.
After waiting for some time for the barrage to stop I re-entered
our lines through No. 2 Company's position. The barrage had cut
off all access to the right end of no-man's-land. Privates Didier
and Lejeune were undoubtedly caught by the barrage and killed."

"I'll bet you're sorry I wasn't," said Didier. "It makes a nice
story, though. How are you going to fix all those lies up?"

"Oh, drop it, will you? As for the report, that's easy. I'll add
a postscript, like this: 'It seems Private Didier was not caught in
the barrage but returned safely to our lines and reports as follows.' All right, now tell me what you did."

"After you killed Lejeune . . . You did kill him, you know. I
went over to see him and he was lying well inside the barrage
line, and so near the mound he wasn't in range from the machine gun either. The bomb must have landed right beside his
head. It was a pulp. . . ."

"Then how d'you know it was Lejeune?"

"I brought his identity tag back. That satisfy you?"

"You don't think I believe you did all this travelling around
right under a machine gun, do you?"

"I don't care what you believe, but I did. If you knew as much
about patrols as I do, you'd know that if you keep calm you're
often safer right near a machine gun than you are running away
from it. Especially where we were there, to the rear of the gun
and in dead ground even if it swung in our direction. All the base
of the mound there was dead ground. They might have dropped
bombs on us, but their attention was all to their front, not to
their flank. So I crawled over and had a look at Lejeune while the
barrage was going. There was nothing I could do for him, so I
moved back to the Boche wire and worked my way along it to
the right. It was easy, as they were all fixed on the uproar around
the mound. Well, I took my time, as I was alone. I didn't want to
run into anything. I got to the old communication trench just

about the time Number 8 sent up the first flare. The trench had fresh tracks in it so I gave it a fairly wide berth. Then I ran into some new wire and I moved farther away, but not before I heard some voices. I got into a shell-hole and threw a couple of stones into the wire. Just as I thought, a machine gun opened up. It was about thirty metres from the German line, in the same communication trench that our post Number 8 is. Don't forget to put that in your report and to say that it was heavily wired."

"Then what did you do?"

"I'd located the post, so I came in," said Didier, simply. It would not have been like him to notice that he had been manœuvred into the position of giving gratuitous explanations, however slight.

"Then that's settled. I'll finish this report and send it to headquarters. And if you know what's good for you . . ."

But Didier was already climbing the dugout steps. He stood aside at the entrance to make way for Captain Charpentier who was on his way down.

"Good morning, Didier," the captain said, pleasantly.

"Good morning, sir," said Didier.

"How was the patrol?"

"Not bad, sir," said Didier, unable to refrain from shooting the captain a look which stopped just short of being a wink. "The lieutenant is down there. He's written the report."

"No doubt," said Charpentier, drily, then went on down wishing his tone had been less dry, his words less caustic.

Didier smiled. "A good chap," he said to himself. "And he knows a thing or two. You can't fool him."

Charpentier found himself, down in the dugout, accepting the patrol report from Roget's eager hands, a little too eager, he thought them. He read the report through attentively, then asked for a map and an aeroplane photograph. He borrowed Roget's note-book and wrote as follows, using the regimental code name and referring to the map and photograph as he wrote:

To: Sanglier
Subject: Patrol
    Officer commanding patrol reports as follows: machine-gun post located in ruined houses at 8B-63-24. Another machine-gun

*post located in old trench at 8B-61-24. Enemy wire heavy and
in good condition. Enemy trench apparently well-manned and
alert.*

*Charpentier, Capt.
No. 2 Company.*

He tore the report and its carbon copy out of the note-book
and handed the original to Roget.

"Take that to headquarters," he said, "and wait to see if the
colonel wants to speak to you." He folded Roget's report and
the copy of his own up together and put them in his pocket.
There was something in Charpentier's manner which prevented
Roget from starting a conversation, a conversation which he
had intended to lead around to his part in the patrol. He felt the
need of crystallizing the version he had invented and his instinct told him that there was no better way of doing so than
to put it into spoken words. Instead, however, he found himself
leaving the dugout with more haste and less ease than he had
expected.

Charpentier was thoughtful: "Something funny. One man
killed. Roget coming in one way, Didier another. Was that a
look he gave me upstairs there, or was it my imagination? Getting separated from his officer, that's not like him. And why didn't
the barrage cut him off, too, from finishing the patrol? I'll have
a look into this when I have more time. After the attack."

It never seemed to come into a man's mind that, if he wanted
to look into a thing, it might be better to do so before an attack.

General Assolant and the aide-de-camp followed Colonel Dax
along the Tranchée des Zouaves as it wound its way across the
face of the low hill, the low hill from the back of which Dax had
watched the signal rockets the night before. The trench sloped
gently upwards on the face of the hill. Just short of its high point
they came to an inconspicuous shelter built into its side. They
stooped to enter the shelter, carefully replacing the curtain of
empty sand-bags which served as a backdrop. The place they
were in was an observation post, and it was already occupied by
an observer. The post was built to hold two men comfortably,
three uncomfortably, and the observer was therefore ordered to

wait outside. So, too, was Saint-Auban, after he had handed a map, some aerial photographs, and a telescope over to Assolant.

The side of the post which faced the German lines was constructed of sand-bags, neatly arranged so as to protect a breast-high horizontal slit which was framed by laths. The slit was just large enough to accommodate the big end of a telescope. Its width was a little short of the width of the post and there was a piece of sand-bag hanging down in front of it, obscuring the view. Prudent observers always dropped this flap when the sudden increase in the light inside the post warned them that the curtain behind them was being opened. This care to prevent a small rectangle of background light from showing up might seem excessive. It was not, however, considered so by the man who had to stay in the post. Having himself spotted German posts now and then by similar revealing glimpses of light or sparkle of lenses, he knew himself to be equally vulnerable in this respect. Moreover, in places where the lack of it might mean swift and painful death, prudence, caution, was never considered excessive.

Dax and Assolant spread their maps and photographs on the boards which served as elbow rests, took off their trench helmets and respirators, and settled themselves for a good look at the view which was revealed to them when they pinned back the flap. At first they looked with naked eyes, then they used the telescopes. For ten or fifteen minutes they said very little except to exchange questions and answers identifying the features of the ground.

What they saw was what they had come to see: the Pimple. In general outline and in size it was rather like an ocean liner just after it had been launched, that is to say, a liner with its superstructures but without the added height that its funnels would give it. It lay enough off the line of a flat broadside to the French front to make it look as if its prow were thrusting at the boundary of the 181st and their neighbours on the left, the 183rd. It was brown and smooth-looking to the naked eye. The telescopes, however, showed that it was not so smooth as it seemed— that it was, in fact, scarred by countless shell-holes and well-laced with entanglements. Whatever shrubbery there might have been on it had long since been replaced by shell-holes, and the darker patches were bushes of wire, not of leaves. Through the naked eye the slope of its flank would have been inviting to a man out for a walk, but through a telescope it was formidable.

"Sinister," Dax said to himself. "That's what it is. Or is it because I know it's sinister that I think it looks sinister?"

He tried, without much success, to dissociate it from the war, to appraise it as if it were any hill in any landscape, but he could not get it to exist in his mind untainted by its reputation. The morning sunlight lay bright and cheerful upon it, but still it didn't, it couldn't, look cheerful. An almost imperceptible vapour seemed to emanate from and to cling to it. "If the priest could see that," Dax thought, "he would say it was the ghosts of all the men who have died upon those slopes. It must be the fumes being ventilated from the catacombs. They would be catacombs too, if we ever got foot on the hill. But if it's ghosts, there'll be plenty more by this time tomorrow."

The Pimple was, to Assolant, just what all other hills were to him, topographical obstacles which might have to be attacked or defended. He saw the jumbled mess of no-man's-land and the brown line of the German wire on its farther side. The slope of the hill looked easy to him, though he was quite aware that it wasn't as easy as it looked. Silently, as he reviewed the various features of the terrain, he ticked off percentages of losses in his mind. He was pleased to find that his arithmetic left a substantial margin of numbers to overrun the crest of the hill and to establish themselves on the ground beyond. His optimism increased and, in proportion, the height and the reputation of the hill diminished. Given enough troops and ammunition, he could take anything. It was all a question of percentages. Men had to be killed, of course, sometimes lots of them. They absorbed bullets and shrapnel and by so doing made it possible for others to get through. Say, five per cent killed by their own barrage (a very generous allowance, that). Ten per cent lost in crossing no-man's-land, and twenty per cent more in getting through the wire. That left sixty-five per cent, and the worst part of the job over, the most exposed part.

His reasoning was faulty and his percentages were pure guesswork, but he failed to notice his fallacies in the exuberance of winning a battle in his head. He even failed to notice them when they themselves provided a hint in the form of an idea, an idea which captivated him so that it displaced all others, blinded him to the very light of which it was itself the source. The idea was simply this: after the attack he would have the burial parties make detailed records on maps of exactly where all the dead had been found. He and his staff would then correlate the information, make a report and a critique of it, and send it on up the hierarchic ladder in the hope that it might eventually reach G.H.Q. and draw attention there to the fact that its author was a man of brains as well as of bayonets. General Assolant instantly became impatient for the attack to begin so that he could the sooner put his idea into practice. He was in no mood to remember that a battle is a thing of flux, and that you cannot measure flux by the debris that it leaves behind. Nor did it occur to him that while an operation might be, strategically, a neatly conceived plan, tactically it tended to become more and more a series of accidents.

"Zero hour will be at seven A.M.," Assolant said, more as if he were talking to himself. "I picked that time because we can't attack in the middle of the dawn bombardment and I don't want to attack before it. This business will have to be done in daylight so that we can see what we're doing. There's this extra advantage, too. After the dawn bombardment the Boche will think all danger of an attack is over for the day. We'll catch him off his guard."

"I doubt it, sir," said Dax. "From my own experience and from what I've been told, he's never off his guard there. He knows the Pimple is as important to us as it is to him. His barrages respond to his signals almost instantly. And they're well-registered."

"Furthermore," said Assolant, ignoring Dax's remarks, "since the dawn bombardment seems a well-established custom around here, we can have the artillery cut the wire then."

"Won't the Boche notice that we're doing it, sir?"

"What of it? He can't repair it till after nightfall, and by that time it won't be his any more."

"Yes, but he can cover the gaps with machine guns. It'll tell him just the points at which to expect us."

"Well, the wire has to be cut. Would you rather have it done during the hurricane barrage before the attack? It's only going to be a five-minute one, before starting to creep. This is a surprise attack, you know. He won't be expecting it so soon after the other."

Dax didn't pretend to know what the Germans might or might not be expecting, but he did know that the problem of cutting the wire was always a perplexing one for him. If you cut the wire in advance, you were bound to warn the enemy at the same time that you were going to attack at those points within the next twenty-four hours. If you waited for the preliminary bombardment to do the job, you ran the risk of its not being done thoroughly, especially if the bombardment was to be, as in this case, a very short one.

"On the whole, sir, I think you're right. Better to have the wire well cut in advance. Then the guns will all be free to attend to the Boche when we go over."

"I'll have the artillery do it quietly. I'll have them drop occasional shells in the wire, as if they were falling short. They can make a few registering shots this afternoon. An officer can register them from this post. Which makes me think. This would be an excellent place for me to watch the attack from. Saint-Auban!"

"Yes, sir."

"Go down to Colonel Dax's headquarters and call up Couderc. Tell him to arrange to have telephone wires strung to this post straight from my headquarters." The view of the sloping side of the Pimple had given Assolant another idea, that of directing the attack in person from the observation post. "Wait a minute. Dax, you can fix me up with a line to the seventy-fives back of the hill here, can't you?"

"Certainly, sir."

"Good. Tell Couderc, then, that after the hurricane barrage those two batteries back there, find out which they are, are to come under my personal command. They will carry on with the fire schedule as planned, but they must be ready to shell any targets which I may have for them during the advance."

Assolant was delighted with the way things were shaping up, with the prospect of being able to select targets himself and to stand there and watch them being blown to pieces. This was going to be war as it should be fought. The terrain was just right for such an exploit, an exploit whose novelty, he now felt assured, would go a long way towards making his coveted promotion in the Legion of Honour a certainty. He went back to his telescope and looked at the Pimple again. When he turned to speak, Dax saw on his face an expression of mingled avidity and affection, the expression of a man who has just been contemplating a cherished trophy.

"I want to go down and inspect your front line."

"Yes, sir. But I must warn you it's a hot place."

"I like hot places," the general said, and it was no more than the truth.

Dax felt tired and gloomy as he conducted Assolant along the trenches leading to the front line. It was quite clear to him, depressingly so, that the hour or more he had spent at his headquarters pointing out the difficulties of the attack and the exhaustion of his troops to the general had been wasted. The discussion, moreover, had ended on a note of unpleasantness, a note which had only served to wound Assolant's vanity and to solidify his stubborn refusal to consider the attack in any way a questionable one. Warming to the argument that his troops were in no condition for the job assigned to them, Dax had been led into an indiscretion which had given instantaneous offence. He had said:

"Furthermore, sir, this is really a corps operation, not a divisional one."

The reply had been cold, forbidding:

"Please confine yourself to obeying the orders of your superiors, Colonel Dax, not to criticizing them."

The sight of the Pimple from the observation post and of the ground between had intensified Dax's misgivings. The general's, if he had had any, seemed to have been dissipated by the same sight. "Rarely," said Dax to himself, "does a soldier see with naked eyes. He is nearly always looking through lenses, lenses which are made of the insignia of his rank."

The two men reached the front line and turned to their left. Picking their way through the traverses which plainly showed the effects of the dawn bombardment, they often came upon working parties digging out the avalanches of earth which had been tumbled into the trench. This earth was being carefully put into sand-bags and stored in the traverses, as if it were something precious. It was precious, at that, but the reason it was being stored was that soldiers didn't advertise their position to the enemy by gaily tossing spadefuls of earth over the parapet. Here and there, however, where the parapet gaped too dangerously, sand-bags were thrown or pushed gingerly into the openings. That the Germans also had observers, and that they were alert, was proved by the frequent bursts of machine-gun fire which these efforts to patch up the parapet drew.

Dax was not displeased by this intermittent fire. He hoped Assolant would notice how responsive, how well-aimed it was, and when he thought the general might not be noticing, he drew his attention to it. More than once they had to crouch with their backs to the damaged parapet and watch the little storm of dust spurt on the parados, a foot or so above their heads. Notwithstanding this, Assolant had been constantly jumping up on the firing-steps to take quick looks into no-man's-land. To Dax, these quick looks seemed to be getting less and less quick.

"Please, sir," he said, when he could restrain himself no longer, "that's suicide. You're putting me in an awkward position, for I'm more or less responsible for your safety, you know, and I can't answer for it if you keep that up. You've seen how accurately they sweep our line. We have a periscope a little farther on and I'd feel easier if you'd wait to use that."

In spite of his love of hot places, Assolant found that Dax's urgings had a welcome sound to his ears, so welcome indeed, that he suddenly realized they might also be considered overdue.

The trench periscope was already set up on its tripod when the two men came around the corner. Dax got to it first, as he had wanted to do, and went to work raising it cautiously over the parapet. He searched with it for a while until he found what he had been expecting to find, then focused it and stepped away, offering it with a gesture to the general.

Assolant looked into the binoculars and failed to control the start which Dax had hoped to surprise from him by the sight he had prepared. The telescopic lenses seemed to spring the mass of bodies right into his face. The bodies were so tangled that most of them could not be distinguished one from the other. Hideous, distorted, and putrescent, they lay tumbled upon each other or hung in the wire in obscene attitudes, a shocking mound of human flesh, swollen and discoloured. Here and there the numerals of the Tirailleurs were plainly visible.

Assolant wheeled on Dax, incensed by the impertinence of a lesson which had at last got home to him, angry words crowding to the tip of his tongue . . .

There was a crash, a tinkle of glass, and the periscope toppled over, shattered.

"I shall not detain you any longer, colonel. Good day."

Assolant walked off round the corner of the traverse alone.

Sergeant Picard, who had been in charge of Number 8 Post the night before, came into Captain Renouart's dugout and saluted.

"Excuse me, sir. Is it true that we're attacking in the morning? The rumour is all over the place."

"Yes, it's true, sergeant. And I want to see all the N.C.O.'s here after supper this evening. Pass the word around, will you?"

"Yes, sir. May I have permission then to visit the men? I'm off duty."

"Certainly."

The sergeant fumbled around in his pocket for a moment and brought out a long, narrow strip of purple cloth which was piped with grey. He kissed it and passed it over his head and it hung down in front to his knees.

"My son," he said, and his voice seemed to have taken a gentler tone now that he was wearing the stole, "do you wish to make your peace with God?"

"Yes, father," said the captain. "Where can we go?"

"Why not outside," the sergeant said. He turned to the others in the dugout, half a dozen officers, runners, and orderlies, and added, "When the captain comes down, any of you who want to can come up. I shall wait."

The sergeant sat on the firing-step and Captain Renouart knelt on the floor of the trench and began his confession. A soldier came into the traverse and hurried by without appearing to notice what was going on.

When he had received absolution, the captain got up, brushed his knees off and went back into the dugout.

The sergeant waited, sitting on the firing-step. He waited for ten minutes, then he too got up and turned to face the dugout entrance. He made the sign of the cross in its direction, silently gave the occupants a general absolution, then picked up his rifle and went off along the trench.

During the afternoon, Langlois was sent back to the regimental train with a message for the quartermaster. He delivered the message and went off to look for a friend of his, the corporal who acted as regimental carpenter. The corporal was not there, but the arrangement of his tools indicated that his absence was a temporary one. Langlois sat down on a box outside the corporal's tent to wait for him and to smoke a cigarette. He still had in his pocket the letter which he had written his wife at the Café du Carrefour the day before, telling her he would be out of danger for a week or so. He now had the opportunity to post the letter, but he was unable to decide whether to do so or not. If he posted it and was afterwards killed, the war ministry's notification would be a doubly cruel blow for his wife. On the other hand, suppose he posted it and came through all right. Then he would have done her a distinct kindness by anticipating his fate. Had he the right, though, to gamble with another person's feelings? The reply to that was, yes, if he won the bet, no if he didn't. He was right back where he started from.

His gaze wandered over the corporal's interrupted work: a saw, a hammer, and nails and, piled neatly beside the improvised bench, strips of wood. The laths in one pile were longer than those in the other, and they were shaped to a point at one end only. "What's he making?" Langlois asked himself. The answer eluded him until he had finished his cigarette. He tossed the butt away and followed it with his eyes to the place where it landed, just short of a box of stencils. Instantly the various parts of the

corporal's work fell together and stood completed in his mind—
markers for graves.

Langlois got up and lighted another cigarette. He nursed the
match while he pulled the letter out of his pocket with his free
hand, then set fire to it, dropped it to the ground where he
watched it flame, curl, and lie still.

The day passed quickly for most of the men of the 181st. There
was a good deal of unostentatious activity going on in the sector,
subterranean and semi-subterranean activity which could not be
seen by enemy observers. It was the aim of everybody to preserve,
so far as the Germans were concerned, an appearance of nor-
mality throughout a day which could not be quite normal. The
eve of an attack always seemed to have a quality of newness, of
exciting newness, no matter how often it might repeat itself.

One or two flights of aeroplanes crossed the German lines
some distance to the north, wheeled to their right and returned
to their own lines after having travelled an almost equal number
of miles to the south. The Pimple sector had not, however, es-
caped attention from the observers or their cameras.

In the headquarters dugout, in the Tranchée des Zouaves, Adjutant Herbillon had spent most of the afternoon doing his paper work. The last thing he did before going up for a breath of
the evening air was to make out the requisition for the next
day's rations for the regiment. This he did, easily enough and as
a matter of routine, by taking the preceding day's requisition
and cutting it by fifty per cent.

An artillery officer, followed by a man who was stringing a
wire, came to the observation post. For some reason he did not
care for its location and so moved off to find a place better to his
liking. There he registered a number of shots in the German
wire, using a mysterious jargon of his own, then packed up and
left, taking his wire with him. Everything he did was done with
precision and self-assurance and, if he had to address himself to
an infantry-man, even of higher rank than himself, there was a
faint condescension in his manner.

Perhaps the reason the artillery officer had disliked the observation post was that it had, since the general's visit, become an

unusually active rendezvous. First, the regimental telephonists had arrived to install the telephone wire to the seventy-fives. They were not yet through with their work when other telephonists showed up, bringing the private line from divisional headquarters with them. The co-operation between these two groups was not an enthusiastic one. The owners of the divisional wire considered themselves entitled to priority, while those who actually possessed the priority were disinclined to yield it. Their squabbles showed every evidence of transforming themselves from oral to physical ones when regimental officers began arriving at the post in pairs to familiarize themselves with their objectives and boundaries, easy to identify now that the declining sun shed its light full on the slope of the hill opposite. The telephonists were, therefore, forced to compose their differences and to complete their work with a proper regard for correct behavior when in the presence of authority.

All this and other activity was merely a projection of the intense activity at the source—divisional headquarters. The energy spread from the source, fanwise, down the various communicating and dependent centres, losing some of its intenseness in direct ratio to the distance it travelled. Zero hour would reverse the flow of energy and the centre of activity would be shifted in one bound from the rear to the front, giving point to one of Assolant's chief complaints against modern war: that a general was condemned to days of intensely busy preparation before an attack, but that once zero hour was at hand, he might just as well turn in and go to sleep.

Just at present, however, all was relatively relaxed and quiet in the ranks except for those detailed to fatigues, mainly the lugging up of small-arms ammunition, grenades, and explosive charges for dugouts. Men slept in funk-holes or dugouts, or sat in the entrances or in the traverses, tinkering with their equipment, delousing themselves, smoking, thinking, or talking.

Sergeant Picard had just left Captain Sancy's Number 4 Company lines. The sight of the sergeant, but more particularly that of his stole, had had the effect of transforming the prevalent rumour of an attack into a certainty. A group of Number 4 Company men were talking.

"When the priests come around you always know there's death in the wind."

"Yes, and you're the first one to run to them."

"Naturally, I always take every precaution."

"Including the permanganate of potash?"

"Don't blaspheme." It was said sarcastically.

"Listen to who's talking about blasphemy! The Jew!"

"Well, there's nobody knows any more about it than those two."

"What d'you mean by that?"

"Well, you've done time in Cayenne, haven't you, Meyer? And Férol has served in the Legion. They're not seminaries, those places."

"You've said it. You've got to be a man to go through the dry guillotine," said Meyer.

"And you've got to be two men to be in the Legion," Férol retorted. Meyer and Férol were started again on their everlasting wrangle, a wrangle which always removed them from the general conversation and which quite often ended in blows.

"They're off again. Who gives a curse which is tougher, Algeria or Guiana?"

"You're right. This war's tough enough for me. I'd swap places right now with any convict or legionary, anywhere. . . ."

"That's because you're afraid of going over the top tomorrow, afraid of being killed."

"I'm not going to be killed."

"Don't say that, it's bad luck."

"Bad luck nothing. This war is bad luck."

"I know I won't be killed because I'm not afraid of it. It's always the ones who are afraid of it who get it. You've seen that."

"That may be true. I don't know. But I'm afraid of it and they haven't got me yet. What's more, they're not going to. They haven't got my number."

"Don't say that, I tell you. That's a sure way to get it."

"If you stay here long enough, you'll get it. That's sure anyway."

"What time's zero hour?"

"Usual time. Dawn, I suppose."

"They say the general was down here today."

"Which one? There's millions of generals. This army is all generals and privates."

"Joffre, of course."

"Say, he couldn't get that carcass of his into a trench."

"And he wouldn't if he could."

"They must feed well down at G.H.Q."

"Generals and priests are always fat."

"I've never seen a picture of a fat English general. And Assolant isn't fat."

"Who's Assolant?"

"You tell him."

"He's the divisional mascot. A pet tiger. He can kill you with a look."

"Well, anyway, generals and priests always mean death. That's sure."

"If those colonials would ever shut up, I'd take a nap."

"Colonials is good. . . ."

Langlois got back to his section in time for the evening meal, breakfast for some of the men who had managed to get some sleep during the day.

"Hey there, Langlois, what's new at the regimental train? Any papers?"

"No papers, but it's going to be an attack all right."

"You're telling us! It's been official around here for hours."

"Yes, the general was through here . . ."

"And the priest . . ."

"And look at those extra packages of ammunition . . ."

"Yes, I know. The carpenter was making wooden crosses."

"Did they look pretty?"

"He didn't make one for me."

"Don't say that. That's a sure way to get it."

"Stay here long enough, that's the sure way to get it."

"Was he making one for you, Langlois? Did you print your own name while you had the chance?"

"I don't know and I don't care much. I'm not afraid of dying, only of getting killed."

"That's as clear as trench mud."

"Well, which would you rather be done in by, a bayonet or a machine gun?"

"A machine gun, naturally."

"Naturally—that's just my point. They're both pieces of steel going into your guts. Only the machine gun is cleaner, quicker, less painful, isn't it?"

"What does that prove?"

"That proves that most of us are more afraid of getting hurt than of getting killed. Look at Bernard. He's in a panic when it comes to gas, but gas doesn't mean anything to me. He's seen photos of gas cases and it looks bad to him. Now that doesn't bother me a bit. But I hate like the devil to be without my tin hat. But I don't mind not having a tin hat for my tail. Why's that?"

"Well, you ought to, since that's where your brains seem to be. Why is it you don't want a tin hat for your tail? You tell us."

"Because I know a wound in the head will hurt much more than one in the tail. Your tail is just flesh, but your head is all bone . . ."

"Speak for yourself."

"I am. Now you tell me, apart from bayonets, what are you most afraid of?"

"High explosive."

"Me too."

"And me."

"Exactly. It's the same with me," said Langlois. "Because it can chew you up worse than anything else. Just what I'm trying to tell you. If you're really afraid of dying, you'd be living in a funk all your life because you know you've got to some day, any day. And besides, if it's death you're afraid of, why should you care about what it is that kills you? Why are you more afraid of shells than machine guns, or bayonets than shells?"

"You're too deep for me, professor. All I know is, nobody wants to die."

"You mean you don't want to."

"Yes, and you too."

"That's where you're wrong," said Langlois. "Personally, I'd rather like to. It's the only absolute thing in life. It has a mystery and perfection all its own. I have a strong curiosity about it. So strong at times that I've thought quite seriously of suicide."

"Well, hang on to your curiosity for a few hours more and it will be satisfied without the danger of losing your immortal soul."

"Don't invoke fate. It's bad luck."

"But how d'you know my soul is immortal?" Langlois liked to discuss these things.

"I just do, that's all."

"Well, I don't. In fact my intelligence tells me it isn't. Nothing to nothing, why not? It's logical enough."

"Yes, but then why are we here?"

"No reason, so far as I can see."

"We're here to propagate the race."

"That's another phrase that gives me a pain," said Langlois, glad of the chance to express his ideas on this subject, "like 'self-preservation.' They take the instinct not to get hurt and call it the instinct of self-preservation. It's some instinct of self-preservation all right, that makes people continue to live right under a volcano, in the earthquake and typhoon zones! And then they call the business of going with a woman the instinct of self-reproduction, when all it is is the instinct of going with a woman. Do you want a child every time you tear off a piece? You do not, and you take good care not to have one. It's the finest indoor and outdoor sport there is and there's no need for any further justification of it. Why do people have to go round trying to make it a noble thing by saying they are reproducing their species when all they're doing is having some fun?"

"Well, if they acted the way you talk, the race would die out."

"All right, and who'd be the worse off for that? Plenty of races have died out and nobody seems to be mourning them. Ours will too, and I can bet the animals will be delighted when the day comes."

"What about the unborn children?"

"What about them? I wish I was an unborn child this minute. . . ."

"That's because we're going to attack tomorrow."

"D'you think you're doing anybody a favour by creating them out of nothing for the very doubtful joy of living a life of misery and pain in the world of men, the most savage of the predatory animals?"

"It's nature's law. I've got nothing to do with it."

"Take this war," Langlois continued. "Do you think our parents would have had us if they had foreseen the things they were sentencing us to?"

"Probably. There have always been wars and there always will be. They're part of life, like disease, storms, death. There are lots worse things than war to my mind. For instance, sitting on your tail in some bastard's office and making and counting his money for him. It takes a man to make a war, but a louse can make money."

"It takes a fool to make war, if you judge by those who are making this one. This attack they're pushing us into now, it's just plain murder. Look at what the Boches did to the Tirailleurs. Anyway, war never settled anything except who was the strongest."

"Well, that's something."

"It's not enough."

"It's never enough."

"I'm going to get some sleep," said Langlois.

"Good night. And don't oversleep. You'll miss your chance to satisfy that curious curiosity of yours."

During the night working parties cut lanes through the French entanglements, using wire cutters. Four men were killed and nine wounded during this.

II

At zero minus thirty minutes, that is to say at half-past six o'clock in the morning, every man of the division, from the general to the last private, was at his post. Everybody was equipped in attack order, armed and ready. Cannons were loaded and aimed. Watches were synchronized. Maps, boundaries, and objectives were known by heart. Telephone lines were repaired and in working order. Signal rockets were inspected and checked.

The usual quiet which followed the dawn bombardment lay over the front.

Assolant and Captain Nicolas of the artillery were in the observation post. Both had powerful binoculars instead of telescopes, and both were studying a map which had been divided into countless little numbered squares. Squatting on the ground and trying not to touch the artillery officer's knees, was a telephonist corporal. He was talking in a low voice into two receivers he was holding, first into one and then into the other.

"Through to Division, sir," he said. "Through to Polygon," he added, using the code name for the seventy-fives.

Nicolas said nothing. Assolant said nothing. The general was not in a talkative humour. He was, in fact, in the grip of a smouldering anger, an anger which was all the more bitter because he had nothing to vent it on but the weather, an unresponsive target.

A northeaster had started to blow up sometime during the night bringing squalls of heavy rain with it. Just at present it was not raining, but the damage to the ground had been done. Clouds were, moreover, still moving across the sky, flying so low they seemed to just miss catching their dark bellies on the crest of the Pimple, dark bellies from which more water was likely to pour at any minute. "What's your hurry?" Nicolas wanted to ask them, they looked so much to him like workers, pressed for time, hastening to their offices in the morning.

An ugly day had, not without reason, given Assolant an ugly mood. The gas barrage had had to be abandoned because of the wind's direction. The same wind would, if it rained again, blow the water blindingly into the faces of his advancing men. Then there was the mud. Mud and rain, as Assolant knew, had taken the sting out of more than one attack. But what annoyed him the most was, perhaps, that his dream of directing some target shooting might be spoiled by a sudden squall. Visibility had already been lowered by an atmosphere which was laden with humidity. If the rain started to come down again it would be reduced still more and his horizon might be no wider than his own front line, four or five hundred metres away.

"Get the latest weather report," the general ordered out of pure irascibility and nothing else. This was the third one the corporal had been told to get since Assolant had arrived at the post, and it was the first and the same report which he was quoting again:

"Northeast winds, rain, and squalls for the next six hours."

But the general had already forgotten he had asked for it. He was looking through his glasses and the lenses pulled at his eyes a bit.

"Zero minus fifteen minutes," the corporal announced, repeating what the voice in the divisional ear-piece was telling him. "Everything quiet. All units report themselves ready."

The front-line trench was crowded, more crowded, so it seemed, than when it had been filled with the double congestion of the relief two nights earlier, crowded with men whose uniforms were slate-grey with moisture and whose thoughts were slate-grey with apprehension. They stood in the jumping-off positions quite silently and almost motionlessly, staring in front of them. Each man carried two extra packages of rifle ammunition and a small bag of bombs. Here and there a man would be fairly well loaded with what looked like satchels, giving him the appearance of a traveler waiting for a train. His satchels were explosive charges for use on the galleries and dugouts of the Pimple. He looked rather taller than the rest, but this was a deception caused by the dwarfing effect of the other men's rifles, elongated as they were by the disproportionately long bayonet.

A cruel-looking thing, a bayonet, Langlois thought. And the cruelest-looking of all, the French one. Perhaps because it was the most slender, the purity of its lines the most perfect, its intrinsic proportions the nicest. Or, perhaps, because it had the reputation of making the wickedest wound, the quadrangular wound that was so difficult to heal. Langlois had never used his bayonet, and he never would unless he was caught with an empty magazine in front of an oncoming German. He asked the time of Lieutenant Bonnier who was standing right beside him.

"Zero minus twenty minutes," the lieutenant said. He was in command of the company and he was feeling a slight nausea in the pit of his stomach.

Langlois looked at the men around him. Some of them were condemned to be dead within the half hour. Perhaps he was one of them. The thought passed through his head, a strangely impersonal one, as if it had not been a thought of his at all, but some story he was reading. He noted the unusual self-possession of these men but he had seen it before and accepted it as granted. The thought kept returning: this one, or this one, or that one, would actually, inevitably be dead in a few minutes. He tried, half-heartedly, to guess which. Then: a number of lives right there next to him, within touching distance, some of which he had been on intimate terms with, were rushing with incredible speed (yet a stationary one, too) towards their ends. No, the ends were rushing towards the lives. Thirty minutes more to live, and then the totally unknown, apotheosis. The idea had a force so poignant at that time and place that it suffocated and extinguished itself.

His mind, having been emptied of a thought the power of which it was no longer capable of bearing, reverted to the more commonplace and personal subject of his own flesh. There were three wounds that Langlois dreaded: in the eyes, in the genitals, and in the feet. When he thought about this, as he did now and then, in places of safety, it was the wounding of his genitals which he abhorred the most. Night made him wish that his eyes might be spared above all else. But now, on the eve of a hand-to-hand encounter with the enemy, it was his feet which obsessed him, the feet without which he would be helpless to move. That was the way he felt, and that was all there was to it. Yes, his feet would not be of much use to him if his eyes were gone, but still he would rather have it so. If he had his feet he could move, grope, he would manage. Above all, he could move, move, move. . . .

"Zero minus fifteen," said Bonnier, without anyone having asked him.

"I'll get it this time," Didier said to himself. He did not actually picture himself as dead, for that would have been beyond him. "Seventh time over the top without a scratch, that's too much to expect." What he would have said, had it been in him to reason about the signs he was so good at reading, was: "I ought to get it this time." He felt that his run of luck had built up a cumulative weight of probability against him. The weight oppressed him, and he felt vaguely that there was something unfair about it, that he was now handicapped. Langlois would have been able to tell him that his chances, whatever they were, say fifty-fifty, were the same for each attack no matter how often he had previously benefited from those chances. Didier would have followed the reasoning easily, once it was made for him, but he would have none the less gone over convinced that he was a marked man.

He looked at his watch and saw that it was a certain time. The man next to him asked for the time and Didier had to look at his watch again.

"Fifteen minutes to go," he said.

Captain Charpentier had developed a blister on his heel which was so sore that it made him limp. It was sore enough, too, to have taken almost complete possession of his mind. He stood in the trench and cursed it endlessly and repetitively. He cursed the weather, too, for having added to the difficulty of walking just at the time when he wanted the greatest bodily ease, when he wanted, in fact, to be as unconscious of having a body as it was possible to be.

He looked at his wrist watch for the twentieth time, but what he saw on the dial was the raw spot on his heel, that exasperating blister which obtruded itself upon everything. Charpentier was in a rage. . . .

At zero minus six minutes it began to rain again, a slanting, hostile rain, maddening and penetrating.

"That settles it," Dax reflected with some bitterness. "The weather's always on the side of the Boche. It's going to be bad." He yawned, a nervous, uncompleted little yawn.

General Assolant was fidgety. His wrist watch seemed to have stopped. He compared it with the artillery officer's and found that it hadn't. The powerful binoculars pulled at his eyeballs, and yet he could not lay them aside for more than a few seconds at a time, so great was his eagerness for his victory to begin. That was the way he was now thinking of it, his mind frankly supplying the word victory instead of attack.

Nicolas did not keep looking at his watch. He had learnt to let time alone. He knew that the moment it felt itself to be under observation, it began to show off. It slowed up, played tricks on you.

"Zero minus one minute," said the corporal, still quoting the information which came over the wire.

Assolant picked up his glasses, but he had to take them away again almost at once as they had clouded with the moisture of his brow. He wiped them on a handkerchief and this time held them just clear of his face. The view jiggled, but it was better than seeing nothing, and he could fit them to his sockets by a motion of the wrist as soon as things started. Nicolas, who wanted to spare his eyes from the pull of the lenses, let three-quarters of a minute go by, counting it off on his pulse beats, before picking up his.

The concentration of both men had become so intensely focused on what they would see that they never heard the thunderclap of the first discharge. A wall of dark smoke shaped itself suddenly in the lenses of their glasses, and it startled them. Nic-

olas laughed out loud at himself for being surprised by something which he had done nothing but plan and work for during
the last thirty-six hours.

"There it is . . ." he said.

"There it is," said Captain Charpentier as the sky behind him
filled with the piercing whine of countless shells. The roar of the
discharge, like that of a huge, long-pent force which has burst
its bonds, blotted all thought from his mind. Silence behind him,
for a moment, while the guns were being reloaded, in front of
him the crash of the barrage as it struck the ground and burst
two hundred metres from the trench. The earth trembled with
the shock of the impact. Clouds of dark smoke leapt upwards,
then bowed before the wind. The pungent smell of explosives
was everywhere, all at once. Shovelfuls of mud were hurled into
the air, then fell back again, scattered. The place buzzed and
sang with flying metal. Men crouched a little and moved closer
to one another.

Charpentier looked at his watch. It was already zero plus
forty seconds.

The earthquake continued. The barrage seemed like an ele-
mental upheaval, terrifying alike to those it was meant to protect and to those it was meant to destroy. S O S rockets were
bursting all along the enemy line, rising, bursting, and falling
with their absurd deliberateness, aloof from the turmoil below.

Machine-gun bullets began to clip the French parapet and to
splash mud around.

At zero plus three minutes the German counter-barrage was
adding to the chaos, tearing up the French wire, moving back
and forth across the front line. Already there were cries for
stretcher-bearers in the trenches, but nobody could hear them.
At the same time the enemy's heavy machine guns were coming
into action along the whole sector and the parapets were under
a steady spray of bullets.

At zero plus five there was a momentary lull while the French
guns were being re-aimed for the rolling barrage.

Whistles sounded along the jumping-off line.

Charpentier climbed onto the smoking parapet, shouting and
waving to his men to follow. He stood there, waving and shout-

ing, an heroic-looking figure, fit for any recruiting poster. He did not feel heroic, though. All he felt was the blister on his heel and the intoxication of the vibration all about him.

Men started to scramble over the parapet, slipping, clawing, panting. Charpentier turned to lead the way. The next instant his decapitated body fell into his own trench.

Four other bodies followed right after his, knocking over some of the men who were trying to get out. Three times the men of Number 2 Company attempted to advance, and each time the parapet was swept clean by the deadly machine-gun fire. It couldn't be done, that was all. The men, with one accord, decided to wait.

Number 1 Company got as far as its own wire, but it was driven to earth there by the German barrage. Unable to advance, the men crept back, one by one, to the less meagre protection of their trench. Captain Renouart was the last to go. He had given up ordering his men forward. It was useless.

The two companies on the left made a bit better showing to begin with. About fifty men of Number 4 Company managed to get beyond their wire, but only a half dozen survived, among them Meyer and Férol.

Number 3 Company, Lieutenant Bonnier leading them, got away from their jumping-off position with less trouble than the other had had. But they missed some of the lanes and got tangled up in their own wire, and it was there that the sweeping German machine-gun fire caught them. Everybody was shouting, unheard by anyone else. They seemed to be dancing a crazy dance in their efforts to disentangle themselves . . .

"Get down! Get down!" Bonnier shouted, himself standing waist deep in the wire. "Get down! Get down! . . ."

His shouts turned to gurgles. Blood sputtered in his mouth. His legs gave way under him. The din faded out of his ears with astonishing speed. Silence. Darkness. Lieutenant Bonnier sat down in the wire. He sat there as if he were attentively reading a book. He had taken a burst of machine-gun bullets full in the chest.

By zero plus thirty-five minutes the third attack on the Pimple was all over, stopped in its tracks, smothered.

Adjutant Herbillon's paper work on the ration requisition had been estimated with some accuracy.

———————

Telephonist-Corporal Nolot had a good story to tell. That was obvious to his mess-mates back at Division and they accordingly gave him the seat of honour at the table and set a bottle and a mug within his reach.

"The best day of my life," he began, almost squirming with delight. "Old Sharkface told where to get off. And by a mere captain! I heard the whole business. I couldn't close the wire because he was talking through the open extension. You can't run a switchboard in an observation post, you know. And anyway, I'd have heard his side of—"

"Never mind all that . . ."

"Yes, begin at the beginning . . ."

"And don't leave out anything . . ."

"But don't put in anything, either."

"Make it short, I've got to go."

"Never mind him, tell us everything."

"Well, I was squatting on the floor. I had the receiver to the seventy-fives in one hand, the other in the other. Ernest, here, was on the other end of that one. The general had asked for the weather report three hundred and seventy-nine times . . ."

"Sixty-nine," said Ernest.

"Oh, get your mind off it for a while . . ."

"Yes, don't interrupt. I've got to go in a minute and I want to hear it."

"Well, I kept on giving him the weather reports. They were all the same one. The last time he asked for it was about zero minus fifteen. We fiddled around there, Ernest telling me the time every minute and me repeating it. Wasted breath though, because all Sharkface looked at was his watch and the Pimple. One eye on each, so to speak."

"So then, after a while, Ernest says 'Zero.' I know it was zero all right. Hell had just broken loose. Zero for the Boche and for plenty of the boys, too . . ."

"Never mind the accompaniment . . ."

"Sharkface and Nicolas, that's the artillery officer, were glued to their glasses. And they stayed glued too. Then Ernest says, 'Zero plus five,' and you could hear the fire slacken for a moment while they fixed the guns. Ernest starts to tell me a dirty story. By the way, where did you say the flea woke up . . . ?"

"Oh, come on."

"Well, suddenly I hear Sharkface yelling, 'Name of God! Where are they?'

"'There, on the left, sir,' Nicolas yells back at him.

"'But that's only a handful. Where's the rest? Zero plus six and they're not out of the trench yet. . . .'

"Then a couple of minutes later from Sharkface, 'Any reports yet?'

"Ernest says there aren't any reports yet. As if there could be! I start to yell this to Nicolas but Sharkface is already doing some yelling of his own:

"'The dirty cowards! They aren't advancing. The barrage is getting away from them. . . .' Then he thinks it over I suppose and what d'you think he says next? He's in a terrible rage. He says, 'By God, if they won't advance behind a barrage, they will in front of one! Captain, order the seventy-fives to fire on the jumping-off positions. That'll blast them out.'"

"Jesus! You don't mean it?"

"Just as sure as I'm sitting here."

"What does the captain do?"

"He looks as if somebody had shot him. He says, 'Sir?' Question-like, see?"

"And what does Sharkface say?"

Nolot was letting them drag it out of him, and enjoying doing so.

"He says, 'You heard me,' and he gives the captain a look that would spike a gun. So Nicolas picks up the map and the extension receiver to the seventy-fives and says:

"'Hello, Polygon. General orders both batteries to fire on 32, 58, and 73. End. Repeat.' Those were the squares marked off on the map. The fellow down there repeats it right and then I hear him passing it on. A couple of minutes go by and the voice comes back:

"'Polygon speaking. Battery Commander says there must be some mistake. Those indications are our own front line. Please verify. End.'

"So Nicolas tells that to Sharkface and he says, 'Tell them there's no mistake and to obey at once. The troops are mutinying, refusing to advance. Fire as ordered until further notice.' And he can swear worse than any trooper I've ever heard.

"There's another wait, a bit longer. Then the voice says—now listen to this—it says, 'Battery Commander respectfully reports that he cannot execute such an order unless it is in writing and signed by the general.'

"'Give it to me,' says Sharkface and grabs the receiver out of Nicolas's hand. He roars like a bull, 'Get the Battery Commander on the wire at once. General Assolant speaking.'

"I can hear the fellow at the other end falling all over himself. Pretty soon another voice begins:

"'Battery Commander speaking, sir.'

"'Are you going to obey my orders?' Sharkface bellows at him.

"'Not that one, sir, with all respect, unless it is in writing.' Calm, just like that.

"'For the last time I say, will you obey my order, Name of God!'

"'With all respect, sir, no. Unless it is in writing and signed by you.'

"There's a pause for a moment. Sharkface is fuming and looks as if he's going to burst. Then the voice begins again:

"'With all respect, sir, you have no right to order me to shoot down my own men unless you are willing to take full and undivided responsibility for it. I must have a written order before I can execute such a command. Supposing you are killed, sir, then where will I be . . . ?'

"'You'll be in front of a firing-squad tomorrow morning, that's where you'll be. I'm running a battle up here, not a bank. D'you think I carry an office around with me? What's your name?'

"'Pelletier, sir.'

"'Hand over your command and report yourself under arrest to my headquarters.'

"'Yes, sir.' He says it just like that. Sounded a bit tired.

"It was about zero plus thirty then and Ernest starts buzzing in my other ear, 'According to first reports attack has apparently

failed all along the line.' But Sharkface interrupts, 'Tell my chief
of staff to arrange for the immediate relief of the 181st Regiment. Send them to Château de l'Aigle. Tell him to assemble a
field court martial and have it ready to sit at noon.' Then he
goes on, talking to Nicolas, 'If those bastards won't face German bullets, they will French ones.'

"'What are you going to do, sir?' says Nicolas. He's so flab-
bergasted he starts questioning the general. But Sharkface
seemed glad of the chance to talk.

"'I'm going to have a section from each company shot for
mutiny and cowardice in the face of the enemy, that's what I'm
going to do.'

"'Jesus!' says Nicolas. 'A section from each company! Jesus!
Why, you'll have to use a machine gun.'

"'That's a first-rate idea, my boy,' says Sharkface. He was so
pleased with it that he was feeling better already. And he didn't
seem to notice that Nicolas didn't say 'sir,' talked to him just as
if he was his pal.

"'Come on,' says the general. 'There's no use staying here.
But I'll teach them a lesson they won't forget. Playing a trick on
me like that. But I can play tricks too.'

"So they pick up their stuff and go out. Nicolas keeps saying,
'Jesus! Jesus! Holy Mother!' But Sharkface only smiles, if you
can call that look a smile. That's a good name for him, too,
Sharkface. I've never seen it fit him better than when he walked
out of that observation post. What a day!"

Telephonist-Corporal Nolot squirmed with delight.

There were three reasons why Assolant had directed the 181st
Regiment to the Château de l'Aigle. Later he was glad to dis-
cover that there had been a fourth. Retrospective reasons were
normal by-products of the general's decisions, and he always
accepted them as additional tributes to his sagacity without ever
recognizing their spuriousness as such. On the contrary, he welcomed them all the more for having come to make a sound piece
of judgment, as he thought, sounder.

Chief of the three genuine reasons, however, which had flashed
through his mind in the observation post and which had made
him fix instantly on the Château de l'Aigle, was the fact that the

château happened to possess the best parade ground in that part
of the country. There was, as the general knew, on the northern
limits of the estate, a spacious and level tract of land, bounded
on two adjacent sides by woods, on the other two by the avenue
of poplars which went out from the buildings and the highway
to which it gave access.

How was it, though, that in the tenseness and bitterness of the
situation in the observation post, the general's mind had remained
so well-ordered that the minute he had decided to relieve the
regiment, he knew exactly where he wanted to send it?

Surprised at such a question, he would have told anybody
who asked him that it was perfectly simple; he knew the place
well. He had reviewed troops there more than once.

Below the perfectly simple explanation there was, however, a
deeper, if equally simple reason for his unusually retentive memory of the detail of a parade ground. That parade ground had
become, ever since he had first seen it, a permanent fixture of his
day-dreams. It was the place where the President of the Republic, no less, would pin the star of a Grand Officer of the Legion
of Honour on General of Division Assolant's right breast. What
more fitting then, than that those who had cost him his star
should pay the debt on the same ground? The woods would
make a good backstop for the execution posts and there was
plenty of room for the regiment to form in three-sided square so
that no one would miss the spectacle.

The other two reasons for the selection of the Château de
l'Aigle were its convenient distance from both the line and Divisional Headquarters (it was about ten kilometres from each)
and the general's feeling that a château would be a more digni-
fied and, therefore, a more appropriate place for a court martial
to sit in than some tumbledown billet nearer the line.

In its day the estate had undoubtedly been one of some charm,
of a decorous charm which still was evident in places in spite of
its having been in the zone of the armies since the beginning of
the war. The château itself was in the centre of a good-sized
park. Most of the park was now overrun with huts which had
been built there under the trees for concealment. These were the
officers' billets and messes. Beyond the park there were fields,

and beyond the fields, woods. Sections of the woods to the north and to the west had been cleared of underbrush and thinned out to allow the construction of two cantonments for the troops, Camps A and B. The one nearest to Assolant's parade ground was Camp B, and this was the one that the 181st Regiment was now approaching down the avenue of poplars.

The men were talking.

". . . I heard the colonel committed suicide."

"He got over it quickly enough, then; I just saw him go by in that car."

"That's right. He was in the car with the general."

"Maybe he's under arrest."

"He ought to be, for sending us into that slaughter house."

"They say he threatened to shoot an officer."

"Who did?"

"The general."

"He ought to shoot the colonel for sending us into that attack."

"He ought to shoot himself then. The colonel didn't have anything to do with it. He was just obeying orders."

"That's right. The colonel said he'd resign if they went ahead with the attack."

"Who told you that?"

"I heard it."

"And I heard one of the headquarters runners saying the telephonist had said that there was a devil of a scene somewhere and they threatened to shoot each other."

"Who did?"

"Dax and the general."

"Suits me if they do."

"There's something in the wind, all right. This sudden relief . . ."

"Nobody could advance against that fire. Georges, you know Georges, stuck his head up to climb the parapet and the machine guns took the top of it clean off, right through his eyes."

"Machine guns don't slice that neatly."

"That one did. I got his brains splashed all over me."

"Funny, I never thought he had any."

"More than you, anyway."

"No. I had brains enough not to get killed."

"It doesn't take brains to hide in a dugout, only cold feet."

"Well, his troubles are over. He was always saying they didn't have his number. That's a sure way to get it."

"If you stay here long enough you'll get it."

"Somebody's going to get it for this fiasco, that's sure."

"Get what?"

"Well, if you're a general it'll be a medal. They always get medals, no matter what happens. But if you're a trooper you'll get a kick in the face. And they get that, too, no matter what happens."

"There's something queer going on. I can feel it. All this bustle to get us out of the line. And the officers, they don't act natural. Hello! Dragoons . . ."

The regiment had turned off the avenue of poplars to the right and was making for the woods, fifty metres or so away. They could see the nearest huts just beyond the line of the trees and, in front of the entrance to the camp, a group of mounted Dragoons. The cavalry had very much the look of a reception committee, but not an effusive one, it must be admitted.

The column passed between the ranks of the Dragoons, who stared at them with a cold curiosity, then disappeared into the wood. They soon found out what the guard of honour was for when they lined up in their company areas before being dismissed to their billets. Company commanders read out the following order:

> The regiment is under collective arrest and will remain confined to quarters until further notice. The camp is under guard and any man attempting to leave it without a pass will be shot at sight.

The presence of the Dragoons was Assolant's fourth and retrospective reason for being satisfied with the Château de l'Aigle.

Captain Pelletier finished his coffee at the Café du Carrefour and asked the old woman how much he owed her.

"Five sous," she said.

Pelletier put the money down and lighted a cigarette.

"Going on leave?" she said as she picked up the coins. It was the first purely conversational question she had asked anybody in several weeks.

"Yes," said Pelletier.

"Ten days?" she said.

"No, longer than that, I think," said Pelletier, smiling half at her, half to himself. He looked very young, very tired, and very dirty. The old woman saw his pallor, the taut muscles around his mouth, the glassiness of his eyes. She noticed, too, that his movements and gestures began jerkily and ended listlessly.

"Been in a long time?" she asked.

"Too long," he answered.

"Have another coffee with some cognac in it," she suggested.

"No, thank you, I must be going."

"If you wait a half hour, the empty ammunition trucks will be passing on their way back to railhead."

"Thank you, but I think I'll start walking. The exercise will do me good."

"It's a bad day."

"It is indeed."

"Well, good luck to you, young man."

"Thank you, I shall need it. And the same to you."

"Au revoir, captain."

"Adieu, madame."

When General de Guerville, chief of staff of the Fifteenth Army, entered Assolant's office at Divisional Headquarters shortly before noon, he had the feeling for a moment that he was interrupting a court martial, so much did the scene resemble one. He found General Assolant seated behind the long table which served him for a desk. On his left was the divisional chief of staff, Colonel Couderc, and on his right an empty chair. In front of the table stood a group of officers, in much the same attitude in which Assolant himself had stood two nights before to express his misgivings about the attack to the Army Commander. Whatever was being said was silenced by Assolant's rising to greet de Guerville. Everyone clicked his heels and saluted.

"Good morning, general. Good morning, gentlemen," said Guerville affably as he advanced into the room towards the empty chair which Couderc was holding for him. "A nasty day. Please don't let me interrupt you."

"Good morning, sir," said Assolant. "Allow me to present these officers. Colonel Couderc, I think, is known to you. Colonel Dax, commanding the 181st Regiment of the line. Colonel Labouchère, one of my staff. Captain Herbillon, Colonel Dax's adjutant."

There was more heel clicking and saluting, even by Saint-Auban and two other junior officers whom Assolant had not bothered to introduce.

"Please don't let me interrupt you," said de Guerville. Dax took him at his word and addressing himself to Assolant, from whom he had received a nod, plunged right in again where he had been stopped.

"I repeat, sir, I insist it was not mutiny."

"I order an attack and your troops refuse to attack. What's that if it isn't mutiny?"

"My troops did attack, sir, but they could make no headway."

"Because they didn't even try. I saw it myself you know, from the observation post. Three-quarters of the regiment never left the jumping-off positions."

"Two-thirds of the regiment was in support, sir. Not even in the front line."

"I mean battalion, of course. Please don't quibble. By the way, where's the battalion commander? He ought to be here."

"Major Vignon? He was killed. By our own barrage. Several shells fell short. I'm going to make a report of it as soon as I have time. That was another thing, sir . . ."

"Will you please stick to the point, Dax, which is that your First Battalion failed to advance as ordered and that, as I've already repeated several times, I'm going to have one section from each company executed. I call that lenient. The whole battalion should by rights—"

"Lenient, you cannot mean it, sir. And the men did advance. By God, we had almost fifty per cent casualties . . ."

"Yes, in our own trenches, Dax. For that many we should have been on the other side of the Pimple."

"It seems to me, Assolant," de Guerville put in, "that the casualties prove the fire was heavy, even if most of them happened in the jumping-off positions."

"Yes," said Assolant, "but the point is that the men failed to advance. They should have gotten themselves killed outside the trenches instead of inside."

"They weren't choosing where to be killed," said Dax. "The Germans were doing that for them."

"They didn't advance. Can't you understand that?" said Assolant.

"Yes, sir," said Dax. "But you say they refused to advance and I say they couldn't advance. It was physically impossible. In spite of that, many of them did manage to go a few metres. Some of them were literally blown back into their own trench." Dax, thinking he had found an ally in de Guerville, had turned and finished his remarks to him.

"Oh," said de Guerville, hastily disclaiming the alliance, "we must have some examples."

"Absolutely," Assolant agreed. "A section from each company."

"That's somewhat excessive, I think, general," said de Guerville.

"Well, what do you suggest, sir," said Assolant.

"Oh, say ten men from each company. Forty."

"That's practically a section," said Dax, "with the strength of the battalion what it is now."

"Aren't you exaggerating a bit, colonel," said de Guerville, smiling pleasantly.

"If it's an example you want, sir," Dax went on, "one man will do as well as a hundred. But I wouldn't know how to choose him. I'd have to offer myself. After all, I'm the responsible officer."

"Come, come, colonel," said de Guerville, "I think you're overwrought. It isn't a question of officers."

"Well, why shouldn't it be?" Dax asked. He had noticed that de Guerville was disquieted by the suggestion, and he was pressing the point. De Guerville, in truth, didn't like the turn the discussion was taking at all. He quickly decided on the paradoxical manœuvre of retreating from and at the same time ignoring Dax's attack. He turned to Assolant and said:

"Suppose we make it a dozen. We won't say it was mutiny. It would be just as well, I think, to keep that troublesome word out of it. Just cowardice in the face of the enemy."

"I was talking about four sections," said Assolant, "and here we are down to one squad already . . ."

"I implore you, gentlemen," Dax broke in, no longer wishing to restrain himself now that he felt he had de Guerville on the run. "A dozen men! A dozen men, like a dozen head of cattle. It's monstrous! Either the whole battalion is guilty or I alone am. But think of our record, of our *fourragères,* of what we've just been through at Souchez. Of the condition of the men. Of the rain. And of the murderous Boche fire. The general sampled some of it himself, yesterday. If it's an example you must have, will not one man do? But twelve men! Who knows which ones they will be? Where they come from? What connexions they may have? Poor devils, they tried to advance. It was impossible. On my honour, gentlemen, they weren't cowards. Far from it. They were heroes . . ."

De Guerville interrupted again. One of Dax's remarks had struck his ear and had remained there: "Who knows what connexions they may have." De Guerville did not like the possibilities evoked by that phrase. The chances were, he was forced to admit, that a dozen men would have more connexions than a lesser number. And those connexions would be more widely scattered too. Also, there were deputies in the ranks. An interpellation in the Chamber would . . .

"I think on the whole, Assolant, that we'd better fix on one man from each company. That'll make four."

"But, sir . . ." Assolant began.

"No buts, general. My mind is made up."

"If you insist, sir, then I'm forced to yield. But only because you speak with higher authority."

"Yes, I must insist, Assolant. No more than four."

"Very well, then, I'll have to content myself with four. A man from each company, Dax, to be shot tomorrow. Is that clear?"

"But without trial, sir?"

"Oh, no. The court martial will meet at the château at three this afternoon. That'll be convenient for you, won't it, Labouchère?"

Dax turned to Labouchère who was standing near him, then back to Assolant.

"I don't quite understand, sir," he said. "Am I relieved of my command? Colonel Labouchère . . . ?"

"Not at all," said Assolant. "Colonel Labouchère is to be president of the court martial, that's all."

"Then I beg to protest formally," said Dax, "and most emphatically against Colonel Labouchère serving on the court martial after having been present at this discussion."

"Let me remind you, Dax, that I'm giving orders . . ."

"Yes, sir. But I respectfully submit that it is improper for you to do so to an officer who is going to serve in a judicial capacity . . ."

"Silence, Name of God! No more observations!"

"May I inquire, sir," said Dax, speaking through clenched teeth and tight lips, "which four men you want executed?"

"That's immaterial to me. All I want is four, one from each company to give the others a lesson in obedience and duty."

"I have no candidates for the honour, sir."

"Then get somebody else to find them."

"But how? They're all equally innocent . . ."

"Name of God, colonel! Are you trying to obstruct me? If you are you're putting yourself in a very bad position. Let the company commanders choose the—er—er—culprits. That's an order, and it's final. You may go gentlemen. General, I hope you can stay for lunch."

"I shall be glad to," said de Guerville.

A half hour later, during which time de Guerville had explained his reasons for reducing the number of executions to Assolant, the two men left the office. They were met in the hall by two captains who halted and saluted. One of them looked very young, very tired, and very dirty.

"What d'you want?" said Assolant in a tone which lacked any invitation to express a want.

"You ordered me to report to you here, sir," began the one whose complexion was the most pallid, whose jaw muscles were still quite taut, and whose eyes were glassy. "Pelletier, battery commander of—"

Assolant didn't let him get any farther.

"Yes, yes. I wanted to speak to you about some of your shells falling short. The colonel of the 181st Regiment has made an oral report of it, and it may be a case for court of inquiry. I haven't time to go into it now. Report back to your command till further orders."

Assolant's face was under perfect control and the expression on it did not encourage further conversation. Pelletier glanced at de Guerville, saw the Army staff band on his sleeve, and stood aside to let the generals pass.

When they were out of earshot, de Guerville began:

"That's serious, firing on his own infantry. You must punish that sort of thing with the utmost severity, Assolant."

"I quite agree with you," said Assolant. "And the worst punishment for him would be shelving. Say to Macedonia, or a colony. He's an ambitious man and troublesome. I'll put the order through at once. Will you see that it's confirmed as soon as possible?"

"Certainly, if you wish it. But what about the court of inquiry?"

"Well, in cases of firing on your own troops I always try to avoid an inquiry. It gets around among the men and makes a very bad impression. Shelving will be the best discipline for him. I'll send the order transferring him through today, and if you will be good enough to speed its confirmation . . ."

"Just as you say, Assolant. You probably know more . . ."

"Yes, sir, for the good of the service."

De Guerville noticed the gratuitous explanation, also that the general seemed unusually well acquainted with a mere artillery captain, but he made no comment.

The men were talking. They were always talking. They even seemed to be talking when they were silent, as on a march, or on parade, or standing to in the trenches. That is, they seemed to be communicating. A look, the movement of a hand or of a foot, the expression on a face or the tilt of a head, the very angle at which the headgear was worn, often had an extraordinary implication of a conversation in progress. What did they talk about? Mostly themselves, of course, but also everything, everything in relation to themselves and vice versa. The talk was, inexplicably, always the same and always new. It seemed to be part of a larger conversation which had been begun way back in the past and was going to be continued monotonously into a future whose duration no one could guess. It had a strange quality of self-perpetuation which made one feel that, while men might die or go away, the talk never would, because other men would come to give it fuel, negligently and in passing.

It had stopped raining and the men were gathered near the cookhouse, eating their noonday meal, standing.

". . . the Dragoons."

"A sour bunch, all right. You'd think we were Boche prisoners."

"Wish we were, then we'd be safe."

"We're safe enough, except from the night bombers."

"That's not what's worrying me. It's the officers. Are we safe from them?"

"We always have been. What are you driving at anyway?"

"There's a rumour around there's going to be some executions."

"Oh, balls! This isn't a cinema."

"All right, balls then! But you'll think different when you find out it's rifle balls."

"He's right. There's something in the wind."

"Maybe somebody knocked over a latrine."

"Sure he's right. Or why are we under arrest? The whole regiment. It's unheard-of, a whole regiment."

"I suppose you think they're going to shoot the whole regiment?"

"Why not? They can do anything they want."

"Don't talk crazy."

"What's crazy about that?"

"It's just crazy, that's all."

"I suppose it wasn't crazy to send us into that attack then?"

"That's different—an attack."

"Well, anyway, I don't like it. It's too quiet around here. There's something dirty going on. There always is when it's quiet."

"Yes, and where are all the officers? No inspections, no parades, nothing."

"They didn't come to sample the soup, either."

"Just read the order and walked off."

"They've got their own soup, that's why."

"And we'll be in it, I'll bet."

"One of the Dragoons said it was court martials."

"Field court martials mean field executions."

"Well, they haven't ordered the grave-digging details out yet. That's something."

"What's the use of fooling yourself? I tell you . . . ."

Meyer, who had contributed nothing to this conversation but his attention, finished his meal and walked off towards his hut. He put his mess kit away without cleaning it, then stood in thought for a few minutes. His eyes, like his thoughts, began to rove. Pretty soon his body was in motion too, unhurried, purposeful. He got out his pocket-book and verified the contents: five francs and three obscene pictures. He got his knife and a bar of chocolate out of his haversack and put them in his pocket. He hunted for a pair of socks, but finding none in his own things, he searched the packs near him until he found a dry pair. He changed his socks, taking his time about it. His eye lighted on a tunic hanging from a nail half-way down the hut and he went to it and started to go through the pockets. He found a letter, which he began to read, but no money. A man came into the hut behind him and Meyer turned. He saw at a glance that the man had his tunic on so he went right on with what he was doing. Meyer was like that, cool. It was one trick he had to thank the army for teaching him. His drill sergeant had been profanely emphatic about it: "If you are out of order, hold it, keep still. Don't draw attention to it by trying to retrieve yourself." It was a good dodge and it worked. The man went out of the hut without giving Meyer a thought. Meyer finished the letter and went back to his own stuff. He wondered about taking his overcoat with him. It would come in handy for sleeping out in fields. Then he decided against it. So much more to carry, and it might make him conspicuous. Nobody was wearing coats now, except when it rained.

Meyer went out and wandered about the camp, mostly near the edge of it, where he could see the Dragoons. He spoke to one or two of them but did not get much of a response. "Surly swine," he said to himself, mistaking their embarrassment for surliness, the embarrassment of simple men acting in the unaccustomed and uncongenial role of jailers.

Meyer got nearer and nearer to the upper end of the camp, the end which was deepest in the woods. He pulled a cigarette out, then put it back for future use. He unbuttoned his tunic, stuffed his cap into his hip pocket and felt that he was giving a good imitation of aimlessness. He couldn't see any Dragoons around so he moved off into the wood, walking slowly and spreading a vacant expression on his face . . .

"Halt!"

Meyer pretended he hadn't heard.

"Halt there, or I fire!"

Meyer turned and saw a dismounted Dragoon a few paces away. He was bracing his rifle against a tree and Meyer saw that he was the target at which the rifle was aimed.

"If that's the way you feel about it . . ."

"Yes, that's the way I feel about it. Orders are orders. Get back to your lines."

"Look here, old sport, I'm just going over to the village for a bit of fun. I'll be back in an hour. Nobody'll know the difference."

"You'll know it if you go one step further. Orders are to shoot . . ."

"What's all the shooting about, anyway?"

"You fellows are under arrest. There's going to be plenty shooting tomorrow . . ."

"What for, for Christ's sake? What have I done?"

"You should know. You're trying to run away from it."

"I'm not running away. Just going for a stroll . . ."

"Nature lover, eh?"

"Yes."

"You look it. Well, pick your daisies over here. It'll be better for you than pushing them up there." The Dragoon jerked his head towards the camp. Meyer noted that he did so without jerking his rifle, which continued to be aimed at his chest.

Meyer weighed the chances of making a get-away. There was a tree near him but it was too thin to step behind. On his other side there was a good-sized tree from behind which he could safely put distance between himself and the Dragoon. But it would take four steps to get there, three to many. Meyer saw the Dragoon was wearing spurs and cursed himself for not having that cigarette in his hand. He could have thrown it at the Dragoon and made him lower his aim just long enough to jump in the tree and run for it. Spurs didn't help anybody to run, especially in a wood. But his hands were empty and spurs had no effect on bullets.

"All right, eater of horse dung," he said, and started walking back to camp, looking over his shoulder.

The Dragoon pivoted around the tree against which he was bracing his rifle and he kept Meyer in the sights until he was gone.

Regimental Headquarters
181st Regiment of the line

No. 13934-CD-19.
Confidential. Urgent.

To: Capt. Renouart, O.C. No. 1 Company
Capt. Sancy, O.C. No. 4 Company
Lieut. Roget, Acting O.C. No. 2 Company
Sergt.-Maj. Jonnart, Acting i/c No. 3 Company

You are hereby ordered to select and arrest one man from each of your companies and to have him at the regimental guard-room at the château not later than 14.30 o'clock today ready to appear before a court martial on charges of cowardice in the face of the enemy.

By order:
Herbillon
Capt. Adjt.

"How's that, sir?" said Herbillon, handing the piece of paper to Colonel Dax.

"Hmm," said Dax. "That seems to cover the situation. And yet it doesn't. What I mean is, I want these men to know what it is they are being called on to do. That in all probability they will be choosing a man to be shot, not just court-martialled."

"Why not call them in and explain it to them, sir?"

"I can't, Herbillon. I couldn't face them. I won't have Assolant's role forced on me. I couldn't stand their reproaches . . ."

"They wouldn't dare, sir . . ."

"No, I'm talking about the unspoken ones. They would be the hardest of all to bear. I am literally unable to do any more arguing about the matter. An order is an order, by God! I've been fighting this thing ever since they sent us into the line. Protests, protests, protests, all beating up against a stone wall, the stone wall of Assolant's stubbornness and vanity. He's a bit mad all right, and I know it. But I'm afraid lots more men have got to be killed before they find it out higher up. Why, do you know what he did? He ordered the seventy-fives to fire on our jumping-off positions to make the men advance! Pelletier refused, unless the order was given in writing. Assolant wasn't cracked enough to do that, however. Pelletier's forward observation officer told me about it. So you see what I'm up against. I'm tired out. I've just spent about two hours with the general arguing about it. And I'll be shelved for my pains, that was obvious."

"Oh, I hardly think that, sir . . ."

"Of course, I'd forgotten you were present at the meeting."

"Please let me explain the situation to the company commanders for you, sir," said Herbillon who really wanted to do something to ease the distress of his chief.

"No, it's no use. They'd just insist on seeing me and on shoving the responsibility on me too. They've got to take their own responsibility and act as best they can. Those were the general's orders anyway, and I'm going to take full advantage of them. Also, if there's any justice to be gotten out of this mess at all it will probably be obtained better by letting the company commanders act on their own initiative. They know their men, or at least they know them better than I do. The general wanted a section from each company shot. Think of it, a section! The man is insane. I beat him down to four men, with the help of the

Army staff officer. I've done all I can. It was a degrading piece of
bargaining, I assure you. No, let things take their course. I'll appear at the court martial to make a final plea, though it will
probably be useless. You heard how Assolant practically gave
Labouchère orders to condemn the men. If the worst comes to
the worst, I'll appeal to the Army Commander, right over Assolant's head too. But I want these officers to know the serious-
ness of the choices they've got to make."

"Well, shall I put in something about executions . . . ?"

"No. That's taking too much for granted. I really can't believe
they're going through with this, though I know they are. And it
would never do to admit that we expected something of the
sort. It would be unfair to the men. There's always some hope,
you know, until they're actually dead."

"How about a phrase like this, sir: 'Orders concerning firing
squads will be issued later . . .'"

"That's practically the same thing. I tell you what though. Put
'summary court martial' instead of just 'court martial.' That
should bring the gravity of the affair home to them. Also they
will know that there is no appeal. And by the way, change the
beginning. If Assolant is going to give such orders, I want them
to appear in the record. Start it off this way: 'You are hereby
instructed, according to the orders of the general commanding
the division, to select and arrest, et cetera.' That'll show them
that I'm not trying to avoid responsibility by passing it on to
them. It also ought to show them that the order is final and that
there's no use trying to argue about it with me. I'm going to try
to get a nap, but if anybody wants to see me about this business,
you must wake me up of course."

After Dax had left, Herbillon took back the draft order and
rewrote it himself on the typewriter, making the changes Dax
had wanted and using four pieces of carbon paper. He signed
each copy, put it in an envelope and sealed it. Then he addressed
the envelopes, marked them "Personal and Urgent" and called
for a runner.

"Take these around and give them into the hands of the officers they're addressed to," he said. "And get receipts."

The runner saluted and went out. As soon as he was safely
away from the door, he looked at the envelopes and tried, un-

successfully, to pry each one open. His face fell, then brightened again at the sight of the one for Sergeant-Major Jonnart. That meant a trip up to Camp B, a nice little walk. Also a chance for some gossip with the boys. Being a runner had its advantages. But it had its disadvantages, too. Sitting outside the office, doing nothing, sometimes for a whole morning. Not allowed to smoke either. And jumping up and saluting every time an officer passed. No one to talk to, except the other runners, and you knew as much as they did, if not more. Of course, you usually got wind of what was going on around headquarters, and that made you a person of some importance. Even sergeants would listen to you, or try to pump you. But you missed being with your own kind and talking about familiar things, freely. You had to be careful what you said around the office. And, no matter how decent an officer might be, he was still an officer and you weren't. Officers talked a different language. They even ate different food . . .

The runner went off into the park to deliver the letters.

"Silly of Herbillon to say get receipts," he reflected. "You always get receipts. Fussy old fool. But adjutants are always fussy. Think they have the weight of the world on their shoulders. Now for a cigarette on the way up to Camp B. Sergeant-Major Jonnart, eh? Not a bad sort, but thick. Sergeant-majors are always like that. Perhaps he can tell me what's up. Headquarters is certainly quiet about it. They talk in the office so you can't hear them outside. Maybe the Dragoons will know something. A whole regiment under arrest! Thank God for a chance to smoke. Seems as if it might be a nice day after all. The country looks fine. It'll be just right for when I go on leave next month. Maybe I can wangle a drink at the canteen on the way back . . ."

The runner took his time. He inhaled the cigarette smoke deeply, giving his lungs the nicotine they had been deprived of and for which they were grateful. He was delighted to be sent on an errand.

III

Captain Renouart tore the envelope open, took out the thin sheet of official paper, and looked at his wrist watch. He spread the paper out and wrote across the right-hand top corner:

"Received 12.48" and signed it with an R. While he was doing this his eye was already at work extracting the message from the typewritten lines. So practiced and selective was his glance that he knew what the order contained almost before he had signed his initial. His eye had acted telegraphically, giving him the message thus: "Renouart . . . arrest one man . . . guardroom . . . 14.30 . . . court martial . . . cowardice."

At last! There it was. They were going to do it that way, then. He had been expecting something to happen, though not quite of this kind. There had been a good deal of loose talk around the mess at luncheon about executions. Renouart, disagreeing with the others, had been inclined to think that, if any disciplinary action was going to be taken, it would be against the officers, himself among them probably. As far as the men were concerned, he was sure they would be deprived of leave and would be given some extra tours of duty in nasty sectors instead. But this was different.

Renouart put an end to his now useless speculation about what might have been done and read the order through, word for word.

Select and arrest a man. He repeated the phrase out loud and started to repeat it again, but found himself lingering over, repeating the word "select" only.

His decision took shape at what seemed a very great distance from him, minute shape. In the same instant it had grown to a thing of gigantic but intangible size and had moved in upon him with terrific speed, overwhelming him with its absolute finality.

No. He couldn't and wouldn't select a man. A summary court martial, he knew what that meant. Nobody had the power to make him do that. They could shoot him first. But they wouldn't dare. Better go and see Dax, talk it over with him. No, better not. Dax would only have to order him to obey and he could only refuse. That would bring it all to a head and would probably make it worse for everybody all round. What about getting the priest in? No use in that either. He knew what he'd say. Thou shalt not kill. Poor piece of translation, that. Should be, Thou shalt not commit murder. Better still, Thou shalt not commit individual murder. The church ought to get that changed before the next war. Make it much easier for good Catholics to answer embarrassing questions. Why bother to go on thinking about it? His mind was quite clear on this particular problem and besides it was already made up. . . .

Renouart reached for a piece of paper and started to draft a reply.

Col. Dax:

As I have already reported to you, my company left the jumping-off position to a man and attempted to advance. In the face of a fire which was, without exaggeration, decimating, they reached their own wire where they were literally driven to earth. Twice I ordered the men forward, and twice they obeyed, each time many of them, too many of them, rising only to be shot down. They had already displayed superhuman heroism. That, however, was no protection against machine-gun and shell fire. I therefore permitted them to seek whatever shelter they could find in their own trench, pending an opportunity to begin a fresh assault.

There were no cowards in No. 1 Company. I can personally take my oath on that for I was right amongst them and saw their actions with my own eyes.

There is, therefore, no man in my company against whom I can bring charges of cowardice, much less charges which would be tenable.

Moreover, and with all respect, I consider that it is not within the prerogatives of the military authorities to order me to act in a way which would be a violation of my duties as a citizen and my scruples as a Christian and practicing Catholic. As an officer acting in a judicial capacity I would be guilty of dereliction of duty by bringing charges which I knew to be false. As a Christian I cannot take a step which would brand me a murderer in my own eyes as well as in those of God and my fellowmen.

I make this reply with the deepest respect for your person and your rank, and I do so fully aware of what the consequences may be for me. My sense of duty as an officer and as a man does not, however, permit me to act otherwise.

Renouart drafted two more replies, each shorter than the preceding one. Then he wrote the final one:

From: Capt. Renouart, O.C. No. 1 Company
To: Col. Dax, O.C. 181st Regiment of the line

Sir:
In reply to your No. 13934-CD-19 of today's date, I have the honour to report that I am unable to comply with your instructions because there is no member of my company against whom charges of cowardice in the face of the enemy can either be made or be found tenable.

(Signed) Renouart
Captain.

"That's better," Renouart said to himself. "It sounds like a routine reply to a routine order. Glad I thought of using the word instructions instead of orders. Makes the refusal sound less of a refusal. A good job all round. The others were argumentative, this one isn't."

Pleased with the bland note he had managed to introduce into his answer, Renouart decided to extend it to his actions by putting himself out of reach until the court martial was over. Delay, he knew, even in a military trial, helped to thwart the aims of the prosecutors. It would also give the red tape a chance to tangle itself up, a chance it never failed to avail itself of. He sealed the note, marked it personal for Colonel Dax and put it in his pocket, then called his orderly.

"Have my horse here in half an hour," he said. "I'm going for a ride." He added the explanation of his intention on purpose, hoping thereby to convey, and to have it passed on, that his absence would be a temporary one only and that he was, therefore, not bothering to delegate his authority to anyone else.

Renouart walked slowly over to the château. The assistant adjutant was alone in the office.

"Where's everybody?"

"I don't know. Sleeping, I suppose," said the assistant adjutant, who looked as if he would like to be doing the same thing himself.

"Here's a note for the chief . . ."

"Well, I know he's sleeping, and he's not to be disturbed unless . . ."

"Who's asking you to disturb him? Just give it to him when he comes in, will you? I'm going for a ride. Won't be back till about supper time."

"Say, ask her if she's got a sister or a friend who wants . . ."

Lieutenant Roget, acting in command of Number 2 Company, read the order from regimental headquarters, found Didier's name present in his mind at the end of the reading, and promptly rejected it. He was rewarded for the rejection of a thought so unworthy by feeling a glow of self-admiration. This was no new experience for Roget, but the genuineness of the glow was. For a while his mind remained stationary, that is, the thoughts it contained all seemed to have taken seats, like people in an anteroom who realize the time has not yet come. It was then that he discovered that his rejection of Didier's name had not been followed by its ejection too. It was still there, and there to stay, he knew, although he was not yet quite ready to admit it in so many words.

There was no getting round it, however. He had to choose a man. That was an order, and it came straight from the general. Not that that made any difference. An order was just as much an order, no matter what rank it came from, as long as the authority was there. Roget got the bottle of cognac out of his things and set it on the floor near the bunk where he had been lying. It was a characteristic move and, had Roget had the curiosity to examine and define his psychological processes, he would have described them thus:

"Alcohol clarifies my mind and lubricates its functioning. It simplifies my perplexities, makes them more remote and less consequential. That is, the right amount of alcohol. The first two or three drinks are always the right amount, or, at least, proportions of it. Liquor takes the vaporous and roaming thoughts I already have and solidifies and fixes them. It also seems to make their quality better and cleans them of their non-essential growths and erosions. At the same time it creates another set of vaporous and roaming thoughts which are always a distinct improvement on the old ones because of their originality. Stupid, therefore, not to draw on this reservoir of originality when the key to it can be found in almost any bottle. In addition to this, alcohol has the property of conferring courage and impelling to action. What does it matter that this is an illusion, that it does not really increase courage but reduces fear through its anæsthetic quality? The result is the same. I am now about to choose a man—to be shot, undoubtedly. That will take courage. But it will take infinitely more courage to choose the man who is my enemy, who could be my destroyer, and to put him out of the way in the coldest of cold blood, namely, without the slightest danger to myself. On the contrary, it's my duty to select a man, and I'm going to have the guts to select a particular one. Such cynicism will take courage. . . ."

All this did not pass through Roget's mind as so much conscious thought. He just knew that a drink would help and he took it, a long one, then lighted a cigarette. He smoked without thinking for a few minutes, during which time the alcohol was making its way to his brain. Then his conscious thinking began, conscious enough to be reflected in the silent movement of his lips and in vague, half-completed little gestures, characteristic enough to be oblique at the very first.

"It would not be fair to the other man, whoever he might be, to be penalized because I'm bending over backwards about Di-

dier. The fact that I want to get rid of him mustn't be permitted
to give him the slightest advantage of immunity. On the contrary, my reasons for wanting to get rid of him are sound ones,
absolutely legitimate, any one of them alone being enough to
send him in front of a firing-squad. The fly in this ointment is
that my personal wishes coincide too closely with my duty."

Roget took another swallow of the cognac, a smaller one. The
coincidence between his wishes and his duty was already beginning to fade from his thought.

"A man has to be chosen to go before the summary court
martial. That'll certainly mean execution. Didier wasn't killed,
not even wounded in the attack. Where was he then? Certainly
not on the parapet, for all the men in our company who scaled
it were killed. Practically all, anyway, or wounded. So that
makes him a candidate at once. He didn't get out of the trench.
On top of that, his actions on the patrol are enough to get him
shot three times over. I'll bring that out at the court martial, if
necessary. And if he starts to talk, he'll only make it worse for
himself. They'll realize it's a man in desperate circumstances making insane accusations in his efforts to save himself at another's
expense. Make a very bad impression. Thank God Charpentier
got it. He never liked me, and I didn't like the way he acted
about that report of mine. I've certainly had some luck. It would
be the height of stupidity for me to do anything but assist events
on the road they seem to be taking anyway. Later, perhaps, I can
get transferred out of this regiment. Get clean away from it . . .
maybe a nice little wound . . ."

"Runner!"

"Sir?"

"Is Sergeant Gounod around?"

"I think so, sir. I'll see."

"Tell him to come here at once."

Roget took a third drink, put the bottle away, and lighted a
fresh cigarette. He felt quite pleased with himself for having
reached and taken his decision, a decision which now seemed
logical, dutiful, inevitable. The alcohol had effectively anæsthe-
tized him from his scruples and had removed his irresolution.
Unconscious that he was doing so, he paid it tribute, gave it

credit for its assistance: "Sufficient unto the crisis is the alcohol thereof," he said to himself, and laughed.

"You wanted to see me, sir?" said the sergeant, saluting in the doorway of the hut.

"Yes, Gounod, come here. Read that. Understand? All right, go up to the camp and arrest Private Didier and take him down to the guard-room as ordered. But do it quietly, without anybody knowing, if you can."

"It will be difficult, sir, with all the men around."

"I tell you what. Better do it this way. Just tell him to come along with you, you've got a job for him. Don't arrest him formally until you're clear of the camp. And don't tell him anything. If he asks questions, say you don't know. By the way, do you know which is Didier?"

"Yes, sir."

"Well, don't make any mistakes."

"Hey! Look at this, Arnaud. Who says there's nothing new in this world? I've had some experiences in my life, but this is the first time I've had the role of fate or God or whatever you call it thrust upon me. This is going to be interesting."

"Interesting, that's a queer thing to call a responsibility such as this order places on you, Sancy."

"Don't be so solemn, my boy. To a man of my temperament everything is interesting. And this is more interesting than anything. Up to now, in my scientific work, I've never played God to anything but microbes, monkeys, or rats. But now I've got to play God to my own kind, to men. What a chance to exercise my intellectual faculties!"

"You speak of yourself and God as if you were messmates. It's in poor taste, to say the least. And after all, the role is not an unusual one. Every officer who has commanded troops in the line has been responsible for the fate of his men at one time or another."

"Oh, but that's quite different. It's more or less predetermined or collective responsibility. You're only a link in a chain of responsibility. And you can't measure your own part in it with any accuracy. But this is different. Here am I, Captain Sancy of

Number 4 Company, probably the only man in the world who is being called upon to pick a fellow-man for destruction. To select him, mind you. In other words, to put my intelligence to work upon a problem which involves not a sum of money, not an ordinary question of life nor even a military one, but a man's existence. I move my finger over a row of men and when it stops and points, that point is fatal."

"You're a strange fellow, Sancy. You seem to enjoy the job. But you're wrong about one or two things. First, you're not the only man in the world playing God, as you put it. Don't forget the other company commanders have to do the same thing. Second, it's very much a military problem. Third, surgeons are every day in the same position you're in . . ."

"Not the same at all. They're using their intelligence to preserve life. I, on the other hand, will be taking it."

"I think you're a bit cracked sometimes. Now I'm delighted it's you who has to do the choosing and not me. I wouldn't know how."

"Yes, I suppose you'd draw lots. No imagination."

"Well, aren't you going to?"

"Certainly not. Besides, if I did that, I'd be disobeying. The orders are that Captain Sancy, not chance, is to select a man. And the first intelligent order I've seen come from above. Of course the company commander is the one best qualified to pick a man to be shot, because he knows his men."

"I've never seen you so pleased since the day they put you in charge of that raid . . ."

"I like to use my head, Arnaud. The beauty of this case is its freedom from complications because all the men are equally innocent. None of them showed cowardice in the face of the enemy, but one of them's got to be shot for it none the less. Now the point is, which one?"

"One man's got to be shot for a crime he didn't commit, which nobody committed. Do you call that justice?"

"Who said anything about justice? There's no such thing. But injustice is as much a part of life as the weather. And you're getting away from the point again. He isn't being shot for a crime he didn't commit. He's being shot as an example. That's his contribution to the winning of the war. An heroic one too, if you like."

"So you figure that the man who is shot as an example is as much a part of the scheme of an offensive as the man who calculates the barrages, the infantryman who goes over the top, or the quartermaster who doesn't?"

"Of course, why not? Discipline is the first requisite of an army. It must be maintained and one of the ways of doing it is to shoot a man now and then. He dies, therefore, for the ultimate benefit of his comrades and of the country."

"In other words, then, you think the general ought to come down and invest the victim with the *médaille militaire,* then step aside and let the firing-squad do its work?"

"Excellent, my boy, excellent!"

"There are shirkers in every company. I've got a prize one in my platoon, if that's the way you're going about it."

"No, no, you're off on the wrong track."

"What track are you on then? Don't you want to narrow it down to the ones who are the poorest soldiers?"

"Citizens, my boy, citizens, not soldiers. This war isn't going to last for ever, and when it's over we'll be glad enough to be rid of the soldiers and to have some citizens for a change. Besides which, what you call a poor soldier is often a good citizen. Take me, for instance. From the point of view of a soldier, I'm a poor one. That's why I'm only wearing three stripes instead of three stars. As a matter of fact, however, I'm a very good soldier. But I'm an even better citizen. I'm intelligent, industrious, educated, in good health mentally and physically. And I contribute my talents to the betterment of the world I live in. Not out of smugness, you understand, but out of intelligence. The better the world, the better for everybody and therefore the better for me and mine."

"Well, who've you got on your mind?"

"Easily and instantly answered: the two incorrigibles, Meyer and Férol."

"But they're the best soldiers in the company. And as a matter of record they got farther in the attack than anybody in the regiment."

"Which adds one more proof of their stupidity. Now listen, Arnaud. Try to get this straight. If the whole regiment had been made up of Meyers and Férols, would it have done any better, got any further? No. Shells kill good and bad soldiers without discrimination. So even speaking militarily, they aren't worth any more than anyone else. We're all cannon fodder. Are you going to ask me to preserve the life of one of these brutes and sacrifice instead some man who might be of some use to society, who may only be of a negative use but who, at least, will not be a positive danger to it the way these two have already proved themselves? No. It's either Meyer or Férol then, and I'll let you know which in a few minutes, after I've thought about it carefully."

There was silence for some time while Captain Sancy pondered his problem. He walked up and down the hut, stopping every so often to make a note on a piece of paper which was lying on the table. Lieutenant Arnaud, sitting nearby, could see that the captain's notes were gradually taking the shape of two columns. One column was longer than the other and it held its lead throughout Sancy's deliberations. Arnaud tried to read the names at the tops of the columns, but he couldn't make out the captain's small writing at that distance. After about twenty minutes Sancy tossed the paper over without saying anything, and this is what Arnaud read:

MEYER	FÉROL
sexual crimes, some against minors	*Robberies*
Suspected of murder	*Mental defective*
Syphilitic	*Chronic alcoholic*
History of drug addiction	*Absolutely untrustworthy*
Absolutely untrustworthy	
Brutish	

"Those are the high spots," said Sancy. "A fine pair, eh?"
"It looks as if Meyer's elected," said Arnaud.
"Why do you think that?"
"His list is longer, isn't it, and blacker too?"
"Yes, on the face of it, it would be good riddance. But there's another circumstance which you've overlooked. He's a Jew."

"All the more reason for . . ."

"That's where you're short-sighted. This is one time when being a Jew is going to save a man his life instead of costing him it."

"What? I don't follow you . . ."

"I'll explain. I'm really using my head about this. Do you remember the Dreyfus affair? . . ."

"I've heard about it, of course. But what's that got to do with it?"

"It's a lesson, that's all, a lesson against exposing yourself to the same thing over again."

"But this isn't going to be a Dreyfus case . . ."

"No one thought the Dreyfus case was going to be one either. They didn't dream, when they picked on that quiet little Jewish officer, that the whole world would ring for years with his name, that ministry after ministry would fall and war loom because of him, or that the whole of France would be kept in a constant state of disturbance over him and his fate."

"But Dreyfus was an officer. This Meyer is just a common criminal, an ex-convict . . ."

"Well, half the world thought Dreyfus was a criminal too. One of the worst, a traitor to his country. And they made an ex-convict out of him at that. No, my boy, I'm not going to touch Meyer. In the first place, you never know what connexions these Jews may have. Secondly, even if he hasn't any, and this business gets out as it undoubtedly will, the cry of anti-Semitism will go up instantly. And once that cry is raised, no one can tell when or at what price it will be silenced. This is where I'm using my head, being foresighted."

"It's tough on Férol, though, that Meyer's a Jew and that you're so foresighted."

"It's always tough on somebody, Arnaud. Life is. The world is an immense graveyard, getting perpetual care from the survivors who are living off it."

"But Meyer is a much greater danger to society than Férol is. He can, with his syphilis alone, cause untold havoc to society, and most probably will."

"I grant you. But I'm saying he might be an even greater danger to society, cause even more havoc, by being dead—that is, executed by a firing-squad. Besides, he may be killed any day. No, there's no two ways about it. My mind is clear on this point. So go up to the camp, will you, and tell one of the sergeants he's to arrest Férol and bring him down to the guard-room at once."

"Since you order it. But I can't help thinking . . ."

"What I really would have enjoyed, Arnaud, would be to have a man in the ranks who had high connexions—really high, like G.H.Q., or who was a deputy or something. I'd have picked him out of pure mischief, just to watch the court martial and the brass hats squirming out of that dilemma. It would have been most interesting. . . ."

"Yes," said Arnaud, putting on his cap. "Probably more interesting for you than you had bargained for."

Sergeant-Major Jonnart belonged to that class of men which is said to form the backbone of an army, namely, the N.C.O. of long service. He was thick of body, it is true, but not as thick of head as the runner had implied. It was just that he was incurious, unimaginative, methodical, and taciturn. Army life suited him perfectly. He liked the routine and, as it had long since become a part of his blood, he would not have known what to do without it.

Colonel Dax's order didn't surprise Jonnart in the least. Nothing surprised him in the army because it was all part of the routine, and routine was merely another name for the channels through which authority flowed. Sergeant-Major Jonnart, therefore, went to work methodically to obey the colonel's order. He got out the company roster, which he had already corrected for the morning's casualties, and saw that the ration strength of the company was one hundred and fifty-eight men. He crossed out the names of three sergeants, seven corporals, and thirty-six men who had been assigned to special duties for the attack or who had been left at the regimental train as a nucleus, but who, in either case, were not part of the attacking wave. Then he sent for his three sergeants, read the order to them, and explained his intentions.

"You will," he added, "assemble the whole of Number 3 Company outside the sergeants' mess hut. That's large enough to hold them, isn't it?"

"Plenty."

"Two of you will go into the hut and stand at either door. The other one will stay with me. I've a list of the names here and as I read it out the men will pass one by one into the hut. You will count and check them off as they come in. When they are all in I will follow and the ones whose names were not called can be dismissed."

"Why not get them all in the hut first and then send the ones you don't want out?"

The sergeant-major looked at the speaker but made no comment.

"All right, get busy then! Not a word to anyone about this order. I'll be out in ten minutes."

When the last man had entered the hut and the rest had been dismissed, Jonnart was vexed to find that he had forgotten something. "After all," he excused himself, "this is the first time in my career that I've had to do a job like this." He went back to the company office, got two pencils and a refill pad for a notebook, then walked over to the sergeants' mess hut.

"Attention!" shouted the sergeant at the door. The buzz of conversation stopped as if cut off by a knife. Jonnart was pleased with the company's snap, and he knew whom to credit it to. He walked the half length of the hut briskly without looking into the eyes of any of the men, climbed over a table and turned to face them from the other side.

"At ease! Rest!" he ordered. "But no talking. I have an order to read to you as follows:

"Regimental headquarters 181st regiment of the line one-three-nine-three-four-c-d-nineteen to captains etcetera and sergeant-major Jonnart acting in command number three company you are hereby instructed according to the orders of the general commanding the division to select and arrest one man from each of your companies and to have him at the regimental guard-room at the château not later than fourteen-thirty o'clock today ready to appear before a summary court martial on charges of cowardice in the face of the enemy by order signed herbillon captain adjutant."

The sergeant-major came abruptly and a little breathlessly to a stop in his headlong reading of the order, and found himself in

the midst of a stupefied silence. This silence was broken at last
by an incredulous guffaw which came from the rear of the
crowd.

"Shut your face!" ordered one of the sergeants. The laugh
died.

"This is no laughing matter, men," said Jonnart, and the slight
tone of kindliness in his voice awoke uneasiness in more than
one of his audience. "In fact it's very serious. You all know what
a summary court martial means. It means one of you is going to
leave this hut with only a short time left to live . . ."

"Which one?"

"They're mad!"

"I don't believe it."

"I was no coward!"

"It's a joke."

"And not a funny one, either."

"Which one?"

"Silence! Silence everybody!" Jonnart shouted. "How can I
tell you which one unless you stop this noise? Now listen to me.
I've gone over the company roster carefully and all you men
who are in this hut were in the attacking wave this morning. All
those of our company not in the hut were on special duties or at
the regimental train—"

"I wasn't in the attack . . ."

"Who's that? Come up here. Where were you then?"

"Don't you remember, chief, you yourself sent me down to
the dump to get detonators for that case of bombs we found
didn't have any?"

"That's right. You can go then."

"I think I'll stick around and watch the fun."

"Get out, you bastard, before I change my mind and keep you
here for the draw . . ."

"Jesus! He's going to draw lots."

"Draw lots . . ."

"I won't draw any lots . . ."

"Me neither."

"They have no right . . ."

"Married men should be exempt."

"Men with mothers . . ."

"Certainly with widowed mothers."

"Or sisters . . ."

"I was the farthest one in front."

"Only those who lagged behind . . ."

"My three brothers have already been killed."

"I was no coward. I won't draw."

"Ha, ha. Watch the shirkers step up . . ."

"There were no cowards."

"The colonel doesn't agree with you."

"Where are the corporals? Are they any . . ."

"I have four children . . ."

"I've been cited in Divisional and Army Orders. . . ."

"That's enough, men!" Jonnart cut in. "Silence, I say! Everyone has a good reason for not wanting to die. Orders are orders and one of you has got to be the victim. So you're going to draw lots. There are one hundred and eleven of you in this room. I'm going to make one hundred and eleven pieces of paper. One of them will be marked with a cross. The man who draws it will go before the court martial. I'm giving orders here, but since it's a serious matter, I'm willing to hear any objections anybody may have to this method."

"Yes, I object. The paper's thin and we'll see through it if it's marked."

"That's stupid. The slips are going to be folded up and put in my cap. Each man will be blindfolded before he comes up to draw."

"A blindfold never prevented anyone from looking down his nose."

"Besides which, the fellow who gets it might erase the mark, or substitute another piece of paper for it. We most of us carry some of it around. It's thin and comes in handy for . . ."

"All right then," Jonnart conceded. "We'll do it this way, though it will take longer . . ."

"We aren't in any hurry, chief . . ."

"We'll write out two sets of numbers from one to one hundred and eleven. One set will go in my hat, the other in Sergeant Darde's. Each man will come up in alphabetical order, draw a

number and open it at once. It will be entered against his name.
When all are drawn, Sergeant Darde will draw one number from
his hat. The man who has the corresponding number will be the
one chosen. Yes, that's better. All the papers will have markings
on them and the unlucky man cannot be known until after all
the numbers are drawn."

"Unlucky is right . . ."

"All right, Darde. Here's some paper and a pencil. Tear each
sheet into four equal pieces and write the numbers on them,
from one to a hundred and eleven. Print them carefully, but
don't fold them up until I tell you."

It took Sergeant Darde about twelve minutes to do the numbers, while Jonnart needed an extra five. The men watched them
in silence, fascinated by the work.

"Finished, Darde?" Jonnart asked when he was himself
through. "Now, as I count each number, you pick it up, call
it, and fold it and put it in your cap. I'll do the same with
mine. One."

"One," said Darde.

"Two."

"Two . . ."

"Say, chief, can I have number thirteen?"

"No, you cannot," said Jonnart, "unless you draw it.
Sixty-two."

"Sixty-two . . ."

"I'd like number one," said a voice.

"Why one?"

"Because I never heard of number one being drawn in any
lottery."

"You're a wise one! I'll take one hundred, then . . ."

"You'll take what you get, all of you," said Jonnart. "One
hundred and three."

"One hundred and three . . ."

"Say, chief, can I go out for a smoke?"

"One hundred and eleven."

"One hundred and eleven."

". . . and finish," said Jonnart. "No. No smoking, and no going out. Nobody leaves the hut until this business is over. Now

let me see, where's the nominal roll? Ah, yes. First, Aboville. Step up, Aboville. Not so fast. Wait till I've finished mixing them up. Now, now draw a number out of my cap here. Be careful not to pick up two. What is it? Let me see it. Twenty-two.

"Aboville, twenty-two. Got it, Darde? Enter it there, right in front of his name. Next. Who's next? Ajalbert. Come on, step lively. Don't pick up more than one. Let me see it.

"Ajalbert, fifty-nine . . .

"Lalance, one hundred and three . . .

"Be careful, they stick to your fingers. Langlois, seventy-six . . .

"Ravary, forty-seven.

"Richet . . . Richet . . ." Jonnart hesitated over this number, realizing suddenly that he had overlooked something—something which might turn out to be troublesome. *"Merde!"* he said to himself. "If I'd only written them instead of printing them so carefully! But it may come out all right if I can keep my memory of the numbers already drawn working quickly and correctly.

"Richet, six . . ."

One by one the men came up to draw their numbers and to have them recorded against their names. One by one they joked, swaggered, whined, argued, affected unconcern, or acted as if they were picking hot coals. They were all doing just what they were told, but each one felt that this was one time when he could allow his mannerisms to be seen in his obedience to an order. There was not one of them who did not have an increased sense of self-dramatization, of individuality—above all, perhaps, of power, that curious feeling of power that a man has when he votes.

The drawing and recording of the numbers took, in all, about three-quarters of an hour. When it was ended, Sergeant-Major Jonnart checked the list and read it over out loud. So far his memory had served him well.

"Now, Darde," he said, "mix the slips in your cap thoroughly and then turn your back and draw one."

"If you don't mind, chief, I'd rather not be the one to . . ."

"Do as I tell you!"

"All right, but I don't relish the job."

"Who d'you think does relish this job? Get busy."

Darde mixed the pieces of paper in his cap. He mixed them with both hands, as if he were inspecting grain. He mixed and mixed and mixed. . . .

"For God's sake, draw!" said a strangulated voice from the crowd.

Darde stopped mixing. He did so with reluctance.

"Turn your back to the men," said Jonnart, "and put your hand behind you."

There was absolute quiet in the hut, that intensified quiet which seems to prevail over a body of silent and motionless and expectant men. Darde turned and looked at the wall of the hut. He found a nail there and rested his gaze upon it. Jonnart took the sergeant's cap and pushed it up so that Darde's hand was plunged into the pieces of paper. Darde looked at the nail and felt the paper all around his hand. He moved his fingers, took hold of one piece of paper, let it go, took hold of another and let that go too. . . .

"Draw, for the love of Christ, draw!"

It was the same strangulated voice.

The sergeant's fingers closed on some paper. He felt two pieces and he released one. He pulled the other out and held it over his head.

Jonnart took the slip from Darde's hand, unfolded it and flattened it out on the table with his palm.

"Sixty-eight," he said.

He turned to the company roster, but even before the name was announced a man was pushing his way through to the table.

"Fasquelle."

There was a sound of many breaths being released in the hut.

Fasquelle, in front of the table, looked at the slip of paper, then looked at Jonnart.

"What makes you think that number's sixty-eight, sergeant-major?" he asked quietly.

"Look at it. Can't you read?" said Jonnart with a harshness which was really nothing more than his vexation with himself.

"Luckily for me, I can," said Fasquelle. "From where I stand the number's eighty-nine, not sixty-eight."

"But you can see the sixty-eight is right on the line, can't you, whereas the other way the eighty-nine isn't?"

"Are you going to have me court-martialled because of a line, sergeant-major?" Fasquelle was still speaking quietly.

"Well, no. No, I'm not," said Jonnart. "The thing to do then, obviously, is for you to draw against the man who's got eighty-nine. Who's got eighty-nine? Poujade. Come up here, Poujade. You've got to draw against Fasquelle."

"Nothing doing," said Poujade. "The number's clearly sixty-eight. And my number's a long way from it."

"The number," said Fasquelle, "is not clearly sixty-eight."

"Anyway," said Poujade, "I refuse to draw against you. I refuse to be forced into a one-out-of-two chance after having already taken a one-out-of-a-hundred-and-eleven chance."

"Don't let me hear any more talk about refusing," said Jonnart.

"Well, you're going to," said Poujade, "if you try to put a one-out-of-two draw on me when I'm entitled to one out of over a hundred. Furthermore, the number's clearly sixty-eight, and the draw has been made. I drew the same as everybody else did and without any fuss about it. It's a question of my life, sergeant-major, and I'm going to have my rights."

Jonnart was nonplussed and angry with himself for having failed to foresee the possibility of this sort of thing. He was convinced the number was sixty-eight, but still he didn't want to send a man to the execution post on a mere conviction. He wanted to do so even less because Fasquelle's behavior about the matter had earned his approval. An idea suddenly came to him.

"Darde, open all the numbers in your cap and get me eighty-nine."

The impasse remained, however. Number eighty-nine, when found, was so written that it didn't rest on a line whichever side up it was held. It could have been either eighty-nine or sixty-eight.

"The only thing for it," said Jonnart, "is to make the draw again . . ."

Instantly a chorus of protests broke out.

"How many times, Name of God!"

"We've drawn once . . ."

"That was final."

"Let those two fight it out."

"It's an outrage."

"I took my chance with the rest, and I won't draw again."

"Silence, all of you!" Jonnart roared. "You'll do as you're told. No more observations, or I'll draw some extra numbers. The draw will be made again. You'll keep your same numbers, but I'll fix the others so there won't be any confusion this time."

Jonnart went over Darde's slips one by one, picking each up and looking at it from top and bottom. When he was through, he had underlined the following pairs of numbers thus:

$$\underline{6}\ \underline{9} \qquad \underline{66}\ \underline{99} \qquad \underline{68}\ \underline{89} \qquad \underline{86}\ \underline{98}$$

There were other numbers containing ones, such as eighteen and eighty-one, which might have been subject to the same confusion of inversion had not Darde been a Frenchman. Because he was French, and because he had printed the figures, the sergeant had made his ones with two distinct strokes and there was no doubt about which side up the numbers should be read.

"All right. Attention, men! We're ready. And there won't be any mistake this time. Darde, mix the slips again. All the numbers that might be confused are underlined. The line shows that the number is to be read with the line at the bottom."

"Please, sergeant," said a voice, "my pal and me would like to swap numbers . . ."

"No," said Jonnart.

"What's the idea?" said Darde.

"Well, we sort of figured our numbers had been good to us once and we didn't want to ask too much of them again. . . ."

"If they've been good to you once," said Jonnart, "you'd better stick to them. Ready, Darde?"

Darde turned his back to the men again, again placed his hand behind him and felt the cap come up and the papers close over his hand. His fingers again felt for a piece of paper, caught a small wad of them, released them all except one which he withdrew and held at arm's length over his head. Jonnart took it.

"Number seventy-six."

The crowd parted to let the owner of number seventy-six through, but there was no need, for Langlois had been standing near the table all the time.

The guard-room had been set up in one of the outbuildings of the château, in the coach house, to be exact. The coach house itself served for the guard while the harness room, leading off it, had been converted into a prison by the simple means of constructing a low, sloping, and man-length pallet of boards along one of the walls. This was so that the prisoners would not have to sleep on the cement floor, and it was the only furniture the place contained except for a urine bucket near the door.

Férol was the first of the three men to be let into the clink. One glance showed him which was the best place in the room, the corner near the window and farthest from the door, and he went straight to it and took possession. Férol made himself at home in a place in which he felt quite at home. He had been in many clinks in various parts of the world, and this was by no means the worst of them. He took off his tunic and his boots, unbuttoned his trousers, and stretched himself out on the bare boards, resting his head on his tunic which he had folded into a wad for a pillow. In a few moments he was asleep.

Within the next half hour Didier and Langlois had each in turn been escorted into the guard-room. They woke Férol up, and it was the first time the three men had spoken to each other. They exchanged names and established the fact that none of them had any cigarettes.

"What are you here for?" Didier asked Férol.

"How should I know? This is my headquarters. I'm always here. And, sooner or later, I always find out why. Either of you got a pack of cards?"

"What are you here for?" Langlois asked Didier.

"It's a long story and I'll save it for later," said Didier. "There's a little bastard of a lieutenant who's out for my hide, that's all. I know this is his work, all right. And you, what about you?"

"Well, I'm here for the same thing you two are, though you don't know it. There ought to be a fourth showing up soon. Then we could play bridge, if we had some cards . . ."

"Bridge, what's that?" said Férol.

"It's a game," said Langlois.

"But what's this game, that's what I'd like to know," said Didier.

"Oh, this game," said Langlois, "this game's much simpler than bridge."

"Well, what is it, if you know what you're talking about?"

"It's just this. We're here under charges of cowardice in the face of the enemy and we're going before a court martial this afternoon, a summary court martial," said Langlois.

"How d'you know?" said Didier.

"Because I heard the order read out."

"And what did the order say? Come on, loosen up, will you."

"Just what I told you. Each company commander was to select and arrest a man to go before a summary court martial on charges of cowardice in the face of the enemy."

"But what cowardice? Whose cowardice? I don't understand."

"This morning," said Langlois. "Because the attack failed, I suppose. The staff wants to make some examples, and we're the examples."

"Why us?" said Férol.

"I don't know why you," said Langlois, "but I know why me. Because our company drew lots and I drew the wrong number. Wrong for me, that is, right for all the others."

"Jesus!" said Didier. "Drew lots, eh? That looks serious."

"Yes," said Férol, "that looks like something, all right. But my company didn't draw lots. The sergeant just comes up to me and says, 'Come with me.' As soon as we're out of the camp he tells me I'm under arrest. Just as if that was a novelty for me. . . ."

"That's just the way they did with me," said Didier. "They didn't draw lots in my company either. Ah, now I begin to see it. Select and arrest a man, you say the order said? The dirty, stinking little bastard! Talk about cowards! But I'll tell the court martial a thing or two. I won't let the little swine get away with . . ."

The door of the clink was suddenly thrown open and the sergeant of the guard entered. "Prisoners, attention!" he ordered. "Up on your feet, there. Snap to it!"

An officer, a captain, walked in and the sergeant went out, closing and locking the door after him. The captain looked at a piece of paper he was carrying.

"Private Didier?"

"Here, sir."

"Langlois?"

"Here, sir."

"Férol?"

"Here, sir."

"At ease, men. Sit down, if you wish. This is serious and I haven't got much time, so listen to me carefully. . . ."

"Got a smoke on you, captain?" said Férol.

The captain passed out a package of cigarettes and watched it, after making the rounds, disappear into Férol's pocket. He gave Didier a match and the men lighted up.

"You all know," the captain continued, "that the attack this morning was a failure. Division insists that it was because the attacking wave failed to advance on account of cowardice. They can't punish a whole regiment so they've decided that one man from each of the first-wave companies is to go before a court martial on charges of cowardice. I can't argue about the right or wrong of this now, I haven't time. And anyway it wouldn't get us anywhere. Colonel Dax has personally done all in his power to prevent this, but he's up against a stone wall. Orders are orders. My name is Etienne. I'm in command of Number 7 Company of the Second Battalion and the colonel has appointed me to defend you at the court martial because I'm a lawyer in civil life. What good that'll do me at a court martial remains to be seen. I'll do my best, you can be sure, but I don't want to give you any false hopes or take anything for granted. A court martial is quite a different thing from a civil court, even a criminal one.

"Now, first, I want to ask each one of you a question and I want you to answer it with absolute honesty. It will be for your own good if you do. If I am to defend you, I must not be in the dark about anything. And remember that whatever you tell me here is in the strictest secrecy. It is just as safe with me as if it were said to a priest in the confessional.

"Did any of you three men do anything, show any sign that might be construed by witnesses as cowardice in the face of the enemy?"

"No." The word was spoken three times with varying degrees of emphasis.

"If you did, I beg of you to tell me so that we can work out a defence. I don't want them to spring any witnesses on me and not have an answer ready."

"I was way through our wire," said Férol. "Meyer can tell you that, he was with me. So can Captain Sancy."

"I was right near to Lieutenant Bonnier in the wire when he was killed," said Langlois.

"And I was climbing onto the parapet," Didier said, "when Corporal Valladier's body fell on top of me and knocked me back into the trench. It knocked the wind right out of me. By the time I was on my feet again, my company was all back in the trench. They couldn't advance."

"That's good," said the captain with a cheerfulness he didn't feel. "My advice to you is to stick to those stories and not to let the prosecutor shake you out of them. I'll help you all I can, but the rules of evidence do not obtain in courts martial the way they do in other courts. You must expect to find the whole business very arbitrary.

"Now, one or two hints about your behavior. Remember that you will still be soldiers in the presence of your superior officers, not litigants before a bar of justice. Make your bearing respectful but in no sense cringing. Act like what you are, soldiers and brave ones at that, but don't overdo it to the point of seeming to be arrogant or lacking in a sense of discipline. I've looked at the room where the court will sit. You will have the afternoon light in your eyes. Don't let this disconcert you and above all don't let it make it seem as if you were dropping your eyes, hang-dog. Just brace yourselves to the light. Keep your chins up. Repeat it to yourself, if necessary: 'I must keep my chin up.' When you are speaking, look each of the judges in the eye. Don't whine or plead or make speeches. Just make statements in a soldierly manner. Make them short, but make them so they can be heard all over the room. Try not to repeat yourselves. I'll do that for you when I sum up. I'll emphasize the points you brought out in your testimony. Confine yourselves to answering the questions that are put to you and leave the speech-making to me. Is there anything you want to say to me now?"

"Yes," said Férol. "Will you leave us a few matches before you go?"

"Yes," said Langlois. "I was drawn by lot for this business. Wouldn't that point be an excellent defence? It shows obviously that there was no coward in my company whom the sergeant-major could put his finger on."

"Yes," said Didier, and he began to tell the captain the story of the patrol. He told it to him quietly, not omitting anything, not even that he had fired at Roget to prevent him from killing Lejeune. The three men listened to him intently and, when he was through, each one, to his own capacity, felt anger in his heart.

"You believe me, sir, don't you?" Didier asked, passionately desiring to be believed.

"Yes, I believe you, Didier, but who else will? Who else will want to? I'm afraid your story won't do you much good, and it might do you a lot of harm. In the first place, you've got no witnesses. That's very bad. Secondly, even if you had, I think the story would only antagonize the court. They couldn't very well tolerate a private soldier bringing such accusations against an officer. And they would be bound to suspect and to believe that you were trumping them up in order to save yourself. That would react against you in the worst way. Take my advice and don't say a word about that affair at the court martial. If things go wrong, I'll see what use can be made of it later, in private conversation with one of the judges or someone."

"Do you think things will go wrong? What chances have we got?"

"Frankly, men, I must tell you that this is a very serious matter for you. Division wants examples. What makes it serious is that apparently they don't care who the examples are."

"But drawing by lot . . ." Langlois began.

"Yes, I know. But it's an accepted practice in the army. I'm afraid that just because you were drawn by lot, your position will be the weakest. I'll have to see how the trial is going before I make up my mind what to do about that. What about you, Férol? How did they decide on you?"

"They always decide on me, that's all."

"Well, I've got to go. Keep up your courage, show them a brave front. We'll do the best we can for you, you may be sure. The colonel himself is going to put in a plea for you. I've talked to him about it and we're going to bring out your record as a regiment and as individuals . . ."

"Leave mine out," said Férol.

"I mean your record as attack troops. Then we'll make a strong plea for mercy, or for imprisonment at most. Don't forget what I said about a soldierly bearing. I attach a lot of importance to that. The court will sit in about half an hour. Sergeant! Open the door, please!"

"The matches, captain . . ." said Férol.

A sergeant put his head into Colonel Couderc's office at Divisional Headquarters.

"I've got Colonel Dax, sir," he said. "He's on the wire."

Couderc nodded and picked up the receiver on his desk.

"Hello! Dax?"

"Dax speaking."

"This is Couderc. About the men to go before the court martial. I find the names of only three in your report. There should be four. Where is the fourth? Who is he?"

"I don't know."

"What did you say?"

"I said I didn't know."

"You don't know! But it's your business to know."

"I have merely obeyed instructions, Couderc. I gave the company commanders the orders the general gave, namely, to each choose a man for the court martial. One of them didn't, that's all."

"One of them didn't, you say? Why didn't he? Did he refuse?"

"Oh, no, he didn't refuse. He merely said there was no man in his company against whom he could bring such charges."

"When did he say that?"

"Well, he didn't say it. He wrote it."

"You should have sent me a copy."

"Didn't I? I'm very sorry. I must have overlooked it."

"Have you got his note there, Dax? Read it to me."

"He says: 'In reply to your et cetera I have the honour to report that I am unable to comply with your instructions because there is no member of my company against whom charges of cowardice in the face of the enemy can either be made or be found tenable.'"

"That's nothing less than a refusal. Have you drawn his attention to that?"

"I can't. He's gone off for a ride and won't be back till the court martial is over."

"That's clearly a case of refusal then. You must put him under arrest immediately upon his return. What's his name?"

"Captain Renouart, of Number 1 Company."

"Spell it."

"R-e-n-o-u-a-r-t."

"Well, arrest him at once when he gets back and I'll let you know what's to be done with him. Is Colonel Labouchère there?"

"Did you get his name correctly? Renouart?"

"Yes, I understand: Renouart. Now, Dax, let me speak to Labouchère."

"I beg your pardon, I don't think you do quite understand . . ."

"What don't I understand?"

"That Renouart is an officer of the utmost independence and courage . . ."

"There's no place for independence in this army."

"That may be quite true. But Renouart is not the type of man who is going to take anything meekly. He is a man of strong principles and he will fight for them to his last breath. I'm merely warning you, Couderc, that you are dealing with a spirited personality who may turn out to be more troublesome than you think. I'd go slow about this, if I were you, especially in view of all the circumstances surrounding this court-martial business. It's all been a little hasty, to say the least . . ."

"Well, I can't worry about that, Dax. It wasn't my doing. But no officer in this division is going to refuse to obey orders with impunity. You've got to arrest him. There are no two ways about that."

"There's another thing you seem to have overlooked, and that is that there's a Senator Renouart who is a member of the Parliamentary Commission for the Army. I don't know that they are in any way related, but I thought you might like to look into that side of the affair before . . ."

"Oh, well, that's different. Why didn't you say so before? You're quite right, Dax, we must be careful. I tell you what you do. You send me a copy of your order to him and his reply in the original. I'll take the matter up with the general and see what he says. I'm glad you mentioned the point, even though there may be nothing in it. Now let me have a word with Labouchère, will you?"

"Here he is."

"Labouchère speaking."

"This is lucky, Labouchère, my being able to get hold of you. You heard my conversation with Dax?"

"Yes, I did."

"Then you know there will only be three men to be tried, after all. As president of the court, please see that the question of the fourth man does not come up at the trial. What I wanted to speak to you about was this. The general has given me a note for you but I'll have to read it over the telephone as there isn't time to send it to you now. He wants you to pass it on to the other judges before the proceedings begin. It is as follows: 'The accused are to appear before the court martial as soon as possible. I have no doubt whatever that the court will know how to do its duty. Signed, Assolant.' Is that clear?"

"Perfectly."

"When is the court martial going to begin?"

"In a few minutes."

"All right then. Ring me up as soon as you have passed sentence, then report back here. Au revoir."

The salon of the château was a spacious, high-ceilinged room which faced the west and a view of lawn that seemed to have been spread there like a carpet for the declining rays of the setting sun. The room had, ever since it had been built in the late eighteenth century, seen its share of war and of warriors. Napoleon had spent two nights at the place, and it was in honour of this that its name had become Château de l'Aigle. Later, Wellington had danced there into the small hours of another night. Because it happened to be too far to the west, it was neglected by the soldiers of the Franco-Prussian war. Forty-four years later, however, its polished hardwood floors and courtyard flagstones again resounded to clinking spurs, and its mirrors reflected glittering uniforms, uniforms which glittered less as time went by. Von Kluck had lunch there one day not long before he made his fatal blunder at the gates of Paris. That was three days after Sir John French had dined there. A bandy-legged officer with bristling moustaches, wearing a general's oak leaves on his cap, had stopped there to telephone on his way up to see the King of the Belgians. "Foch speaking," he had said. At one time or another most of the higher officers of the allied armies had stayed there. Joffre had dined there, silently but with gusto, and then had gone to bed and slept undisturbed by any nightmares of Verdun. Haig had sat his charger at the lodge gates and had taken the salute of Canadian regiments on the way up to the Passchendaele butchery. Clemenceau had stopped at the same lodge to ask directions.

"I'm jealous of you," he had said to the old woman who lived there.

"Why, *monsieur le minister?*" she had asked.

"Because you have a better moustache than I."

Curiously enough, the line of high-ranking officers and celebrities who had visited the place was destined to be ended, as it had been begun in this war, by the presence of a German, a tall, cold, sorrowful man who sat in that spacious room with a little group of his countrymen, eating a frugal supper, late on a night of November, 1918. This was General von Winterfeldt, military member of a delegation which was going to ask Foch for armistice terms the next morning.

Just at present, however, the highest-ranking officer in the room was Captain Etienne of the 181st Regiment of the line. He was seated at a table which faced a longer table opposite to him and parallel to the western wall and windows of the room. Behind the captain sat three men on a bench. They were hatless, unarmed, and seemed not to know what to do with their hands. They looked like just what they were, prisoners. Right behind the three men a sergeant and six others stood. These were helmeted, equipped in parade order, namely, with ammunition pouches and rifles with fixed bayonets. They had their rifles with which to occupy their hands, but they, too, didn't seem to be quite at ease.

The room began to fill up. Officers drifted in and took seats towards the back. Regimental Sergeant-Major Boulanger came in, put some papers on the long table, then looked the whole scene over carefully, moved one or two chairs around and re-spaced the sentries at the doors and along the wall.

The tension in the room was increasing. Every time someone came in, it seemed to ease a bit, then it would return with added force.

Another officer entered, carrying a large envelope. He went over and shook hands with Etienne, smiled and exchanged a few words with him without looking at the prisoners, then went to a neighbouring table and pulled some papers out of the envelope. Etienne felt slightly encouraged when he noticed how scant their bulk was.

"The prosecutor," said Etienne, turning to the prisoners. Didier and Langlois both looked at him, studied his profile, the back of his shoulders, neck, and head. Férol, apparently, wasn't interested.

The prosecutor was looking around for someone.

"Orderly, get me the sergeant-major!"

In a minute Boulanger was bending over the prosecutor's table.

"Most irregular," said the prosecutor. "Take the prisoners out. They are not to come in until the court is sitting and orders it."

The sergeant-major gave some commands. The prisoners were surrounded by their guards and marched out. Hope instantly began to rise in them.

The sergeant-major came in again, motioning to the sentries to throw the doors wide.

"Attention!" he roared. "Guard, present arms!"

There was a scraping of chairs, the rattle of accoutrements, the clicking of spurred and unspurred heels. The petrifaction of the salute.

Three officers walked in in single file, Colonel Labouchère leading. The one in rear, a lieutenant, was out of step, but he picked it up before he was half-way across the room. The colonel went straight to the centre seat at the judges' table and stood behind it, then waited while the captain and the lieutenant disposed themselves respectively to his right and left. Labouchère saluted the group that faced him and said, "Rest!"

The bodily tension of the room subsided, but the emotional didn't.

"The court martial is open," said the colonel. "Bring in the accused."

Commands were shouted in the hall outside and the prisoners were tramped in again.

"This is a summary court martial," said Labouchère, when it was quiet again, "and we shall therefore dispense with most of the formalities. However, the order appointing the judge should be read. The clerk will please do so."

A lieutenant, sitting at one end of and at right angles to the judges' table, got up and began reading:

> "The general commanding the division orders that the Summary Court Martial assembled at the Château de l'Aigle to judge the cases of four men accused of cowardice in the face of the enemy shall be composed as follows:
>
> "President: Colonel Labouchère;
> "Judges: Captain Tanon; Lieutenant Marignan;
> "Prosecutor: Captain Ibels;
> "Clerk: Lieutenant Mercier.
>
> > "(Signed) Assolant
> > "General of Division."

ETIENNE (*rising*): May I request that the service status of the officers composing the court be stated?

PRESIDENT: What is the purpose of the request?

ETIENNE: To determine whether they are in the services of the rear or whether they are officers of the line. In other words, combatant officers.

TANON (*the only combatant officer on the court, moving so his collar will show*): You can see that by looking at our insignia.

PRESIDENT: Quite irrelevant. Please don't take up our time with stupid technicalities. We shall omit the reading of the indictment. It is lengthy and it states that the prisoners are accused of having shown cowardice in the face of the enemy during this morning's attack on the Pimple. Accused, stand up!

ETIENNE (*rising at the same time*): Mr. President! The indictment is an important document in the case. I myself have not even seen it yet. I request that it be read out.

PRESIDENT (*who hasn't seen the indictment either, for the good reason that there isn't any*): The request is refused.

The expression on ETIENNE's *face is one of bewilderment, of horror even. He does not like the tone of this beginning and he feels that every effort will be made to maintain it.*

ETIENNE: But, Mr. President, the indictment is of capital importance. We have a right to know what the accusations are which—

PRESIDENT: The request has been refused. Please don't delay proceedings. The accused will give their names.

LANGLOIS, DIDIER, *and* FÉROL *look at each other, hesitating.*

ETIENNE: From left to right. You first. Speak up!

The prisoners tell their names.

PRESIDENT: Where's the fourth—? I withdraw that. All right, sit down. The prosecutor will call his first witness.

This is the moment ETIENNE *has been anxiously waiting for. The calling of the first witness will give him a much-needed hint of what the prosecutor's tactics are going to be. He is surprised and baffled when he hears the name.*

IBELS: The accused, Private Férol!

Two guards detach themselves from the group and lead FÉROL *to a place opposite the clerk at the other end of the long table and turn him to face half-right towards the judges. The* PRESIDENT *consults some notes, then begins to question* FÉROL, *without looking at him at first.*

PRESIDENT: Were you a member of Number 4 Company during the attack this morning?

FÉROL: Yes, sir.

PRESIDENT: Did you refuse to advance?

FÉROL: No, sir.

PRESIDENT: Did you advance?

FÉROL: Yes, sir.

PRESIDENT: How far did you advance?

FÉROL: To about the middle of no-man's-land.

PRESIDENT: Then what did you do?

FÉROL: Well, the Boche machine guns were like a hailstorm and I saw that—

PRESIDENT: No. Answer my question. What did you do?

FÉROL: Well, sir, I saw that me and Meyer—

PRESIDENT: I didn't ask you what you saw. I asked you what you did.

FÉROL: Yes, sir.

PRESIDENT: Did you advance?

FÉROL: Not after I saw that me and Meyer—

PRESIDENT: Did you turn round and go back?

FÉROL: Well, when I saw that—

PRESIDENT: Attention! Answer my question. Did you turn round and go back? Yes or no?

FÉROL: Yes, sir.

PRESIDENT: Any questions, Mr. Prosecutor?

IBELS (*with a smile which is meant to convey that the* PRESIDENT'*s adroit questions have made any others superfluous*): No, sir.

PRESIDENT: The accused may go back to his seat.

ETIENNE: Just a minute, Mr. President. I'd like to question the witness.

PRESIDENT: You mean the accused?

ETIENNE: Yes, sir.

PRESIDENT: Say so then. But make it short.

ETIENNE: Férol, when you reached the centre of no-man's-land, tell the President why you turned back.

PRESIDENT: Is that a question?

ETIENNE: Yes, sir.

PRESIDENT: Then put it in the form of a question.

ETIENNE: Yes, sir. When you reached the centre of no-man's-land, were you and Meyer alone?

FÉROL: Yes, sir.

ETIENNE: Address yourself to the court. What had happened to the rest of your company?

FÉROL: I don't know. Those near us were all killed or wounded. The rest had gone back, I suppose.

ETIENNE: So, finding yourselves alone, you decided the only thing to do was to go back and get in touch with your company?

FÉROL: Yes, sir.

ETIENNE: Was the fire heavy?

FÉROL: It had already done in half of our company.

ETIENNE: If you had advanced then, you would have been two men advancing alone?

FÉROL: Yes, and we wouldn't have gotten two metres farther. We had to crawl back, at that.

ETIENNE: That's all.

PRESIDENT: Mr. Prosecutor?

IBELS: So you retreated?

FÉROL: Well, when we saw that—

IBELS: Did you retreat? Yes or no?

FÉROL: Yes.

IBELS: Yes, what?

FÉROL: Yes, sir.

PRESIDENT: The accused may go back to his seat. Call your next witness, Mr. Prosecutor.

ETIENNE's *heart sinks. The prosecution's tactics are now clear to him, sickeningly so. They aren't going to bother with witnesses, not even with primed witnesses. They are simply and cynically going to force the prisoners to inculpate themselves. He mutters under his breath: "Jesuits! Steam-roller! Assassins!"*

IBELS: The accused, Private Langlois, to the bar!

LANGLOIS *faces the judges, his guards at his elbows. He faces them a little more than half-right because he wants his* médaille militaire *and his* croix de guerre *to show.*

PRESIDENT: What company were you a member of during the attack?

LANGLOIS: Number 3, sir.

PRESIDENT: Did you refuse to advance?

LANGLOIS: No, sir.

PRESIDENT: Did you advance?

LANGLOIS: Yes, sir, I did, sir.

PRESIDENT: Why are you here then?

LANGLOIS: Because we drew lots and I—

PRESIDENT: The question is withdrawn. How far did you advance?

LANGLOIS: I was right near Lieutenant Bonnier when he was killed in the wire.

PRESIDENT: The enemy wire?

LANGLOIS: No, sir. Our wire.

PRESIDENT: Our wire is close to our trench, isn't it?

LANGLOIS: Not so close, sir. There's a space between the wire and the trench.

PRESIDENT: But it wasn't the enemy wire?

LANGLOIS: No, sir.

PRESIDENT: Then you didn't advance more than a few metres?

LANGLOIS: I advanced as far as I could, sir.

PRESIDENT: I see. And then what did you do?

LANGLOIS: Lieutenant Bonnier was killed. A lot of men were killed. There didn't seem to be anybody in command. I didn't know what to do.

PRESIDENT: Did you take command, urge the men forward?

LANGLOIS: There were no men to urge forward.

PRESIDENT: Answer my question. Did you take command?

LANGLOIS: No, sir. There was nothing to take command of.

PRESIDENT: Did you stay where you were?

LANGLOIS: Yes, sir.

PRESIDENT: So you didn't advance any further?

LANGLOIS: I couldn't. The fire was too heavy. The attack seemed to have faded away.

PRESIDENT: So you retreated to your trench?

LANGLOIS: I went back to it when I found the advance had been stopped.

PRESIDENT: But if the advance had continued, it wouldn't have been stopped, would it?

LANGLOIS: . . . ?

PRESIDENT: Answer my question.

LANGLOIS: Yes, I think it would. It was already stopped by the German fire which—

PRESIDENT: Or by the French cowardice. Anyway, you failed to advance, didn't you?

LANGLOIS: No, sir.

PRESIDENT: What do you mean, "no, sir." You said yourself you didn't get further than your own wire.

LANGLOIS: I couldn't, sir.

PRESIDENT: Because you were afraid.

LANGLOIS: Because it was useless.

PRESIDENT: Ah, I see. You, a soldier of the line, decided it was useless. Any questions, Mr. Prosecutor?

IBELS: No, sir.

PRESIDENT: Any questions, Captain Etienne?

ETIENNE: With the court's permission I'd like to read the citations for bravery this man has already earned on two occasions. First, citation in the Orders of the Army for—

PRESIDENT: Quite immaterial, captain. The accused is not being tried for his former bravery, but for his recent cowardice. Medals are no defence.

ETIENNE: May I, then, call witnesses to his character and to the fact that he is on the list for promotion to an officer's training school?

PRESIDENT: You may not. But you may, if you can, call witnesses to the fact that he reached the German wire.

ETIENNE: I am unable to do that, sir, because there wasn't anybody in the whole regiment who could get anywhere near the German wire.

PRESIDENT: That is a matter of opinion. You will permit me to disagree with you, captain.

ETIENNE: I expect it, sir.

PRESIDENT: I am grateful to think that I won't disappoint you. The accused may go back to his seat. Next witness, Mr. Prosecutor.

IBELS: The accused, Private Didier!

PRESIDENT: You've heard the questions put to the other prisoners. I presume that you, too, were part of the attacking wave, that you did not refuse to advance, that, in fact, you did advance, undoubtedly the farthest in your company?

DIDIER: Yes, sir, I tried to advance.

PRESIDENT: You tried to advance. Am I to understand that you failed?

DIDIER: Well, sir, I got farther than some at that.

PRESIDENT: Explain yourself.

DIDIER: We were standing three or four deep in the trench. I was with my back up against the parados. When the whistles blew, the ones in front started to climb the parapet. Captain Charpentier was first and he was killed at once. My turn came and I started to climb the scaling ladder. Just at that moment, Corporal Valladier's body was blown back on top of me. It knocked the ladder backwards with me on it. Valladier was a heavy man, and he and the ladder came down like a load of coal on top of me. It knocked the wind clean out of me. When I came to and pulled myself out from under, the attack was all over.

PRESIDENT: So you never left the jumping-off trench?

DIDIER: Yes, I was practically out of it.

TANON (*interrupting*): Were your feet on the parapet?

DIDIER: Well, almost, sir.

PRESIDENT: How much of you was actually on the parapet?

DIDIER: Well, none of me was on the parapet. As I said, I was on the ladder. But from the waist up I was above the parapet.

PRESIDENT: But your feet were on the ladder, not on the parapet?

DIDIER: Well, they had to be on the ladder so as to get onto the parapet.

PRESIDENT: Yes, I quite understand that. As a matter of fact, however, your whole body remained in the space delimited by the walls of the trench, didn't it?

DIDIER: I don't understand what you mean, sir.

PRESIDENT: Is it not a fact that you never got out of the jumping-off trench at all?

DIDIER: Well, as I was saying, sir, I was just getting out when Valladier's body—

PRESIDENT: Answer my question. Did you or did you not get out of the jumping-off trench?

DIDIER: I was trying to tell you, sir—

PRESIDENT: Answer yes or no.

DIDIER: . . .

PRESIDENT: Answer me, I say.

DIDIER: No.

PRESIDENT: Any questions, Mr. Prosecutor?

IBELS: No questions, sir.

PRESIDENT: Captain Etienne.

ETIENNE: I would like to call witnesses to the conditions which prevailed in the Number 2 Company trench. I would like to show that—

PRESIDENT: Quite unnecessary. The accused himself has told us that he never left the jumping-off position.

ETIENNE: Just the same, I want to prove that—

PRESIDENT: The request is refused.

ETIENNE: May I then call witnesses to the accused's record, character and—

PRESIDENT: I told you before, we're not trying the accused for his character. I wish you would stop attempting to introduce these irrelevancies. The accused may go back to his seat. If you wish to make your pleading, Captain Etienne, you may do so now. You can have five minutes.

ETIENNE: Yes, sir. First, then, I consider it my duty to respectfully protest against the manner in which this trial has been conducted. I protest with the gravest formality against the fact that the indictment was not read. I consider that this is an omission the illegality of which renders this court martial null and void. Second, I protest against the fact that no stenographic notes of the trial were kept. This deprives the accused of an instrument with which to back up an appeal for pardon to the President of the Republic—

PRESIDENT: You are overlooking the fact that the presidential pardon no longer exists, Captain Etienne. It was precisely because these cases of cowardice and insubordination were increasing that the President relinquished his prerogative of pardon and that the summary courts martial were re-established. There is, therefore, no need for keeping stenographic notes.

ETIENNE: Nevertheless, sir, I take exception to their omission. I do so all the more emphatically because of my third protest, which I am about to make. I respectfully but none the less formally protest against the manner in which the accused were questioned and forced into admissions which were so distorted that they became incriminating. I draw the attention of the Court to the fact that the examination of the witnesses was grossly unfair and that the cross-examination was blocked, if it was not dispensed with altogether. As I said, I would consider myself lacking in my duty to the men I have been appointed to defend if I did not make these formal protests to the court.

Let me now, with the Court's permission, turn to the three men sitting here under the stigma of one of the worst accusations that can be made against soldiers—cowardice.

Gentlemen, I say to you that these men were not cowards. They were heroes! They belong to a famous regiment of assault troops, a regiment whose standards are weighted down with the decorations which a grateful country has heaped upon them, a regiment to which it is my own greatest pride to belong. Within the last month, only, they again distinguished themselves in the fierce fighting in the Souchez Valley and the neighbouring ridges where so much French blood has been spilled. Decimated, weary, sleepless, and shell-shocked, they were finally relieved, what was left of them, two or three days ago for a well-earned period of rest and re-equipment. While actually on the march out to the rest area, they were diverted and sent into the Pimple sector with orders to capture that notoriously formidable obstacle, so formidable indeed that two attacks made on it by fresh troops, fresh troops, I repeat, had recently failed. Without a murmur, they put their fatigue aside and found themselves in the trenches again on the very night they were to have been in billets. For thirty-six hours they submit to a devastating enemy harassing fire. The ground around them is covered with the corpses of their comrades who have fallen in the previous attacks. The air is heavy with the stench of death and noisy with the sound of death.

Zero hour comes, and the barrage opens. The German counter-barrage replies at once, registered to a metre. Deadly machine-gun fire sprays the parapets almost as thickly as does an impenetrable rain. Do they falter? They do not. They advance into the frightful inferno, their numbers thinning out so heart-breakingly fast with each step forward they take.

Férol gets the farthest, way out into the middle of that avenue of death called no-man's-land. There, he finds himself alone. Is he expected to attack the Pimple by himself? No, no one would ask that of a man, it is too senseless. Gentlemen, the accused Férol was no coward!

Langlois, wearing his *médaille militaire* and his *croix de guerre,* is right with his company commander, inextricably caught in his own wire which is ringing to the sound of the enemy machine-gun bullets. His company commander is killed, his company cut to pieces. As he testified himself, he did not take command because there was nothing to take command of—except the dead. He is stopped, he cannot go farther. Gentlemen, the accused Langlois was no coward!

Didier has bad luck, I'll admit. But is he to be branded a coward because a man's body falls on top of him and knocks him out? I wanted to bring witnesses to the conditions which existed in the Number 2 Company frontage, perhaps the worst spot in the sector. They would have told you that the attacking wave was literally mown down like wheat on the lip of the trench by a withering fire. Didier was trying to advance when he was prevented by one of those accidents which might have seemed funny under other circumstances but which, under these, was too significant to be anything but horrible. I also wanted to call witnesses to the fact that he had, prior to the attack, carried out single-handed a dangerous and daring patrol along the enemy wire, that he was considered an ace at that sort of thing by his company commander, unhappily killed a few seconds after he had gallantly led his men to the assault. Gentlemen, the accused Didier was no coward!

What more is there for me to say . . .

PRESIDENT: Nothing. You have already overstayed your time.

ETIENNE: If you please, gentlemen. I know that some examples are wanted, but these men are the wrong ones. Surely it will not be you, honourable judges of a court of military justice, who will contribute to the grotesque irony of condemning these men for a crime which is the antithesis of the qualities they actually displayed and for which they should be decorated?

Gentlemen, convinced of the strong sense of duty which animates your consciences as officers, of the profound sense of justice which rules your consciences as judges, of the pervading feeling of compassion which moves your consciences as men, I commend the destinies of the accused to your generosity of spirit, assured that three French officers of your integrity will not find it possible to act in such a way as to be accessories to what might become a frightful and revolting judicial crime. Thank you for your attention and patience.

PRESIDENT: Mr. Prosecutor.

IBELS: Mr. President and judges of the court martial. I have not my opponent's gift for oratory, and, if I had, I would not use it at this time, considering it, from the point of view of the case for the prosecution, as unnecessary. The accused, one by one, came up and admitted to a failure to advance during an ordered attack. In military law that is, at the very best, called cowardice in the face of the enemy. I therefore confine myself to requesting the court to act in accordance with the provisions of the Code of Military Justice, to find the accused guilty of the charges as stated, and to impose the penalty which is prescribed by the Code.

PRESIDENT: Accused, stand up! Have you anything further to say in your defence?

The prisoners look at ETIENNE *and he whispers with them.*

ETIENNE: The accused Férol says that he is innocent and begs for the mercy of the Court. The accused Langlois says that he is innocent. He asks the Court to take cognizance of his decorations. The accused Didier says that he is innocent, that he is married and has four children, and begs for the mercy of the Court.

PRESIDENT: Very well. The accused will be escorted back to the guard-room. The hearing is closed. The Court will now retire to deliberate.

A small group of men were lined up in the courtyard outside the coach house of the château. The sun had dropped behind the buildings and the pigeons were making their pleasant liquid sounds under eaves which were in shadow. Three men, hatless and unarmed, stood in a line at attention. Behind them the guard

was at the present arms. Facing them was the prosecutor, flanked
by the clerk of the court martial and the sergeant-major. Captain Ibels was reading from a piece of paper.

"In the name of the French people.

*"On this day the Summary Court Martial of the Château de
l'Aigle, deliberating behind closed doors,*

"The President put the following question:

*"'Are the soldiers Férol, Langlois, and Didier, of the 181st Regi-
ment of the line, guilty of having shown cowardice in the face of
the enemy during the attack by that regiment on the part of the
enemy line known as the Pimple?'*

*"The votes having been taken, in accordance with the law, sep-
arately and beginning with the lowest in rank, the President of the
Court recording his opinion last,*

*"The Court Martial declares unanimously to the question: 'Yes,
the accused are guilty.'*

*"Following which, and on the motion of the government pros-
ecutor, the President put the question of the penalty to be inflicted
to a vote, the votes being taken in accordance with the law, separately and beginning with the lowest in rank, the President of the
Court recording his opinion last,*

*"The Summary Court Martial, therefore, by a vote of two to
one, condemns the soldiers Férol, Langlois, and Didier to the penalty of death by shooting as provided for by the Code of Military
Justice,*

*"Instructs the government prosecutor to read this judgment
without delay to the accused in the presence of the assembled
guard under arms.*

"(Signed) Labouchère, President of the Court
"Tanon, Judge
"Marignan, Judge."

Regimental Sergeant-Major Boulanger had had some arrange-
ments to make, some orders to give. He had made his arrange-
ments with competence and now, in his office, he was giving
his orders with precision to a selected group of First Battalion
N.C.O.'s.

"As you know," he said, "the court martial found the accused guilty and sentenced them to be shot. The executions will take place at eight o'clock in the morning, sharp. The colonel insists that everything must go off without a hitch and with the least possible delay. It is not to be hurried, but there mustn't be any fumbling around. I have been put in charge and made personally responsible for any lack of order or for any mistakes. You can take it from me that I shall pass on any blame, and with interest, to any of you who fail in your duties. These duties, incidentally, are simple enough. Get your note-books out and see that you put down what I say to you.

"Sergeant Gounod, you are appointed to command the prisoners' escort from the guard-house to the execution posts. You will have a guard of twelve men under arms, rifles loaded, bayonets fixed, four men to each prisoner. The four men are to be individually assigned to each prisoner and held responsible for that one prisoner alone in case trouble starts. At any sign of trouble the prisoners are to be instantly covered. If the trouble does not subside at once, the prisoner is to be shot on the spot. If any concerted action gets under way, they are all to be shot or bayoneted. But every effort must be made to get them under control without resorting to shooting. Is that clear?

"No, the prisoners' hands will not be bound until they are at the execution posts. The colonel does not wish to have any unnecessary cruelty inflicted on them. Besides, it would make it more difficult for them to walk.

"The escort is not to exchange a single word with the prisoners except words of command. You will be given a litre of cognac with which to fill your canteen. When you go to fetch the prisoners you are to give each one of them a good swig of it and a cigarette if he wants it. But see that they don't take too much. Don't forget that it will be on an empty stomach—a very empty stomach, if my guess is any good. Then, when the detachment reaches the corner of the wood where it turns onto the parade ground, you are to give them each another swig. That will be their last. Is that clear?

"As soon as this meeting is over, Sergeant Gounod will go to the guard-room and, timing himself carefully, he will walk up to the parade ground at a pace a little slower than the usual marching time. You are to make a note of the exact amount of time it took you to reach the centre of the field near its western edge by the trees. That time, plus eight minutes, is to be deducted from eight o'clock, and that will be the time the escort is to leave with the prisoners from the guard-house. Have you got that all clearly in your mind?

"All right. The quartermaster-sergeant will detail a fatigue of two parties, one to rig up the execution posts at spots which I shall show him, the other to dig the grave, one grave large enough for the three bodies, in the woods behind the execution posts. These same parties are to remain under orders until the business is over. The quartermaster-sergeant will see to it that he has a knife, rope, and blindfolds. The rope is for binding the condemned men to the posts. Their hands are to be tied behind them, then their bodies bound to the posts, and tightly enough to prevent them from falling if they faint or if their knees give way. Number 3 Company will supply this detail.

"Now, as to the firing-squads. Orders are that they are to be formed of the new-class soldiers only. No, I don't know why, but I suppose it is to impress them with a sense of discipline and perhaps to avoid any trouble which might arise from some old-timer's refusing to fire at a comrade. Yes, I know the regulations say the firing-squads should be from a different regiment or at least from one of the other battalions. But orders are orders, and these come from Division. They know what they're doing, and if they don't it isn't our worry. Anyway, that's beside the point. Furthermore, the colonel wants it so arranged that the squads shall not be from the same companies as the man they are going to execute. Number 1 Company will, therefore, supply the squad for Langlois; Number 4 Company for Didier; Number 2 Company for Férol. Twelve men and a sergeant to each squad, and they are to march separately to the field and to stand apart at the farther end. I will put them into position as soon as the time has come.

"The whole regiment is to be on the field at seven-fifteen, lined up in parade formation at the eastern end. At seven-thirty I shall take over the parade and move the regiment into three-sided hollow square.

"At seven-forty-five the officers will come on the field and take their posts. I shall turn the parade over to the commanding officer.

"As soon as the condemned men have come onto the field and are being bound to the posts, I shall move the firing-squads into position and then report to the commanding officer that all is ready. At his order, the band will ruffle the drums, and then the adjutant will read out the sentence of the court martial. At the end of the reading the drums will be ruffled again. A warrant-officer will give the order to fire. I don't know yet whether the regiment will have to march past the dead bodies or not.

"Any questions . . . ?

"No, there will be no military degradation ceremony. It was apparently overlooked in the orders from Division and the colonel is going to take advantage of the oversight. Any other questions . . . ?

"All right, dismiss!"

"In the name of the French people . . ." said Langlois.

"He should have said 'in the name of the French butchers,'" said Didier.

"To think," said Langlois, "that, after all, we are the people of France, you and me and Férol, and millions just like us."

"Don't take it so seriously," said Férol. "This is the third court martial I've been up against and nothing ever came of any of them except a bit of prison. And prison isn't at all a bad place to be in, especially during a war. We're safe, we get our three squares a day, and nobody bothers us. All we have to do is to sit and wait. A fatigue or two now and then maybe. I tell you, after Algerian clinks, this is luxury. The way you fellows talk, you'd think the end of the world had come."

"Well, it has for us," said Didier, "only you don't know it."

"How do you know it?" Férol asked.

"I read the signs. First, Langlois here is drawn by lot. When they start drawing lots you might as well start drawing your will. Second, Roget picking me. Clever little bastard, all right, to put me out of the way so neatly. You know, I've never had any wish to kill a man, except in the war of course, but I'd give a lot to have Roget cringing at the point of my revolver. And d'you know what I'd do? I'd fill it with five blanks and the last one would be a live round. I'd fire each one of those blanks at him at intervals, and make him die five deaths before the real one. . . ."

"Say, now that's a clever idea," said Férol, his eyes gleaming with admiration. "How'd you think of it? I must remember it for when I get out. There's a beast of a . . ."

"But can't you get it through your fat head, Férol, that you're not going to get out this time," said Langlois.

"Oh, you're a crêpe-hanger!"

"Well, didn't that court martial, if you can call it a court martial—didn't it convince you that you haven't a chance?"

"To tell you the truth, boys, I didn't pay much attention to it. I was figuring out if I could make a jump for it out that window which was near me. I'd just about made up my mind to take the chance. The captain was making his speech. I looked around the room to see if anybody was watching. And, Name of God, when I looked back again one of the guards had moved nearer to the window and he had his pig's eyes on me."

"You're crazy," said Didier. Langlois accepted this dismissal of Férol as being adequate and he and Didier fell to talking between themselves.

They were apprehensive, deeply so, but, as yet, they were not really afraid. They had relaxed from the strain of the court-martial proceedings, made more than ever an inimical performance by the stiffness of the court, the overwhelming number of officers' uniforms, and the long, slim, gleaming fixed bayonets of the guards. Most of their bodily secretions were functioning normally again and saliva once more moistened mouths which had been dry.

They outdid each other with arguments to prove that death was certain, though at the same time they were convinced that it was life that was certain. They were responding to that curious instinct which impels men to talk themselves out of a situation by talking themselves into it. They heaped hopelessness upon hopelessness and they felt that they were doing their cause some good thereby. They talked for an hour or more in a vain effort to free themselves from the contradictoriness of their feelings. They knew they were going to die and, at the same time, they didn't believe it. Or, they believed they were going to be executed and yet the idea that such a thing could happen to them was unthinkable.

This state of contradictory and tangled feeling received a clarification shortly after nightfall which swept away almost the whole of their laboriously constructed edifice of immunity and left them suddenly and shockingly in possession of what remained, namely, hopelessness. The clarification came in the form of a visit from Sergeant Picard, the priest.

"My sons," he said to them, "you are soldiers and I therefore do not need to beat about the bush. I bring you bad news. You must prepare yourselves for the worst. The colonel told me to tell you so. He has been in telephone communication with Army Headquarters. The Army Commander was out to dinner and couldn't be reached. The colonel talked to the chief of staff, but he said he had no authority to intervene in such a matter. The colonel pleaded with him, and then the line became disconnected. Dax tried to get him back, but when he got Army Headquarters again and said who he was, they kept him waiting for some time and then told him the chief of staff had gone out and couldn't be found. He says you will understand that they don't want to be found. It's the same way at Division.

"My sons, there is nothing for me to say to you just now. But there is something I can do, and I have done it. I have brought you paper and pencil. If any of you cannot write, I am at your service. It will be the same as if it were in a confessional. . . . Very well, then, here are the writing materials. I shall be back later. You can write your letters without fear of the censor for I shall see that they reach your families. The church, as well as the state, you know, has its means of communication."

"Sergeant," said Langlois, "how much time have we got?"

"Not very much, my poor fellow, but I think at least until after it is daylight."

"Why do you think that? Are you sure?"

"Yes, I'm sure, because the whole regiment has been ordered to parade. They wouldn't be parading in the dark. Besides, the firing . . ." Picard checked himself suddenly and was relieved to hear Didier cover the gaucherie with a question.

"Will it hurt very much, sergeant?"

"I don't think you'll ever feel it. Your pain will be now, and not of the body. The—er—that will come as a welcome end to your anguish. I'll be back to help you through these hours, if I can."

"Sergeant," said Férol, "bring us some cigarettes, will you? And don't forget some matches too."

Sergeant Picard went out.

"Not one of them called me 'father,'" he said to himself. "Later, perhaps . . ."

Didier sat on the boards and worked over his letter to his wife. Words came slower for him at first from a pencil than they did from his tongue.

He began at the beginning and told her the story of the patrol, of his arrangement with Roget, of the attack on the Pimple, and of all that followed thereafter with such bewildering rapidity. He became so engrossed in the recital of the military events of his story that, at times, he slipped into the style of a formal report. It was his defence he was writing, the one he had been deprived of. Now and then the injustice of the whole thing would overwhelm him and his words came in rushes of indignation, almost hysterical in their striving to convey his sense of outrage. This was followed by a calmer interval of grief; nor was it an inarticulate one, either, merely because he expressed it in terms of his love for the odds and ends in his pockets, those odds and ends which a wife sent to her husband at the front. He gave detailed instructions about exactly how he wanted his children brought up, what trades they were to go in. In the next sentence he left all that to his wife. He spoke with dignity and with pride about his own life and work. He had always been a man of character and he wanted his wife to preserve his reputation among his friends and acquaintances, more for his children's sake than for his own. He assured her he had never been a coward. He was simply being shot as an example. He had never had any luck and he was resigned to his fate. After all, France was already full of fatherless children and widows. He promised her he would face the firing-squad like a brave soldier. Neither she nor the children need ever hang their heads in shame for him. He returned to the objects in his pockets which he had spread before him, the tobacco pouch, a letter, a lock of hair, all from his beloved Annette. Then, suddenly overcome, he ended his letter abruptly:

"How I love you, my God! And how I weep!"

And Didier wept, silently, turning his face away so the others would not see.

Langlois's letter:

At the front.

My darling wife,

How can I begin to tell you of what has happened to me? It is too cruel, but when you read this letter I shall be dead, fallen under the bullet of a French firing-squad. I am bewildered and so lonely. You must forgive my incoherence. Thoughts and feelings rush in upon me so fast they carry me away.

If Sergeant Picard or Captain Etienne should ever come to you, you can believe them. They were friends, and Picard is the priest who promises to see that you will get this letter. Colonel Dax, too, I think was a friend, though a remote one. They will tell you how it was done. Briefly, this is what happened. We failed to take our objectives in an attack this morning. It seems ages ago now. It was not our fault. No human being could have advanced through that fire. Somebody wanted some examples made, and I am one of them. There are two others besides myself. We have been court-martialled and we're going to be shot in the morning. We were charged with cowardice and the court martial was a steam-roller. I was not a coward, I swear it to you. But they want examples. I don't say I wasn't afraid. There's no man who hasn't been afraid.

Oh, my darling, dearest one. Words, words, how pitifully they fail me. The president of the court was a Colonel Labouchère, and his name sounds like what he was, a butcher, though I suppose he thought he was doing his duty.

The speed of time appals me. At any moment now I may hear the tread of the guards come to take us out. No, that is not true. It is still night and they won't shoot us till daylight. They've got

*to have light to take aim by. It is so difficult to remain honest,
especially in a time of crisis. What I mean is that I feel as if they
might come at any minute. In truth, I have some hours left to live.
They will go so slowly, they will go so fast. Already I feel numb
inside, as if my intestines were filled with lead. They will be, soon
enough. Forgive the cheap and cruel sarcasm. Perhaps in writing
to you I may get some control over myself. I shall try not to inflict
the pain of my heart on yours for, by the time you learn of it, mine
will be all over. I never knew that time could exert such a terrific
pressure.*

*What will become of you, my dearest, what will become of that
new life which must already be stirring within your body, that
body that I loved so much and that I'll never see again? But it is
not of your body that I think now. Already half disembodied myself, I have lost all capacity for sensuality. On the other hand, my
mind feels intensified to a point which is nearer to bursting. My
yearning for you is an anguish which I can hardly bear. Every fi-
bre of me is straining to you in a pitiful, hopeless attempt to bring
you to me so that we might comfort each other. But I am alone,
and my only means of communication is to leave you this sorrowful letter to read after I am gone.*

*That, I think, is the brutality of death—sudden incommunica-
bility. Then rage rises in me and I wonder if I shall go mad. Then
I feel the need of telling life what I think of it, now that I am to be
parted from it. Then I realize the futility of that and my rage sub-
sides and I float out for a while on a serene ocean of tolerance and
resignation. I have just done so, and for twenty minutes before
writing this present sentence, I didn't write anything. I was in a
sort of trance, I think. I watched Didier laboring over his letter. I
watched Férol, lying in his corner, smoking peacefully as if he had
all time before him. Well, he has, at that, although he doesn't
seem to realize the form it will take. I envy him his fatalism. I always thought I had it too, but his kind of fatalism seems to work,
mine doesn't.*

*Now, suddenly, the bitterness returns to me. It is brought back
this time by the sight of a cockroach which is exploring the cracks
in the guard-house floor. That cockroach will be alive, exploring
as he has always done, when I am dead. That cockroach will have*

a communicability with you which I, your husband, am being robbed of—the communicability which is life.

Only yesterday, before the attack, I was talking with the men. I said that I was not afraid to die, only of being killed. That was true, and it still is, though I know that I can face the firing-squad without weakening. But I have learnt now that fear of an appointment with death is a real and terrible thing. And the thought of you, my dearest one, is the only one which gives me strength to live through these hours.

The injustice of this to me is something so obvious that I have no desire to enlarge upon it. Of course, I am in a state of violent rebellion against it. But it is the injustice to you that throws me into a frenzy, if I allow myself to dwell upon it. Here we are, two human beings who have never harmed anybody. We love each other and we have constructed, from two lives, one life together, one which is ours, which is wholly of ourselves, which is our most precious possession, a beautiful, satisfying thing, untangible but more real, more necessary than anything else in life. We have applied our effort and intelligence to building, expanding, and keeping the structure in repair. Somebody suddenly steps in, not caring, not even knowing who we are, and in an instant has reduced our utterly private relationship to a horrible ruin, mangled and bleeding and aching with pain.

Sweet and adored other part of myself, I ramble on. I do not, I cannot, say a half of what I feel or mean. If we could be in each other's arms, if we could look into each other's eyes, that is all the communication that would be necessary. But I cannot bring myself to end this letter. It is the only means I have of talking to you. When I stop, as I shall have to, the silence, for all I know, will be everlasting. Do you blame me for lingering over a conversation which may never be resumed? Do you blame me for trying to delay a parting which will be absolute? Do you blame me for trying to make my inarticulateness articulate?

I love you so.

I was drawn by lot. The sergeant-major bungled the drawing, so it had to be made again. It was on the second drawing that I was chosen. Just a confusion about numbers, and here we are, you and I, put to the torture. I don't try to understand it.

Please, please, get a lawyer and have my case investigated. Your father will help you. Get all the influence you can, borrow money if necessary, carry it to the highest court, to the President himself. See that my murderers pay the penalty of murder. I have no forgiveness in my heart for them, whoever they are, only revenge, a deep desire for revenge which I hand on to you as a duty which you must fulfil.

How I love you, my only one. The pocket-book you gave me is in my hand. I touch it. It is something you have touched. It will be sent to you. I kiss it all over, a sad attempt to communicate some kisses to you. Poor, worn, greasy little piece of leather. What a surge of love pours from me upon this forlorn object, the only tragic, personal link I have with you. Tears rise and I cannot hold them back. They pour upon the pocket-book, make it more limp and ugly than ever. How glad I am I didn't bring that photograph of you. Do you remember, when you gave it to me, how I wept because it was so lovely and your expression was so sad. It would kill me to have it here now, and yet, if I did, I couldn't keep my eyes off it.

The bounds of my soul seem to be bursting. I am choking with grief and longing. Férol goes on smoking. Didier has finished his letter and I must tear myself from mine, too, so that the thought of you shall not weaken me.

Good-bye, my dearest, dearest one, my darling wife. Have courage. Time will help you. I have control over myself now. I am no longer afraid. I shall face the French bullets like a Frenchman. The priest has just come back. How I love you, how I need you. Dearest, I have always loved you, always needed you. You have always satisfied me in every way. Good-bye, good-bye. I don't care what our child is now. I think I hope it will be a boy, for your suffering when you read this letter will be far greater than mine when I wrote it. All my love is for you alone. . . .

Sergeant Picard, the priest, returned to the guard-house soon after midnight. He collected the prisoners' letters and put them carefully away in an inside pocket.

"Haven't you one?" he said to Férol.

"No."

"No one to write to? No family at all? Not even a friend?"

"Yes, I had a friend," said Férol, still stretched out in his corner. "She was a whore in Marseille, but I've forgotten her name."

"So your best friend is a whore whose name you've forgotten?" said the priest. He said it with compassion, reflectively. "Poor fellow."

"You can keep your pity," said Férol. "A man's best friend is often a whore. Better than a lot of wives I've seen."

"Shut your dirty face," said Didier. The priest noticed a queer glint in his eye, then decided it was the saltiness of dried tears.

"All right," said Férol. "Nothing personal."

"Better not be, or I'll do the work of one firing-squad for it right here."

"Keep your shirt on," said Férol, not without affability. "You haven't got much time to wear it anyway, and it's going to need mending before long. Ha, ha!" Férol was delighted with his own wit.

"Leave him alone," said the priest.

There was silence for a while in the guard-house except for the monotonous tramp of Langlois's feet as he paced the length of the room, turned, paced, and turned. . . .

The priest wanted to open up the subject of confession and extreme unction, but he didn't quite know how to go about it. Nor did he seem to be getting much encouragement from the men for whom these rites were intended. Their attitude, he felt, was one of friendliness towards him as a man, of hostility as a priest. He decided he would recite a prayer out loud.

"Hail Mary, full of grace! The Lord is with thee—"

"Look here, sergeant," Didier interrupted, "you're a good fellow and a pal and all that. But don't start unloading that stuff around here. I don't want any of it, see. If the others want it, give it to them quietly in a corner. I'm sick enough to my stomach as it is."

"Didier," said the priest, and there was some sternness in his voice, "you can be an unbeliever, if you want to, but you should have enough respect for my feelings and my office not to be a blasphemous one."

"You and your office! You and your Jesus! A fine fix he's let us into. You make me laugh. You make me vomit."

"Don't, don't, my son. You don't know what you're saying—"

"Yes, I do, by God! I say God and all his works are lies, lies. . . . And I say too that if you don't shut up that tripe, I'll make you." Didier glared at the priest and shook a slightly trembling hand at him. Langlois and Férol both looked at Didier, surprised by his sudden loss of imperturbability.

"You haven't the right to deprive your comrades of the comfort I can bring them."

"Don't fool around with me, though. Go ahead and comfort them, if they want it. God! Jesus! Devils, I say. . . ." Didier subsided, muttering to himself.

The priest overlooked the outburst and accepted the suggestion it contained in spite of its ungraciousness. He turned to Férol.

"My son, would you like to make your confession?"

"No, I wouldn't. Besides it would take too long."

"It's never too late to repent . . ."

"Well, I'll wait a while longer. I have already for over thirty years."

"Don't you believe in God and in Jesus Christ, his only son, who—"

"I may have once. I don't remember. But just now I'd like a big swig of cognac. That would do me more good than all the only sons in creation."

"In spite of you, and in the name of the Redeemer, I forgive your stupid blasphemy."

"And I forgive you for keeping me from taking a nap."

Langlois was still pacing the floor when the priest approached him and put himself in step. Didier, sitting against the wall, watched them go back and forth, a slight sneer on his face.

"Please, please, father," Langlois said before Picard had a chance to begin. "It's quite useless, and I don't want to have to hurt your feelings. I was brought up a Catholic. I know exactly what you're going to say. I respect your faith, but this is no time to try to thrust it on me. I have no use for it."

"But my son, you are an intelligent, educated man. Your mind is therefore open to reason . . ."

"Precisely, father, and the stuff you talk is not reasonable. It's just superstition. Cruelly ironical superstition, under the circumstances." Langlois smiled a faintly bitter smile, then went on. "You can't do a thing for me. Please understand that. I mean it in all kindness, just as I know you do. But I have to live through this night alone. If my wife could only be with me. . . ." Tears came into Langlois's eyes and he quickened his pace for a while.

Helpless, full of profound sorrow, perplexed, the priest moved away from Langlois and went to the middle of the room. He knelt down on the concrete and began to repeat the general absolution out loud.

Didier watched him for a while, then got up slowly and advanced with deliberation upon the kneeling man. Langlois turned in his pacing just in time to see Didier give the priest a vicious kick in the stomach.

"Stop it!" Didier shrieked, then fell upon the crumpled form of the priest. "Get out, you sniveling black pig, and take your mutterings with you!"

He started to drag the priest over to the door, at the same time yelling to the guard to open it. Langlois came to from his surprise at the viciousness and the fury of the attack on Picard and jumped on Didier's back. They went down in a pile upon the prostrate body of the priest and in so doing knocked over the urine bucket. Didier shook himself free of Langlois, pulled him to a kneeling position and gave him a knockout punch on the jaw. Langlois fell backwards, teetering on his calves, his mouth wide open and bleeding, then collapsed into a huddle. Férol sat up and began to take a spectator's interest in the brawl. He wondered what would happen next.

Didier was still shouting: "Open the door, Name of God, you swine, and take this buzzard out of here!" He had stepped back from the door and was now standing with the empty bucket held over his head.

The door burst open under the pressure of the guard, who started to rush in. Didier hurled the heavy bucket into their faces and two men went down. Didier was yelling at the top of his lungs. He looked like a madman, and he acted like one, too, for he charged into the solid mass of men who were pushing through the doorway. He charged heedless of the rifle muzzles, heedless of the leveled bayonets. The men apparently had their orders for they pulled their bayonets upwards so that Didier would not impale himself upon them, then forced him back into the room, clubbing him with their rifle stocks.

Didier fought in a frenzy, clawing, punching, kicking—foaming a little at the mouth.

Suddenly he felt a sharp pain above his knee, started to fall, and instantly thereafter lost consciousness. He had received simultaneously one rifle-butt blow which broke his leg and another on the head which knocked him out.

As soon as Didier was subdued, the guard collected themselves, picked the unconscious priest off the floor, and carried him away without looking at Langlois, who still lay on the cement, or at Férol, who was still sitting up in his corner very much regretting that the fun seemed to be over.

At ten minutes to four in the morning Didier began to come to. By four o'clock he had recovered consciousness enough to be roaring with pain.

The sergeant of the guard came in and saw that there was something the matter with the man's leg, very much the matter, in fact, for it seemed to have developed an extra joint half-way between the knee and the hip. The sergeant went out and sent a runner for the doctor.

Three quarters of an hour later the doctor showed up. He was young, sleepy, and irritable. He looked at Didier and saw at a glance that his left thigh bone was broken.

"Couldn't you have waited a few more hours," he said, thinking of his interrupted sleep. "You fellows have no sense of the fitness of things. Think of managing to break your leg just before you're never going to have any more use for it." Didier never heard the gibe, for his ears were filled with the roar going on in his own head. Férol and Langlois drew near and watched the doctor begin to cut the trouser leg off. He did it roughly, and Didier started to bellow again.

The doctor gave up cutting and went over and got his kit. He took a loaded hypodermic needle out of it, held it up and squeezed the air bubbles and some drops out, then felt around Didier's chest for a fleshy spot and shot the dose into him. He took an indelible pencil out of his pocket, moistened the point on his tongue, and made some symbols on Didier's forehead which would inform the initiated that he had been given a quarter grain of morphine at five o'clock.

"How did this happen?" he asked the sergeant.

The sergeant told him.

"Huh," said the doctor. "Hunt around and get me something that I can use for a splint."

Didier's bellows had already quieted down to groans. He felt, vaguely, that something in him was taking a departure, slowly, pleasantly, fading away like a landscape which is being effaced by an in-rolling bank of fog. He did not have time to distinguish, indeed he did not even try to, whether this soothing erasure which was going on in him with such neatness was mental or physical. All he knew was that it felt good to him. And then he became unconscious.

By the time the sergeant came back with the splint, the doctor had cut Didier's trouser leg off and had pulled and jerked the two ends of the thigh bone into an aligned contact again. He took the splint and bound it on with Langlois's puttees which he found conveniently at hand.

"That'll have to do," he said, rising and collecting his stuff. "Of course he can't stand up with a broken thigh. I'll have to report this to the colonel and let you know. And by the way, have a couple of men come in and swab up that mess there. It stinks."

About an hour later the doctor was back again.

"How is he?" he asked the sergeant.

"Quiet, sir. Seems to be sleeping."

"That's the morphine. Hope I didn't give him too much."

"What are we to do with him, sir?"

"I routed the colonel out and told him about it. He was furious with you for letting such a thing happen."

"Name of God, sir, I couldn't help it. The man was fighting mad."

"I know, I know. But why didn't you complete the job while you were at it? Anyway, the colonel called up Division and got the general out of bed. He tried to get this fellow's execution postponed. The conversation was short and not too sweet, I gathered, and the general hung up on him. The colonel looked like a thundercloud. All he said to me was: 'The general says the medical officer will know how to put this man on his feet so that he can face the firing-squad. Go ahead and do it, if you can!'

"Well, of course, I can't. I can't perform miracles. This is what we'll have to do then. I'm having a stretcher sent over here. It's a folding one, the only kind we have. You must have a solid cross-piece nailed at both ends, just below the handles. Put the fellow on it and rope him to it securely by passing the rope under his armpits and over the cross-piece so that he will be supported when the stretcher is tilted up vertically. Do it as soon as the stretcher arrives, while he's still under the narcotic. I'll probably be here myself when they start out and I'll go up with them. But if I'm not, you will have to bring him to if he is still under. The way to do it is to give him a good slapping. If he doesn't answer to that, give his leg a couple of jabs with your thumb, right here, see, where it's discoloured and swollen. That'll bring him round. For some reason that I've never been able to fathom, a man has to be brought to consciousness before he's executed. Now I'm going to try to finish my sleep. . . ."

"Doctor," said Langlois in a voice which came very close to quavering, "will it be terribly painful? Supposing they only wound us? . . ."

"That's what the sergeant-major's for," said the doctor, and walked out.

"Nice little fellow!" said Férol.

Langlois smiled, a faint, slightly fatuous smile.

Sergeant Gounod arrived at the guard-house with an escort which had been increased by eight stretcher-bearers. He took four of them with him and went into the prisoners' room. Langlois and Férol were standing up, waiting for him. Didier lay muttering on his stretcher, semi-conscious.

"Well," said Sergeant Gounod, and that was all he could bring himself to say for a while. Langlois and Férol looked at him. He looked at them, and what he saw was two terrified animals at bay.

"Well," said Gounod again, "let's get busy. What's the use of hanging around."

"Yes," said Langlois. "Quickly, quickly. Where to? Is it far? Let's run there, what d'you say?" Langlois was smiling and Gounod had to look away.

"For Christ's sake, haven't you got a drink for us?" said Férol.

"Of course," said Gounod, relieved to have the talk brought back from the slightly insane direction he felt it was getting away to. "I almost forgot. Here you are."

Férol took a pull at the canteen, such a long one that Gounod had to grab it away.

"Leave some for somebody else, will you?"

"Yes, for the sergeants as usual, I suppose."

Gounod said nothing and handed the canteen to Langlois.

Langlois took a mouthful and swallowed it with an effort. The cognac descended slowly, warming a column down the centre of his icy, trembling body, past his pounding heart to a point where it began to spread sideways.

Suddenly it was all in his throat again, spewing forth through nose and mouth. He stood there, shocked by the unexpectedness of the reaction, cognac dripping from his face, tears from his eyes.

"I can't hold it," he said, and smiled again through his acrid drooling.

"Well, leave it for someone who can," said Férol. Sergeant Gounod again looked away.

"Here's some cigarettes," said the sergeant. Both men took one and Gounod lighted them. Langlois's was quivering so that the sergeant had difficulty keeping the match near it.

Gounod went over to Didier and bent down to offer him a drink, but Didier didn't seem to understand and turned his face away from the canteen.

"Give it to me, then," said Férol. "I need it. I didn't even taste that last swallow."

Gounod gave him another drink and watched him suck the cigarette smoke deeply into his lungs.

"Come on," said Gounod. "We've got to get going. Pick up the stretcher, there! Come on, you two. Courage. It'll soon be over and you'll be in a better place than what I am."

The stretcher-bearers picked Didier up and carried him out the door. The sergeant of the guard, standing there, saw that his eyes were closed, so he gave him a couple of smart slaps in the face as he passed. Didier opened his eyes.

Férol walked out right behind the stretcher. He had been nursing along an accumulation of flatus, and he let it rip as he passed the guard.

"That's what I think of you," he said, pleased with his timing. Nobody laughed.

Langlois walked out behind Férol. How he loved that guardhouse . . . his last home on earth. He fixed his mouth to whistle, but it was only a sigh that came.

"Oh, my darling . . ."

The regiment was, as regiments always are for parades, and seldom are for attacks, if the military historians are to be believed, ready ahead of the appointed time.

Regimental Sergeant-Major Boulanger was there, busy, competent, as regimental sergeant-majors always are, in the same way that head waiters are busy, competent, or seem to be so, if they are good head waiters.

The firing-squads were there, standing at the side of the field farthest from the place where they had entered it. They looked at the execution posts and they looked at each other. They looked at Sergeant-Major Boulanger and at the entrance to the field. They were themselves being looked at by the regiment. The regiment looked at them as if they were men apart. There was curiosity or speculation in many of these glances.

The quartermaster-sergeant and his details were there, near the execution posts. They were hanging around, ill at ease, talking in low voices, inspecting and re-inspecting the posts, ropes, and blindfolds which Boulanger had already inspected and found correct.

The posts were there, evenly spaced and neatly aligned. They looked stark, lonely, and a little absurd. The absurdity was undoubtedly due to their strangeness. Three such posts were not often met with well out in the confines of the field. They did not look as if they were at home and this aspect was increased perhaps by the little mounds of fresh earth in which they had their roots. Because of what was to be done there, the actual texture and form of the posts seemed different from ordinary posts. Not one of the fifteen hundred men present who looked at them could define the difference, but each one felt that it existed.

The parade ground was alive with a kind of electricity, the electricity of men's glances which were constantly flickering back and forth from the posts to the sergeant-major to the entrance to the field to the firing-squads.

In spite of the sergeant-major's order that nothing was to be hurried, there was a tendency on everybody's part, including his own, to advance or to anticipate the time. At seven-twenty-five Boulanger was already facing the regiment from the centre of the field and shouting commands. For some minutes he manœuvred and drilled the mass of blue around until he had it in the formation he wanted. This was a three-sided hollow square of double ranks with the First Battalion forming the base. The fourth side of the square was empty except for the three execution posts, the men who stood near them, and the long, early-morning shadows which the posts and the men cast. The sergeant-major stood the regiment at ease and walked over to the firing-squads.

He inspected the squads carefully, looking each man in the eye as if taking his measure for the job he was going to have to do. He inspected their rifles equally carefully and cautioned two men to put the elevation of their sights back to zero. He gave the order to load and followed it at once by the order to unload. Thirty-six live rounds fell out on the ground and Boulanger now knew for certain that the magazines would automatically fill all the breeches again and that no man could evade his duty by having an empty breech. Then he spoke to them:

"This is a duty you have to perform. It is like any other duty in the army, and it must be performed properly. The better you do it, the easier it will be for the condemned men. You will not be more than seven metres away from the posts. Aim at the prisoners' chests and fire when the warrant-officer gives the word. Attention! Load!" Thirty-six shells were again clicked into the thirty-six breeches.

The officers were now seen arriving on the field in a group.

Boulanger called the parade to order, then went to meet the colonel and reported that everybody was present and correct.

Colonel Dax stood the regiment at ease again and beckoned the quartermaster-sergeant over to him.

"You know, sergeant," he said, "that one man has broken his leg and will be on a stretcher. Can you prop it up against the post all right?"

"Yes, sir."

"Well, be sure that you do. I don't want anything messy to happen."

Dax looked at his watch.

"The officers will take their posts," he said.

The group moved off, began to spread, then scattered and distributed itself along the front of the three battalions. Colonel Dax started to walk up and down with the adjutant.

"It makes it all the harder, the day being so fine," he said. "Poor fellows! What frightful torture!"

Herbillon didn't say anything. He was worried about reading out the sentence of the court martial. He had an uneasy feeling inside him and he was afraid he might fail to keep his voice under control. He was also obsessed by the thought that when he stopped reading, the prisoners would have only a few seconds left. This seemed to put a responsibility on him, a responsibility which was almost an outrage.

The prisoners and their escort stopped at the clump of trees near the entrance to the parade ground while Didier's stretcher was being pulled out of the ambulance. Gounod offered each one his canteen again, but Férol was the only one who wanted a drink. Gounod had to pull the cognac away from him a second time.

"He's passed out," said one of the guards pointing to the deep-breathing figure on the stretcher. Gounod went over to Didier and pinched his face until he opened his eyes.

"This is solid comfort," said Didier. "Did I get wounded?"

"Yes," said Gounod.

"Where are we going?"

"To the hospital," said Gounod.

"D'you see that thing, up there in the branches of the tree?" Didier went on, talking slowly and more to himself than to the men around him. "Something very funny going on. I can't quite understand it. It's got a name which doesn't seem to belong to it. Whoever heard of a thing like that being called Sambre et Meuse?"

"Like what?" said the priest who was standing beside the stretcher. "I can't see anything."

"Like that. It keeps slipping down, but it never gets any lower. It keeps moving, and yet it's always there," Didier murmured, obviously fascinated by what he saw from under lids which had a tendency to close. ". . . Ah, now I'm beginning to understand. It's got something to do with me . . . It's my pain, that's what it is . . . But why up there in the tree . . . ? Queer sort of pain, too . . . It doesn't seem to hurt in the proper way . . . Strange, but I never felt better in my life . . . I feel wonderful . . . I feel so wonderful I think I must be dead. . . ."

"You soon will be," said Férol, and quickly dodged the blow which Gounod aimed at him. Didier had closed his eyes again. There was an expression of unutterable contentment on his face.

"It's almost a pleasure to take a brute like you to the execution ground," said Gounod, glaring at Férol.

"The pleasure is all yours," said Langlois, and started grinning, smugly, ingratiatingly, a little idiotically.

"Come on," said Gounod. "You with the stretcher, lead the way."

"Oh, faster, faster . . ." said Langlois. He made a faint gesture with his hand, and nothing could have conveyed despair more accurately.

Gounod was feeling acutely uncomfortable, and it was Langlois of the three condemned men who made him feel so the most. Every time he looked at this man, or heard him speak, he was conscious of being on the brink of an unknown horror. He was unable to define what he saw going on, but he sensed that he was watching a mind in the process of losing itself, a human life in the obscure and subtle stages of a lonely disintegration. It made him feel a little sick and more than a little afraid. Gounod crossed himself surreptitiously.

The group left the clump of trees and moved out on to the field, walking slowly. Férol walked next behind the stretcher and kept up a steady flow of profane and obscene invective, loud enough to drown out the muttered prayers of the priest, who was the object of a good deal of his abuse. Férol was just drunk enough to have everything look very clear and near to him, not drunk enough to have things look double. He waved to the backs of the regimental ranks as he approached them and shouted: "Assassins! Watch a hero die!"

Langlois came on to the field staring at his own feet, watching them make the steps, looking at the ground and thinking: "This grass that I am walking over is the outmost boundary of the world I have lived in. I never thought of it before, but the next stopping place after this surface is infinity." He looked up, as if to search for infinity in the sky, but what he saw, all at the same moment, was the regiment, the execution posts, and the firing-squads beyond.

"Will they let me take my jacket off?" he asked, turning quickly to Gounod. "I'm afraid the buttons will turn the bullets into dumdums." Panic lurked just behind his eyes.

"Sure," said Gounod, without returning the look.

"Do you know," Langlois went on, relieved, "it just occurred to me. Lots of things are just occurring to me. It just occurred to me that I haven't had a single sexual thought since they drew the lots. That's rather extraordinary for a man. That's what fear will do to you. Fear and pain are the complete neutralizers of sexuality. Of course fear is pain, the most terrible of all. But just at this moment I don't feel so afraid. Funny, isn't it? It's those posts that did it, I think, those posts marking the end of my life. Few people, I'll bet, have had the ends of their lives marked out for them like that in both time and space. Or maybe it's the motion. Did you ever notice how much harder fear is to control if you are standing still? The time before zero hour is much worse than the time after. Waiting, waiting, that's what's unbearable. But now I can see the posts and those fellows over there. They must be the firing-squads. That means the waiting is coming to an end. That means that this solid lump of ice inside me will soon be liquefied. . . .

"Those posts make it look like the Crucifixion, don't they? And if we keep in this order, it will be Férol who will play the role of Christ. That's the proper touch of irony, all right. Has it ever impressed you how that touch of irony seldom seems to be absent, even in the most trivial happenings? But then this is really a trivial affair for everybody except us. Half an hour after we're gone you'll be back in the sergeants' mess, finishing off that canteen of cognac, figuring out when it will be your turn to go on leave again and be with your wife . . ."

Langlois stopped talking abruptly. He was blinded by a rush of tears, lost his balance a little, stumbled against one of his guards, then recovered himself. The guard gave him a sidelong look. He saw a pale, bruised face, dirty, unshaved, and sopping wet. An under lip that trembled and was utterly out of control. A creased jacket, hanging from a pair of forlorn shoulders, two medals dangling listlessly from the left breast. Baggy trousers, untidy and despondent, flapping around a pair of slightly quivering legs. A tramp. The guard looked away.

"Here we are," said Gounod. "Courage, old man! Show them a brave front. Many of us will soon be joining you. This war . . ."

"Oh, God! Oh, Christ!" Langlois fixed his mouth to whistle, but again all that came was the escaping air of a deep sigh. He felt himself grasped by the elbows and turned.

"Let me take my jacket off," he said. The jacket was taken from him, a little roughly because the men who did it were over-zealous and nervous. Langlois heard his medals tinkle. "Please give me the medals."

The medals were detached from the jacket and handed to him.

"I return these decorations for bravery to the French people. I do not feel brave now."

He said it simply, and flung the medals from him, quite without melodramatic intention. He watched them sail away, glint in the sunlight, and separate, then fall to the ground. His eye followed them, as it had followed the cigarette butt he had tossed in among the carpenter's tools—when was that? In another life? No, day before yesterday only. The medals lay there on the grass, their ribbons gay, evocative of dances when on leave and of the admiring looks of women, the envious glances of men. . . .

When Langlois lifted his gaze from where the pieces of metal had fallen he found that a wall of horizon blue had formed in front of him, so close that it shut off the whole world except for a narrow strip of ground.

He drew a deep breath again, trying to ease the solidified anguish of his spirit. At that moment he felt his wrists gripped, pulled behind him, and tied. Men were all around him, puffing in his face, smelly, clumsy, yet tender. He liked the feeling of them when they brushed against him, he liked the smell of them.

He was forced back a couple of steps, felt the hard support of the post behind him, felt ropes pass round his chest and waist, then a constriction as he and the post were lashed tightly together, so tightly it hurt his bound and clenching fists.

A voice from behind asked if he wanted to be blindfolded.

"No," he said. His sight was the last remnant of freedom which was left to him and he would cling to that until the end.

The little crowd around the post moved away. Langlois stood there, soaked in sweat, panting, alone. The rigidity of his attitude gave him an aspect of defiance which he did not feel. He looked at the line of blue in front of him, but the faces of the men did not seem to have any features.

A man came up and examined him, felt the tension of the ropes, took Langlois's cap off and threw it aside.

"Courage!" said Sergeant-Major Boulanger, then vanished as quickly as he had come.

The unearthly silence in which Langlois seemed to be floating was suddenly broken by the beat of drums. It was a throbbing sound, savage and full of doom, yet it comforted Langlois a little because it absorbed some of the piercing ache of his own throbbing heart.

The drums ceased, and a voice began to drone. He caught some of the words and they sounded familiar to him. He had heard them used in those combinations and cadences somewhere else, somewhere where there was also the sound of running water, or was it pigeons? The faces of the firing-squad were becoming more distinct now. That fellow on the end, where had he seen him before? Ah, yes, the recruit who wanted to win medals. Well, he could have those two, down there near his feet. What was his name? Du-something. Duclos? No. Morval? No, not Morval. Of course, Duval! Same name as the restaurant where Louise and he used to eat before they were married. . . .

Férol stood roped to his post, muttering—muttering, had anybody been there to hear it, an incoherent hotch-potch of autobiography, opinion, prejudice, and blasphemy. The last drink of cognac was now in full possession of his brain and he therefore saw twelve men in front of him who were partially effacing twelve others, duplicate of themselves. Time meant nothing to Férol. Nothing meant anything to him. He had managed unwittingly, through a mixture of hatred, contempt, and cognac, to achieve a state of detachment which made him almost as oblivious of what was going on around him as was the man on his left.

Of the three, Didier more nearly maintained the illusion that a crucifixion was in progress. He hung on his stretcher which had been propped up against the post. He hung there, the shape of his shoulders distorted by the ropes in the same way that the shoulders of cripples are distorted by crutches. The top of the post, pushing through the canvas of the stretcher, thrust Didier's head forward and a little downward. His two arms spread outwards, then drooped at the elbows in a drunken farewell. His mouth was open and his tongue was hanging out. He was breathing with some laboriousness, slobbering a little, now and then choking. When he choked, his head jerked upwards to free the obstruction, but this was merely a reflex action, for Didier was in a morphine stupor of some depth. And he would have died there anyway in the end, because his position made it so that he was slowly strangling. Didier did not know this. Didier did not know anything.

The drone of the voice reading came to an end abruptly.

The drums were ruffled again.

"Let justice take its course!" said a loud, clear voice.

There was some shifting around, the colonel and the adjutant doing an about-face. The regimental sergeant-major walked over to where the warrant-officer in command of the firing-squads was posted off their flank and at right angles to them. Picard, the priest, standing behind this man, saw that Boulanger was unfastening his pistol holster. The warrant-officer drew his sword and held it above his head. A tassel dangled from the hilt. He gave an order. Thirty-six rifles were leveled.

"Take aim!"

The rifles steadied.

"Fire!"

Down flashed the sword. The volley crashed out, smoke spurted, thirty-six shoulders recoiled slightly in unison. The smoke drifted sideways, then quickly vanished.

Already the rigid bodies at the posts were beginning to relax imperceptibly.

Didier's stretcher began to move, stealthily—so it seemed at first—then toppled over to the left and fell with him under it. Didier looked like a pack animal that had collapsed and perished under the weight of its burden.

Férol sank slowly too as the parted ropes slowly yielded their support. He fell forward, providing and at the same time following the line of his own dripping blood, fell to his knees. His head, unrecognizable now, went down and struck the earth. For a moment he was poised like a Mohammedan at prayer, then his equilibrium left him and he tumbled into a heap.

One bullet had struck Langlois in the leg and he began to sag in that direction. His ropes had not been cleanly cut by the volley which had ripped through his intestines and lungs and he was left dangling there, his arms caught to the post. He wavered a little, grotesque and pitiable, as if pleading to be released, then slipped a little farther down so that he seemed to be abjectly embracing and imploring his post.

Sergeant-Major Boulanger was coming along the hideous line, pistol in hand. He had to roll the stretcher over before he could find Didier's ear, put the muzzle to it and give him the *coup de grâce*. Férol was easier to manage but his ear more difficult to find. Boulanger bent down and sent a shot somewhere into that head. He could not tell exactly where because two rifle bullets had passed through it first.

It must be said of Boulanger that he had some instinct for the decency of things, for, when he came to Langlois, his first thought and act was to free him from the shocking and abject pose he was in before putting an end to any life that might still be clinging to him. His first shot was, therefore, one that deftly cut the rope and let the body fall away from the post to the ground. The next shot went into a brain which was already dead.

NOTE

All the characters, units, and places mentioned in this book are fictitious.

However, if the reader asks, "Did such things really happen?" the author answers, "Yes," and refers him to the following sources which suggested the story: *Les crimes des conseils de guerre*, by R.-G. Réau; *Les fusillés pour l'exemple,* by J. Galtier-Boissière and Daniel de Ferdon; *Les dessous de la guerre révélés par les comités secrets* and *Images secretes de la guerre,* by Paul Allard; a special dispatch to *The New York Times* of July 2, 1934, which appeared under this headline: "FRENCH ACQUIT 5 SHOT FOR MUTINY IN 1915; WIDOWS OF TWO WIN AWARDS OF 7 CENTS EACH"; and *Le fusillé,* by Blanche Maupas, one of the widows who obtained exoneration of her husband's memory and who was awarded damages of one franc.

Appendix

SELECTIONS FROM THE DIARY OF HUMPHREY COBB (OCTOBER 1917 TO NOVEMBER 1918)

Annotated by Humphrey Cobb

Monday, October 1, 1917. Inspected by Brigadier General Landry. Medical inspection and dental parade. Downtown in evening. Beautiful moonlight.

At this time I belonged to the 23rd Canadian Reserve Battalion, stationed at Shoreham Camp. This was a depot battalion from which drafts of recruits and rehabilitated wounded men were sent to France. It was commanded by "Twenty-eight-day" Fisher, who was a first class son of a bitch. Colonel Fisher's nickname was due to his habit of handing out twenty-eight days in the guardhouse whenever he could. It was the maximum punishment which a colonel could inflict.

Sunday, October 21. Mass at Guoy-Servins. Women in black. Walked to Mount St. Eloie.

Church parades went on as usual on Sundays, almost up as far as the support lines, and I was a Roman Catholic. I went through with the mumbo-jumbo, although I think my religious feeling had vanished. Anyway, it was under a severe strain at that time. It was difficult to reconcile an Almighty and All Merciful and Good God with what was going on around me. There was something fishy about it, and I felt it. "Women in black." All the women in France seemed to me to be in black, enough to cause me to make a note of it.

Tuesday, January 1, 1918. No. 4 Company refused to go on parade so parades were canceled. Talking to Harrison and Hemming. Made no resolutions as it would be impossible to keep them in the army. I wonder what will happen this year. 1917 was full enough. Wrote letters. Terrific argument about nationalities.

Why No. 4 Company refused to go on parade, I do not now remember. All I know is that we were all in complete sympathy with the movement. On this rest period we were billeted in huts which were northeast of Chateau de la Haie, over near the Guoy-Ablain-Saint-Nazaire road. I remember we were short of fuel and that it was damn cold. We burned hard tack biscuits and they made a very fine fire when we could get them. It was about this time that Dixon (more of him later) swiped Von Berg's boots and sold them for Cognac. He came in stinko and, later on in the night, when he had to piss, he missed the door out of the hut and filled up another fellow's boots. These were the only symptoms of foot fetishism that Dixon displayed, however.

Harrison was a Jew from Montreal. I had known him at Shoreham. He was a bright fellow and I had many discussions and a couple of drunks with him. He is the Charles Yale Harrison who wrote *Generals Die in Bed*—a good book of life in the Canadian Corps in the manner that *All Quiet* represented life in the ranks of the German army.

January 29. Parade. 12-inch gun firing and plane registering. Letter from B.R.

This gun was a couple of hundred feet back of our billet, and I was interested in watching its operations in conjunction with an observation plane. Mysterious business—signals arriving out of the ether, the officer making his calculations, giving orders; the gunners twirling wheels, ramming the shell and the charge home—"Ready, Sir!" Pause. "Fire!" Bang! And away went the shell, whinnying and shuddering up into the sky to its vanishing point. Long pause. Then to the wireless man: "Two hundred yards short, Sir!" or "Direct hit, Sir!" It was a gorgeous day, and while I watched that gun firing I forgot that it would probably draw a load of German cast iron down on our billets sometime.

January 31. Colder. Left Bully-Grenay 5:30 (p.m.), arrived dugout 8:30. One hell of an overland walk. Machine guns pretty close. Scouts went out. Young killed by bomb. Good Christ is it just. Dreamed he was alive again.

We were now in the line again, in trenches on Hill 70, in front of Loos. The overland walk meant that we did not use the communication trenches for going up. The frontline was on the forward slope of the hill facing the Germans. We approached it up the rear slope and seldom used the communication trenches until right back of the brow of the hill as we were out of the line of direct fire. But we were not out of the line of indirect fire, and Fritz had the back slope of the hill well registered by fixed machine guns and he swept that area and its trails thoroughly all night long. We lost quite a few men there.

What happened to Young, no one ever knew for sure. Some thought a Fritz potato masher had landed on his respirator and that it had exploded just as he was brushing it off. Evidence: Face blown in and right hand blown off. It was also a question whether it had been a German bomb at all. The patrol had gone out in two sections, one on the right, the other on the left of our front. Both reported a skirmish with a German patrol. It was soft-pedaled, but the notion was pretty strong that the two sections had met and fought each other in the dark. Anyway that was the last time any of our patrols went out in two sections.

The reason, I think, I was so affected by Young's death was that he was the first fellow whom I knew pretty well and rather liked to get it.

February 1. Hell of a sensation after Young's unexpected death. Took his boots off. Rather an unpleasant job.

"Unexpected death"—a queer phrase to use under the circumstances. What it means, I suppose, is that the death of someone you know well always provokes a sense of outrage in you. It's all right for the rest of them to get it, but a personal friend—that's quite another matter.

The incident of the boots was sheer bravado on my part. I wanted to show them that although I was the youngest and newest in the section, I was tough for all that. Young had been killed just outside the German wire, and when the firing had died down the rest of the patrol went back and dragged his body in—a grueling job over the chewed-up icy ground and through our own wire. They brought him down to the second line, where our dugout was, and stretched him out in a blanket along the parapet. In the dugout there was a lot of hemming and hawing about the boots he was wearing. These were a fine pair of Canadian trapper's knee boots, and why let the lousy burying party get them? We were his pals, and so on. Still, there was some hesitation about who would go up and peel them off. So I said I would. I swung his body around so it was at right angles to the trench with the feet slanting down toward me. Then I started to work unlacing them. Young had already stiffened, so I had a hell of a job getting them off. Finally it was done and, as he was too heavy for me, I left him as he was, with his feet sticking into the trench so that they would kick you in the face as you went by. But then nobody would take the damned boots, although there were three or four fellows whom they fitted. Something about "dead man's boots." And I was stuck with them. In the end, I gave them to a civilian Frenchman at Bully-Grenay, and two years later, when I revisited the place after the war, they were the first things I saw when I tramped into the town.

Later that night I went out for a visit to the latrine. Young had slipped down. In the flicker of the star shells I came upon this figure, wrapped in a blanket, headless, standing in the trench.

February 23. Still on trail of German spy and bottle of Scotch. Found neither. Goddamn the luck. Postponed going to the school till tomorrow.

The spy, I remember, was a toothless individual with a strange accent, possibly due to his toothlessness, who hung around the estaminet connected with our billet for a while. He was in a British uniform but wore no insignia whatever. In general he acted queerly. And the idea was not as absurd as it may sound, for we were right in the middle of a mining area of France and the galleries stretched for miles underground, some of them clear over into the German lines. I never did find out what happened to my spy, but I felt pretty pleased with myself for being on the job.

March 29. Up 3:00 a.m. March to Arras 12 kilometers. Into cave. Flopped again and slept. Good feed. Found blankets, bacon, green envelopes. Left in a hurry. On post 7:30—9:30. Slept.

I shall never forget that march into Arras, nor the days that followed it. It was a nightmare all right. The Germans had made a stab at Arras. The caves, chalk ones, were in the outskirts of the town on the German side and the troops that had been there—Imperials—had beat it, leaving us the above-listed luxuries. The civilians had hurried out of the town, leaving everything wide open. There had evidently been a panic. Our fellows came in there and found complete chaos. Soon other divisions and artillery came pouring in, the artillery merely wheeling their guns into position and starting firing without waiting to dig emplacements. But for two or three days I am sure Fritz could have walked right through the place. For the first day we were too dead beat to put up a fight; for the next couple of days we were too drunk from the civilian wine stores left knocking about. And besides, there was a good-sized gap in the line. And every day at dawn we expected the avalanche of men and steel, and we had no defense works behind which to meet it. Let me go over the top any day rather than stand and let the enemy give it to me in the teeth, when and where he goddamn pleases.

March 31. Easter Sunday. Whizbangs 3 feet over my head. Knocked down and buried. Damn close and good shake-up.

One of these shells was a dud, so it interested me to dope out just how close it had been. What actually happened I shall never know. I was standing in a piece of sawed-off trench, looking away from the line, my rifle leaning against the earth beside me. The next thing I knew I was about 10 feet from my rifle, buried up to the armpits. My rifle looked as if lightning had struck it. Dead silence. Ten minutes later the fellow who was with me came sneaking around a hillock as if he were stalking deer. We hunted out a better hole and we went to it.

April 5. Up for bombs. Shell 15 yards away. Damn good scare and bit the dust hard. Going up the line tonight. Everybody's wind up. Lost on way in the dark. Shells damn close. Floundering in mud. Wet and plastered with mud and all in. Gas sentry. Letter from Mother.

That night I really did give up. We wandered around in circles for several hours, through wire, shell holes, and slimy, slippery mud. Time and again I fell into shell holes full of water. I was caked with mud, exhausted by rage and exasperated to the point of quitting. For about the fifteenth time—literally—I tumbled, sprawling into a shell hole. "Get out of there and come on!" bawled Sergeant MacDonald against the uproar of the night bombardment. I've forgotten what I said. This is the substance of it: "To hell with it. Fuck everything. You don't know where you're going, and I don't care. I'm done for. I'm not going another step. Here I am, and here I stay. Let the Heinies come. I don't give a damn. I'm absolutely all in and I'm not going to move another step. I'll wait till daylight and find you then, if I'm still alive."

April 27. Raid pulled off 1:00 a.m. 22 prisoners. Dixon killed and Jones. Great success. Aven of 188th Regiment, I Battalion. Letters from Mother and Arthur.

The Scouts' job in this and other raids was to reconnoiter No Man's Land and the German wire. The points of entry were chosen and the artillery registered on the wire as inconspicuously as possible. On the night of the raid, the raiding parties from the companies blackened their faces, removed all identification marks, and assembled at the places fixed in the frontline. The Scouts then led the raiding parties out into No Man's Land opposite the places in the wire through which they were to go. At Zero Hour a box barrage was put down on the sector to be raided, theoretically cutting it off from its support line, while other guns fired on the wire and blew holes through it. Not much of this could be done beforehand because it would have given the raid away. After a certain number of minutes the wire barrage lifted and changed to harassing fire. The box barrage continued with intensity. It was then that the raiding parties went through the wire and into the German trench. There were, I think, four parties in this raid, each having its own territory to clean up. All this had been practiced back of the line on ground marked out to scale with tapes in exact reproduction of the German positions. The raid was all over in about half an hour. On the right everything went according to plan. On the left, however, Lt. McKean ran into some unexpected trouble and it was there that Dixon was killed. McKean had to subdue two machine gun posts—and he did it practically singlehanded. Later he got the Victoria Cross for this exploit. McKean was the Scout officer and a decent egg. He was a slight, pale-faced, boyish-looking fellow who had been a schoolteacher. A more frail, less warlike person was hard to imagine—but he had guts and proved it many a time. He had risen from the ranks where he had got the Military Medal. After his V.C. he chalked up a Military Cross and Bar and then got what he probably was the most pleased with—a nice "blighty" through the leg. Losing only two of our men in a raid like that showed damned good work all round, and Jones blew himself up by sticking an ammonal tube into a funk hole instead of a dugout, and waiting to make sure that it went off. No decorations were given to the Scouts on whom the whole responsibility for the raid rested— except McKean. 2 Military Crosses, 2 Distinguished Conduct Medals, and 5 Military Medals were dished out to the others.

August 7. The day of "If." Shelled on assembling. Slept out in open in cornfield. In p.m. operations discussion. Shells again. Up the line at night ready for Zero Hour.

Here we were on what Ludendorff called "the black day of the German army in the history of this war"—or, rather, on the eve of it. "The day of 'If'" I called it, because the "operations discussions" were punctuated with that word: "If it rains . . . If the artillery . . . If the tanks . . . and, above all, If Fritz does or does not do so and so."

We, the Intelligence Section of the 14th Canadian Infantry Battalion, spent the day in an orchard of the village of Cachy, east and a little south of Amiens. Around us was the Canadian Corps; on our left the Australian Corps and to our right the First French Army. Yet the lazy summer day droned on and not a soldier was in sight. Nor was there any sign of the 400 tanks and the 2,000 guns and the rest of that unbelievable congestion which had filled the roads and trails the night before. Everything was out of sight, hidden in woods, in the tall wheat or in folds in the ground. Shells dropped casually here and there. A machine gun would rattle lazily and spasmodically in the distance. Planes and bees buzzed around, making a drowsy noise. We loafed around in the high grass of that orchard. All was certainly quiet on the western front around there.

After nightfall the whole area suddenly came alive again. You realized you had been in the midst of an enormous but invisible and silent crowd. There was a good deal of rumbling going on around. Quite a few planes were up. These were to drown out the noise of the tanks. I moved off with four or five from my section to go down to the first-wave platoons to which we had been attached. We reached the front-line down the slope of the hill from our orchard, and walked along the knee-deep jumping-off trench, which was filled with men. I left Tatton and McLaren at their platoon. McLaren was spreading his rubber sheet over the parapet: "It's to keep me breeches clean when I go over," he said to me. We wished each other luck and I went on up the trench and reported to the platoon officer. I should say it was then about 11 o'clock or midnight. I was sleepy, could hardly keep my eyes open, and found a funk hole. D.R. McClare, who had been detailed to the same platoon with me, said he would route me out when things started. It seemed that I had hardly shut my eyes when he was punching me: "Rise and Shine! The lid goes off in half an hour." I took my place with him in the trench, looked my rifle ammunition over, or rather felt it over, as it was black as hell, and squatted down in the trench with my back to Fritz. A shell or two droned over and burst way back. A cockney voice a few feet away was chanting in a low voice: "Just before the battle, Mother, I was eating bread and cheese." I remember thinking that I must not walk too fast or I'd bump into our own barrage. There seemed to be some rumbling around back of us, otherwise dead silence.

Suddenly a great flash of sheet lightning lit up the western horizon as far as I could see. Then, in an instant the sky was filled with a weird whistling and shrieking. There was a roar and a crash and the ground started to jump about. Then more lightning, the smell of explosives, and, almost on top of us, two or three great hulks—the tanks. One gun was firing right in our trench and the "Stretcher Bearers!" cry was heard before we had budged an inch. (To preserve secrecy no gun had registered for the barrage.) Two minutes went by in this air- and earth-quake. Then whistles blew along the line. We grabbed our rifles and advanced.

November 6. Rain continues.

November 8. Revolver practice.

At nine o'clock this morning the German Armistice Commission met Marshal Foch in his special train in the Compiègne Forest.

November 9. Many rumors of peace.

November 11. Peace declared. Hostilities cease at 11:00 a.m. Ye gods!

December 27. Turn in revolvers. Cologne out of bounds. Some damned idiot been holding people up.

There had been several disturbances in Cologne among the troops themselves. The Guards Division had come in there, and their officers were very touchy about being saluted. The Colonials had decided that the war was over, and they had never been very keen about saluting anyway. Imperial picquets picked up Canadian soldiers, and the rough-houses started. There were several brawls in the pubs, ending up with a big one down in the red-light district in which a few men got killed. The Military Police acted more like sons of bitches than ever, which did not help the general spirit of restlessness that was prevailing. The result was that we were pulled out of there soon after and left the Watch on the Rhine to the Imperial Chocolate Soldiers.

The slowness in demobilization, the constant reports of the great numbers of Americans who were going home ahead of us, the lousiness of the parade-ground yellow bastards who had swarmed out to smarten us up, and the general reaction after the armistice started things humming.

January, 1, 1919. Paid 30 marks. Parcel from Fishers. No resolutions. Band concert in street. Civilians made to take their hats off to national anthem. An example of caddishness and pettiness that should be beneath the British. Goddamned bunch of bullying Prussian bastards there "British Officers and Gentlemen."

What had got my goat was that one of our officers had knocked the hat off a civilian and thrown it in the mud. The victim was an inoffensive old man who probably didn't know what tune was being played. At least, it seemed so. I really felt terribly ashamed and embarrassed about the business, that sort of thing never failing to react upon the perpetrator and making him look damned foolish.

May 19. On draft for *Regina*. Five minutes later taken off. Profanity the order of the day, not to mention blasphemy. Promised to be put on draft tomorrow, but being *on* one draft is worth *waiting for* all the rest. Y Emmas concert party. Pretty good.

May 20. On draft for *Carmania*. Sailing tomorrow. Medical inspection, etc. Grave digging this a.m. for men killed in the riot. I must admit I did not kill myself working. I've set my hand to quite a few things in this army, and the last item is grave digging.

May 21. Left Rhyl 7 a.m. Train to Liverpool. Embarked on *SS Carmania*. Steerage, R Section. Not very bad. Cavalry Brigade onboard and several civilian passengers. Set sail finally at 7 p.m. after a lot of idiotic monkeying around.

May 31. Arrived Montreal 8 a.m. Discharged noon. Bath and change and down to 7:40 train to New York.

Printed in the United States
by Baker & Taylor Publisher Services